THIS LAIRD
of MINE

THIS LAIRD
of MINE

GERRI RUSSELL

Montlake
Romance

Text copyright © 2014 Gerri Russell

Published by Montlake Romance, Seattle

www.apub.com

Amazon, the Amazon logo, and Montlake Romance are trademarks of Amazon.com, Inc., or its affiliates.

ISBN-13: 9781477820308
ISBN-10: 1477820302

Cover design by Visual Quill
Cover photo by Jenn LeBlanc / Illustrated Romance

Library of Congress Control Number: 2013921708

Printed in the United States of America

To my children, Adam, Justin, and Melissa, for your love, your patience, and the incredible happiness you've added to my life.
And to the Montlake team, especially Maria Gomez, for the tremendous skill and enthusiasm you bring to everything you do. You have my devotion and my respect.

Argyll, Scotland

Jules MacIntyre, through no fault of his own and much to his dismay, was now the fourth Earl of Kildare. The father he never knew had a heart died when it stopped three weeks ago, and his troubled brother had drowned himself in whiskey two days later. They both lay dead in the family crypt, alongside the woman who had sent Jules to gaol for sixteen months and twenty-seven days.

He had been blamed for his stepmother's death. A death Jules had always suspected was self-inflicted in order to make him suffer. But at the moment, he did not care about his stepmother's machinations. He was free, and he had more pressing issues to contend with today, such as how he would restore the manor and farmland that had gone to ruin, how he would pay off the debts that threatened to drown him as they did his brother, and, now that he was laird, how he could avoid the burden of marriage. Lady Jane

1

Lennox had been the only woman for him, and she had given her heart to another man.

Jules leaned back in his late father's wooden desk chair and contemplated the fanned display of swords that took up the far wall of the study. If a sword was the answer to his problem, he had many to choose from.

Jules frowned at the multitude of unpolished steel. His desire to learn how to use a sword was what had started all his problems, that and a madwoman who had invaded his father's life. Now, the swords remained and all the other players were gone, and the house echoed with their ghosts.

He was alone in his life and in this house, with only an aged servant and a desk full of mail for company. With a flick of attention toward three stacks of letters on the corner of the desk, Jules stood and paced the room. The largest stack contained dun notices from creditors.

His father and brother had lived extravagantly for the past several years, well beyond their means. And now the estate was in ruin and the creditors had already threatened him with debtor's prison. The memory of his dark, dank cell came flooding back.

He drew a deep breath, trying to force the images away, but they were too overpowering. The smell of rotting flesh filled his senses. Heavy manacles tugged at his wrists and ankles. Darkness weighed heavy on him, stole his breath. It was cold, so very cold . . .

Jules shuddered, the motion snapping him back to the present. With an effort, he forced the memory away. Never would he go back to gaol. He would rather impale himself on one of those swords than allow himself to be cast back into that hell again.

With a sharp breath of the musty air that enveloped Kildare Manor, Jules turned to gaze at the second stack of letters on the desk. They were from his friends, Jane and Nicholas, checking on his welfare, begging him to find a wife, annoying him with their constant prattle about how happy they were and only wanting the same for him.

He released a heavy sigh. The problem was he still had feelings for Jane. He loved her, despite the fact she had married another man. Jules had tried to put her out of his mind for the last seven months, but to no avail. His thoughts returned to her time and again, even though he knew she was happy, that her new husband, Nicholas Kincaid, was a decent sort of man, and that she had married for love.

If such a sentiment actually existed.

Disgusted by the thought, Jules paced the chamber, contemplating the faded walls where paintings had once hung. Even if he ignored his own emotions, he still had a problem with Jane and Nicholas's appeal for him to seek out happiness with a bride.

Did Nicholas and Jane not understand that what they had was special? Most people did not find that kind of happiness ever. And requited love? He didn't believe such a thing could exist, not for him. Not ever.

Jules stopped pacing before the massive display of weaponry. He reached up and fingered the dull tip of one of the swords. The metal was cool to his touch, echoing the cold emptiness of his soul. Happiness was a rare commodity. And wanting something more than what life had offered him so far would only lead the way to more disappointment and pain.

Which was why he had created her.

Jules smiled as his gaze moved to the third letter on the desk. A letter from Claire. His newly *created* wife. She was the perfect woman. She never complained, did not mind his late nights out, or his discreet dalliances. She did not expect his adoration or his love. She never spent money. And best of all, she always kept her opinions to herself.

His Claire was the perfect invention, and his only salvation.

He had created Claire to distance himself from Jane and Nicholas and keep them from interfering in his life. He did not want to be near their happiness, or be reminded of his own unrequited love. But Claire, even if simply on paper and an invention between himself and his solicitor, would help him far more than he had ever imagined at her inception. She would allow him the time he needed to untangle the mess his father and brother had left behind. If he was lucky, she would also keep the creditors at bay. Who wasn't sympathetic to a newlywed couple in their first weeks of life together? It might give him time to find some way to save the estate.

A sound at the doorway brought Jules's gaze around. His father's servant . . . his servant, John Finnie, stepped into the room carrying a tea tray Jules had not requested.

"I brought ye somethin' tae ease yer pain." Fin said, setting the tea upon the carpeted desk.

It would take something stronger than tea to accomplish that. But Jules was not his father or his brother. Whiskey at ten in the morning was not for this MacIntyre. He would not repeat his brother's foolishness and poison himself with whiskey.

"Thank you, Fin," Jules replied, meaning the words. He was grateful for the refreshment and just as pleased not to be utterly alone. Jules studied his companion. The aging retainer was dressed in the same threadbare jacket and breeches he had worn for as long as Jules had been alive.

"Beg pardon, mi—," the old retainer said, coughing before he could finish his words. Fin cleared his throat and tried again. "Beg pardon, milord. A messenger brought these fer ye." He shuffled forward, holding four letters.

Jules frowned at the messages. He recognized the tight and neat handwriting on the top letter as that of his solicitor. The other three were most likely duns or more pleas from Nicholas and Jane for him to pursue happiness and love.

Jules's frown deepened at the lack of a silver salver or even a wooden platter to deliver the messages upon. The silver had long since been sold, along with all of the paintings, most of the furnishings, and anything else that could fetch a price and keep the creditors at bay for a few days more.

Jules reached for the first letter. As expected, it was from his solicitor, Grayson, but the contents were not what he had counted upon at all. Ever since Jules had created his wife, Grayson had stepped into the role of her scribe and had been sending him one letter each week for the past five weeks in the voice of Claire.

Jules's fingers tightened on the letter. He could only focus on a few words. *Your father . . . no money . . . unknown benefactor.* Jules closed his eyes and concentrated on his breathing. Then, very slowly, he opened his eyes and read the letter in its entirety.

He had waited for this information for the past seven months, since his release from gaol. He supposed he could have come home and asked his father himself, but he had hired Grayson to do the investigation instead, wanting nothing more to do with the father who had closed his eyes to his own wife's machinations.

Regardless of his father's past sins, Jules had wanted to know the truth about his release. Grayson had discovered part of what Jules longed to know. His father and brother had not had the funds to pay his ransom and release him from gaol. But they also hadn't come to visit or bring him a scrap of food, or even a blanket, some small comfort to ease his pain. And, to add more misery to his already overburdened soul, Grayson was no more able to discover who had secured Jules's freedom than he had during his own investigation. It was why Jules had gone to Edinburgh after he had left Bellhaven Castle and Jane behind. He needed answers about who had offered him this unknown kindness.

A chill worked its way across Jules's neck. If not Jane or his father, then who had released him? The knowledge that he was indebted to some unknown benefactor shook him to his core. He would be beholden to no one, no matter who that one might be.

Jules drew another slow, deep breath at the blatant proof his father had abandoned him. He stared up at the ceiling, feeling empty inside. God, it hurt to know the man he once loved had not cared enough to rescue him, and had never loved him in return.

But with his next breath, Jules forced that pain and isolation away. He might have been denied a loving and decent family, but something good had come about regardless. Whoever had paid his ransom and released him from gaol had given him a second chance. His life had come down to this moment, when he was broken and alone. Yet, the opportunity to change everything was only a heartbeat away.

This was his moment and his crossroad. He could go down with his family, or fight for the life he wanted, despite it all.

Jules's throat tightened and his palms grew damp.

"Milord," Fin said, bringing him back to the present. When Jules failed to retrieve the other letters, Fin stepped closer, jiggling the folded paper in an attempt to gain his master's attention.

Fin's worn boot caught on the carpet, and he pitched forward. The letters fell to the carpet in one direction as Fin fell to the other.

Jules caught the old retainer as he went down, then guided him to the chair behind the desk. "Sit here, Fin. Catch your breath."

"But the letters—"

"Are probably more debtor notices," Jules said, flexing his right arm as he stepped back, grateful he had regained his strength over the last seven months. His time in gaol had stripped him of more than his soul.

"Nay," Fin protested. "Lady Jane wrote one, but the other letter is in an unfamiliar female hand."

Jules's curiosity won out. He bent to retrieve the letters. He paused for a moment as his fingers brushed the thick, intricately woven tapestry on the table and floors. It seemed odd that when everything else had been sold to pay the estate's debts, the carpets still remained. He frowned and scooped up the letters.

He broke the seal on Jane's letter after tossing the others on the desk.

Dearest Jules,

When I first heard from the lady herself that you had married, I must admit I was hurt. I had so hoped to be included in your celebration. However, after meeting the glorious creature you now call wife, I can understand your haste. She is, in every way, your perfect match. I forgive you and congratulate you on a job well done. I look forward to seeing you in two days when you can introduce all of us to your new bride properly.

Your friend always, Jane

It took the words a few moments to sink in. But when they did, Jules dropped the letter on the desk. How was it possible to meet a person who was merely a figment of his imagination?

"Milord?" Fin's voice broke in.

He looked across the desk at his servant, trying to find the words despite his confusion. "This cannot be."

"Beg pardon?" Fin's eyes narrowed with concern.

Jules reached for the next letter, which was from Claire, the one he knew to be written by Grayson. It was exactly as they had discussed—containing trivialities about her daily life. Isn't that the sort of letter a wife would write to her husband?

He tossed that letter aside and reached for the other letter in the unfamiliar female hand, and broke the seal. Neat and fluid lettering filled the page.

Jules, my love,
I have been to see your friends Lord and Lady Kincaid as well as Lord and Lady Galloway and invited them to visit us at Kildare Manor. The couples as well as Sir David Buchanan have agreed to escort me northward in two days' time. Please have the house readied for our guests. Until then.

Yours truly, Claire

His vision blurred and the room faded from view as a sense of disorientation consumed him. Was this a scam of some sort? Had someone discovered his secret and now intended to take advantage? Who would do such a thing? And how in God's name had they discovered his secret?

Jules swallowed hard, thinking. What madness was this? Was Grayson somehow involved? His solicitor was the only person who knew the truth, the one who had been paid to falsify his new bride. Claire did not exist. Would never exist.

Yet someone claiming to be his wife was meeting his friends, and coming to him in two days' time.

He had known the moment he arrived at Kildare Manor that the immediate solution to his problem was to marry a rich bride, yet even now he preferred a fake spouse to one with funds, because a false bride would never see his faults and could never hurt him. Jules raked his hands through his hair. A wife? A real wife?

"Milord, yer scarin' me. Ye got that look yer brother had right before he drank himself tae death." Fin's voice brought Jules's gaze around.

Jules shook his head in an effort to clear his thoughts. The motion did nothing as questions raced through his mind. For his servant's sake, Jules pasted on a smile. "You need not worry, Fin. I am not so weak a man as that. I have endured much worse than this." At least he hoped he had.

Jules continued. "It looks as though Kildare Manor will have no time for grief. We will be having visitors on Saturday. I will arrange for a few maids to come up from town to help with the preparations."

Fin's brow furrowed. "I mean ye no dishonor, milord, but we've no funds fer food, let alone cleanin' women."

Jules nodded as he dug his booted toe into the thick carpet beneath his soles. "I have a notion of where I can gather a few funds, at least enough to hold off the creditors for a while longer until I figure things out."

Fin stood. "Very well, milord. You'd best enjoy yer tea before it grows cold. That was the last of the tea leaves. If ye need somethin' stronger, there's plenty of whiskey still."

Jules nodded as the servant shuffled out of the chamber, leaving him in silence. Whiskey seemed like a better option, Jules thought as he reached for the tea and poured himself a cup. Perhaps, in time, it would be his only option, just as it had been for his brother. But for now, he had work to do and a fake wife to meet.

What kind of woman pretended to be a man's wife? Not the kind of woman he would take to wife, that was for certain. Would it be better to tell his friends what he had done or to go along with this scheming stranger who would soon arrive with the few people in his life who he trusted? Frustration and despair rose in Jules until he could scarcely bear it.

The truth was he needed Claire, any Claire, to help him move past his feelings for Jane, especially when she arrived in the arms of her husband. Could he, in turn, use this woman to help him in his deception, at least until Jane and Nicholas left?

He had loved Jane from the moment they first met ten years ago. While he had never been certain if she returned that love, over the years he had convinced himself that the lack of chemistry between them was not what mattered. To him, Jane was perfect—ethereal, brave, intelligent, and kind. Seeing her again would only fan his devotion once more, despite her married state. And yet, this very real Claire might be the very distraction he needed.

He could accept the schemer and play along with her, acting as husband and wife. But once they were alone, he would discover what was behind this imposter's game. In the meanwhile, for better or worse, definitely poorer than richer, a living, breathing Claire MacIntyre, Lady Kildare, would soon enter his life.

The carriage rumbled along the dirt road, pitching its passengers left and right as it had for the last hour. The roads this far north in Scotland were rough, just like its men. Claire MacIntyre had barely finished the thought as she hit the squabs of the carriage once more. The padding did nothing to soften the jolt of the wood biting into her flesh. Only Sir David Buchanan rode somewhat in comfort on his own horse behind the carriage.

The heat of the day was behind them, and evening approached as they continued on, only stopping briefly at a roadside inn to allow the horses to rest, and to grab a quick bite of luncheon. The meat pie had seemed like a good idea an hour ago. Now it sat like a leaden weight in Claire's stomach. She pressed her hands over her abdomen, as though holding back the upset.

"Is all well?" Jane asked.

At Jane's concerned look, Claire straightened, then smoothed her gray linen skirts. "It's merely nerves at seeing my beloved again." *Or for the first time.*

Claire was spared from having to elaborate as they hit yet another rut in the road that pitched them all to the left. When the carriage righted itself, Claire put off more discussion by staring out the small window near her.

For the first four hours of their trip, the grandeur of Scotland's countryside with its deep valleys and rolling hills all covered in a thick layer of heather relieved her anxiety. Yet now, as they progressed closer to their goal, Claire's tension became a palpable thing.

The carriage gave another violent, creaking lurch to the right. Claire's shoulder banged into Lady Margaret Galloway's. "My apologies, milady."

"Margaret. Please just call me Margaret. No need for such formality among us. We are all friends," the older woman said with a wink at her husband, next to her, and to Lord Nicholas Kincaid, who sat beside Jane.

"The roads up here are in desperate need of repair," Jane said with an apologetic smile. Jane, Margaret, and Lord Galloway had accepted Claire as Jules's wife without hesitation. Nicholas had been more reserved in his judgment. He studied her even now with a calculating look. Could he know the truth?

Claire straightened beneath his regard just as the carriage gave another teeth-jarring lurch. "The road to paradise is not supposed to be smooth," she said brightly. "Seeing my beloved again will be worth whatever trials await us on this journey."

"I can see why Jules fell in love with you." Jane's smile broadened. "He is a fortunate man, but then again, you are a fortunate woman. Jules is just as his name proclaims, a jewel among men."

An uncontrollable tremor of dread shot through Claire. That was not what she had been told by the dark-cloaked figure who had forced her into this marriage. Her husband, she'd been informed, was a wicked rogue with a reputation for carousing Scotland's local villages as well as its lustiest locales late into the night. He had started as a youth, and had continued his craven debauchery until he had been imprisoned for the mysterious death of his own stepmother. He had been sentenced to hang, but was spared by the proof of innocence Jane had supplied.

And yet, there were still rumors of his gambling and carousing. Claire's skin flinched at the thought of joining her life with his.

She pressed her hand against her chest as if to physically quell the fear that had suddenly arisen. No matter who or what he was, she had no choice but to achieve her goal. She had to make Jules MacIntyre fall in love with her, then abandon him.

That was the agreement she had made. In a fortnight, he had to profess his devotion to her or else Penelope, Anna, and Eloise would pay for her failure.

Claire's fingers rose to the small silver locket that weighed against her chest. Her breath caught as her fingers clasped the cool metal. The three young women—all of whom were abandoned after the death of their parents, just like Claire—were her wards. She'd been told they would be tortured and killed if she did not do as instructed.

"Claire, are you certain you are well?" Jane's voice cut through the dark thoughts swirling through Claire's mind.

She startled, releasing the locket, and forced a nonchalant smile. "You remember what it was like to be a new bride?"

"Yes, I do." Jane reached for Nicholas's hand just as the carriage lurched to a stop at the end of a long drive.

"We have arrived," Hollister, Lord Galloway, said as he and Nicholas exited the carriage first. Nicholas extended his hand to Claire as she made her way out. She accepted his assistance as her knees suddenly became unsteady. How could she make a man she had never met fall in love with her in two weeks' time when she had never even managed a flirtation with the opposite sex in all her life?

Forcing herself to remain calm, Claire took in her surroundings and frowned. This could not be right. The one painting she had seen of Kildare Manor had pictured it as a grand estate set against a landscape of lush green hills and wrapped by the shores of Loch Awe. In that image, the house's cool gray stone had reflected in the sun like polished silver.

It was not entombed by bramble bushes that nearly reached the roofline of the two-story structure, or the dull, sad gray that peeked out from beneath the weeds and dust. Kildare Manor was broken and abused and in desperate need of a caretaker.

Was the estate a reflection of the man who lived inside? Was her supposed husband careless and neglectful as well as a rogue? She shivered. What could Jules MacIntyre have done to someone that was so bad they wanted to break the man's heart, his very spirit?

"Claire?" Jane spoke beside her and gently touched her arm. "Jules will no doubt be anxious to see you. Let us go inside."

Claire nodded. She had no notion of what the man's reaction would be, which was why she had arrived with his friends. At least in their presence he would not refuse her outright.

15

She hoped.

As she had learned from his solicitor, if the man was desperate enough to falsely create a bride in order to stop his friends from interfering in his life, then perhaps he would play her game until it reached the only conclusion she would allow.

Just then, weak summer light broke through the clouds over-head, bathing the manor house in a shimmer of warmth. Claire drew a steadying breath. She could do this. She had to do this.

"I will help the coachman with the horses and meet you inside," David called.

The remaining five progressed toward the crumbling arched doorway just as it swung open to reveal a withered old man with wisps of white hair sticking up at odd angles on his head. "Welcome tae Kincaid Manor," he greeted, then stepped back, allowing them to enter the large, open foyer. "Milord will be with ye momentarily. In the meanwhile, allow me tae show ye tae the drawin' room fer refreshments."

When Nicholas and Hollister hesitated, the elderly man waved them on. "Leave the bags there. I'll take them to yer chambers momentarily."

Nicholas frowned and cast a speaking glance at Hollister. "We will take them up the stairs and leave them at the landing."

The older man shrugged, but gratitude shone in his tired gray eyes before he turned away. "Ladies, this way, please."

Claire frowned as she made her way across the bare marble floor and past the unpolished and slightly sagging wooden stairs. No car-pets dampened the sound of their footsteps in the hallway or inside the drawing room. The floors were bare, the walls unadorned, and the furnishings sparse. Who was the man who lived here? A shiver worked its way across her neck. Chief among the things she knew about Jules MacIntyre was that he had a reckless spirit, but was he also mad to live in such a place?

She stepped fully into the room and searched for her missing "husband." When he was nowhere in sight, she released a pent-up breath. What would he say when he saw her? Would he challenge her outright or play along with her game? Was he absent now in order to build her anxiety? Or worse, would he send her away immediately without even giving her a chance to explain?

The truth was they were married. He had signed the marriage documents himself. The paperwork was official, the marriage was real, binding, forever.

For a girl who had lost everything early in life, she finally had something of her own—a real husband. She would take his name, and as a result she would be afforded more independence and be accepted in society's highest circles. Yet that was all she would keep from this marriage. She would have no protection from him, no financial support when she left him behind.

Claire shook off the dark thought and looked about the room. Faded and tattered curtains were pulled back, allowing filtered sunlight to illuminate the chamber. At odds with the stark interior of Kildare Manor was the fresh scent of lemons and rosemary. The room was free of dust, and the floors were, although bare and aged, polished to a shine. The furnishings were as sparse as in the foyer with only three chairs and a settee, and a small table in the middle of them all, bearing a three-armed candelabra with only one candle.

Kildare Manor was nothing like what she had imagined. Would the man who owned it be as well? Would she have to adjust her plans? Because suddenly, making this notorious man fall in love with her seemed harder than she had expected.

"Greetings, my dearest friends," an unfamiliar voice called from the doorway behind her.

Claire stiffened, forced her chin up, and slowly turned around. Conversation moved around her as the newly dubbed laird of Kildare Manor greeted his friends. Claire saw their smiles and heard the joy in their voices as they reunited until all sound faded, and all she heard was the sound of her own heartbeat as it filled her ears. She waited. She watched. She couldn't take her eyes off him and hoped no one else noticed the fact that he would wait to greet his "wife" last.

But those moments with his friends gave her time to appraise him. She wasn't sure what she expected, never having seen even a portrait of him, but it wasn't the handsome man before her. His wavy blond hair fell to the collar of his coat. He was much taller than she expected, and his body, though relaxed, still hinted at lithe power. His jaw was strong and defined, his cheekbones high, and he had a slight cleft in his chin. Her gaze drifted to his lips—lips that were full and expressive and made for kissing. The thought warmed her cheeks as she met his startling blue eyes.

Those eyes narrowed on her. "My dear, sweet wife." His voice was rough-smooth with the hint of a Scottish burr. His gaze shuttered as he came toward her. Only a slight curl to his upper lip indicated his current disposition. He was angry, but he would not reveal that to his friends. Only to her.

The air between them all but crackled as he took a final step closer to her. He leaned toward her, slid his arm about her waist, and pulled her forward, caging her against his body.

Her nerves flicked and her fantasy of him wrapping her in his arms and accepting her without question shattered about her feet. This close to him, the scent of soap and mint filled her senses. She could feel the tension thrumming through his body, see the challenge in his eyes.

"Jules." She didn't press back or retreat. She held her body erect and tried to force a look of nonchalance into her gaze. He studied her eyes, her lips. Against her will her lips parted.

"Oh, how I have missed you," he said. His voice lowered to a gravelly purr as his gaze fixed on her mouth.

"I've missed you, as well, my dearest husband." The words rang with outright challenge as she met his gaze, dared him to reveal that they had never met. His grip at her waist softened as he pulled her close and lowered his lips to hers.

She knew it was part of the role she'd been forced to play—that he would have to touch her and she would have no choice but to allow it—yet the brush of his lips to hers sparked not only anger, but a surprising stir of passion, and that angered her more. Why had the solicitor and his cloaked comrades forced her into this situation?

The girls. Yes, her wards were her life, and all that mattered to her. And still . . . she had wanted a life of her own someday. She had wanted to choose her own husband. Instead, the decision had been ripped from her. And she was now Jules's property in order to save the only three people who ever cared about her.

With a flash of temper, Claire brought her hand up to Jules's face, smoothed her fingers against his jaw. She wanted to push him away. Instead she tunneled her fingers into the hair at his nape and across his neck, pulling him closer.

He responded with a soft groan that only fueled her pent-up irritation. She put her anger, her frustration, and her fear into her kiss. It felt good to let her emotions loose, to focus all her energy on the one thing that had driven her to this place. If he wanted a kiss, she would give the man, who no doubt had had many kisses before, one more that he would not soon forget.

She put everything she had, everything she was, into that kiss, and he responded. He wrapped his arms about her and hauled her against his chest. His lips firmed, he tilted his head, and his kiss deepened. He was now in charge. His kiss was fierce and hot as he ravaged her mouth.

Claire couldn't think, couldn't move as the scent of mint once again invaded her senses. Never in her life had she ever felt anything like his mouth on hers. Her nerves fired at the feel of his hard body against hers. Indescribable need and desire infused her core, potent and real. And she wanted to lose herself in that torment.

She gasped at the thought and jerked out of his arms. What was she thinking? What was she doing? The man was used to seducing vulnerable women.

"Darling," she said, breathless. "We have guests." She studied his profile. There was something compelling about his face, something she couldn't tear her gaze from. In his eyes she saw not anger and vengeance, but a sense of purpose that sent a chill to her core.

"We understand," Hollister said, pulling Margaret close to his side. "It was not long ago that we were newlyweds."

Margaret smiled up at her husband as her hand drifted down to her slightly rounded abdomen. "Look at us now. Married not yet a year and both Jane and I are with child."

"Now there is an interesting challenge," Jules said, dryly.

Claire's heart thudded in her chest at the prospect of Jules getting her pregnant. Why hadn't she considered that before now?

Oblivious to her sudden terror, Jules turned toward the others, releasing her from his gaze. "My apologies. I forgot my manners. I was eager to greet my new wife properly. Each time I see her, it feels as though I am looking at her for the very first time."

Claire forced a smile as she tried to recover not only from his bold words, but from that devastating kiss. She could not afford to lose her head over one moment of seduction. She had to remain in charge and guide his emotions where she wanted them to go, not the other way around.

But one thing was clear. Her husband would not here and now challenge her claim, at least not in front of his friends. Instead, he would taunt and torment her until she revealed her purpose.

Steel infused her spine. *Let him try.* She would instead mold him to her needs and desires until he proclaimed his love for her. Then the girls would be freed. Claire frowned as another thought occurred to her. What happened after he fell in love with her? She had not thought to ask the dark-cloaked and masked kidnappers who had invaded her life. It was one more thing she should have thought about before agreeing to their terms. Why had she not?

She knew the answer even as the question formed—because until this moment, Jules had been just a faceless entity, an end to a means. If she did what they asked, then Penelope, Anna, and Eloise would be safe.

At least that was what they had promised. Claire clutched her hands together, trying to control the horror that had been her constant companion these last two weeks. One moment she had been in her studio preparing paints. The next, the girls were gone.

All that remained in the room where she'd left them to prepare for their painting lesson was a note, warning Claire not to notify anyone that the girls had been taken or they would be killed.

The next day a darkly cloaked person had appeared, and she'd received the kidnappers' demands. Marry Jules MacIntyre by proxy, make him fall in love with her, and then leave him. She had to break his heart. If she succeeded, the girls would be returned unharmed. If she told anyone what had happened, or failed in her mission, the girls would be killed, and their blood would be on her hands.

The dire warning was all the motivation Claire had needed. And for two weeks she had done everything that had been asked of her. She had married Jules. She had lied to his friends. She had worked her way into the edges of his life. Only one task remained.

At that moment, the aging retainer who had greeted them a short while ago appeared in the room. "Milord," he announced in a gravelly voice. "Another message has arrived."

"Put it on the desk with the others," Jules said with a frown.

"The messenger said it was most urgent," the old man stated, his face growing paler by the moment. When Jules moved to accept the tightly folded missive, the old man hesitated. "It's fer the new mistress."

Jules accepted the letter and turned it over, inspecting the simple white linen. He said nothing as he handed it to Claire, but he gave her an arch look that spoke volumes.

No one but the people in this room, the solicitor, and the kidnappers knew she was here. A chill went up her spine. Turning away from the others, she opened the missive and froze. Inside the folded paper were three thin slices of fabric from the dresses her wards had been wearing when they were taken.

A tremor moved through her, and it took every bit of her self-control not to give in to fear. She drew a sharp breath, trying to maintain her composure. The girls would be unharmed as long as she did what they asked.

Quickly, she refolded the letter, slipped it into her bodice, then turned back to the others. Pasting a nonchalant smile on her face she said, "'Tis a message from my relatives, wishing Jules and me well on our recent nuptials." The lie was bitter on her tongue.

Jules's unamused gaze shifted from her face to her bodice, then back again. He stepped closer to her and offered her a wry, evil grin she knew was meant to intimidate her. And it did.

He lifted his hand to stroke the side of her neck, down to the edge of her bodice, only a hairsbreadth from where she had stashed the letter. The feather-light touch sent chills over her.

Her heart pounded. Obviously, whoever had abducted the girls was watching her. They would know if she did not do as they asked. With an over-bright smile she leaned into his touch. There was no time like the present to get started toward her goal.

3

J ules stared at the woman before him. He had intended to deny Claire's claims privately, then send her away. He had created her. He could uninvent her just as easily. He would simply fabricate some reason for her slipping into the night. But with his senses still reeling from the kiss they had shared, he could do no such thing.

Instead, he reached for Claire's hand, led her to a chair, and bade her sit while he talked with the others—Nicholas and Jane, Hollister, and Margaret. David joined them as well after settling the horses in the stable.

For a moment Jules ached at the sight of Jane and her gently rounded belly. "You look well, and happy," he said to the only woman he would ever love.

Jules quickly forced his emotion deep inside himself. Jane had chosen another. Contentment with her husband shone in her eyes as Nicholas moved behind Jane and pulled her against his chest.

"We are so happy to see you, Jules. Especially in light of your secret courtship, engagement, and marriage," Jane said with a soft smile.

"We were quite concerned after we learned your father and brother both passed away three weeks ago. It could not have been easy to lose them both so suddenly," Nicholas said as he narrowed his gaze on Jules. Did Nicholas still see him as he was seven months ago—weak and physically diminished from his imprisonment in gaol and sorrowful after losing Jane's hand to him?

Jules felt none of those things. He had worked hard over the last several months to rebuild the strength that prison had robbed from him. He was in the best shape of his life, if truth be told. And sorrow? That emotion had shriveled in the darkness of his prison cell each and every day that he had waited for his father to come and release him, until finally it had existed no more.

"Let us not talk of the past," Jules said, perhaps a bit too brightly, for his words brought a frown to Jane's lips. "Sit, relax." He turned to Fin. "Will you bring us some tea and refreshments?"

The aging servant nodded, and was gone only a short time before he returned with the tea. Fin hesitated for a moment as he looked from one woman to the next. A frown pulled down the corners of his mouth.

"Why not allow Lady Kildare to serve her guests?" Jules said, interpreting Fin's hesitation of uncertainty as to which woman should serve. At that suggestion, Fin's frown vanished, and he proceeded toward Jules's supposed wife.

Jules paused at his own admission. His gaze lingered on Claire as she accepted the task of pouring the tea and serving freshly baked scones to their guests. Who was this pretender? This interloper in his life?

The woman was unknown to him, but he could not fault her impeccable manners as she finished her task and returned to her chair. She met his gaze. Her large almond-shaped eyes, their color a mixture between brown and gold, challenged him to publicly renounce her in front of his friends.

He met her gaze with a nod of thanks for treating his friends well for the moment, yet a growing restlessness surged inside him to get her alone and ask her what she was about. Why was she using his friends to get close to him? And why had she assumed the identity of a woman who did not exist?

She dropped her gaze to the delicate teacup in her hands—a teacup he had purchased only a day ago from a widow in the village with funds he had secured by selling every carpet in the manor house. That cup didn't belong in her small hands; she'd no right to make it seem appropriate. But even as she sipped serenely, Jules could see a vibrant energy that exuded from her wide eyes to every line of her svelte and attractive form. She set down her cup, then reached up to brush an errant strand of copper hair away from her high, chiseled cheeks set in an oval of perfect porcelain skin.

He did not choose her, but he could not deny that she was beautiful, despite the tight chignon that pulled her hair off her face. Perhaps the woman had a pleasant form—if her colorless gray dress did not conceal too many faults. The virginal gown marked her as a cosseted, easily dismissed woman of society—a society he wanted no part of.

Jules closed his eyes and took a deep breath. If this woman wanted to be part of society, then why attach herself to him? All he desired was to rebuild what his father and brother had destroyed. He wanted to be left alone to deal with the estate and try to carve out a living for himself. It wasn't that much to ask, was it?

He opened his eyes and, almost against his will, his gaze returned to his "wife's" eyes—eyes that sparked with intelligence. The thought brought a moment's pause as her gaze connected with his. She did not look like a schemer. In fact, she looked very much like someone he and his friends might actually befriend.

She did not react to his bold stare. Instead, she folded her hands in her lap. What secrets lay behind those wide, golden eyes? Why would a woman of her obvious good breeding and education pretend to be the wife of a man she did not know?

He tried to look away from her and the mystery she presented, to shift his attention back to Jane, but something about this woman drew him in. Despite her horrible dress, and her severe hair, she had a presence that was hard to deny. It was as if she were unaware of her own energy, or how the slightest shift of her movements could fix any man's attention.

Jules frowned. What was he thinking? The woman was a fraud. She wanted something from him. Why else would she pose as Claire MacIntyre? He needed to figure out what that "something" was, and quickly, before she attached herself to his friends and his life.

He moved to Claire's side, offered his hand to help her stand. She set her cup aside and accepted his outstretched fingers. When she stood, he slipped his hand about her waist, drawing her against his side. She startled at the contact, but did not object. Instead she tossed him a half smile and released a light laugh.

Jules forced a look of fondness mixed with hunger into his expression. The hunger part was easier to feign as his supposed wife's soft body pressed against his own. It had been years since he had held a woman this intimately. He closed his eyes and drew in a deep breath of lavender mixed with vanilla. The combination sent a jolt of fire to his loins. He snapped his eyes open, no longer having to feign desire for the woman in his arms.

"Friends, if you will forgive us, Claire and I have much to discuss. We have been apart too long." Jules did not wait for an answer from his guests as he guided Claire toward the door and out of the chamber. He shut the door behind him, then guided his "bride" to the main hallway, then up the stairs.

"Where are we going?" Claire asked with only a hint of distress in her voice.

"To your new chamber."

She stiffened, but did not break her stride. "The master's chamber?"

"No, you will have to earn your way there, my dear." Annoyance tugged at him as he drew her down another hallway and toward the rear of the manor. He could not merely send her away, not with his friends here to witness such an act. He was obliged to play along with this farce for a time.

At the end of the hallway, he waved the woman at his side up another spiral stairway and into the tower room. She came to a stop in the middle of the tiny, dusty chamber, so different than the one downstairs, while he moved to the hearth and lit a single candle with a strike from the flint and steel.

Pale, golden light illuminated the room, making it appear less neglected. The only furniture in the chamber was a small, sagging bed. She could find some comfort here. Jules frowned and pushed the thought away. He turned back to the woman. She clutched her hands together, her nervousness palpable. She exuded fragility and weakness.

"You no longer need to pretend with me, Claire. If that is your real name." Jules gazed into her face, searching for the duplicity he was sure to find in her large, golden eyes.

She held his gaze. Met it boldly. "My name is Claire. And I am your wife."

"Yet how can that be? I never stood before the minister. Have you, Claire?" The sound of her name lingered on his tongue longer than it should have. He had pulled that name from the air when he had created his false wife, not from anyone he had ever known or cared to attach himself to.

"Ours was a wedding by proxy, or have you forgotten what you requested of your solicitor?"

Jules frowned. "Of what do you speak?"

She returned his frown. "Our marriage arrangements."

Jules stared down at her. She was as good a player as he had ever seen upon the stage, he would give her that. "We," he paused, allowing the word to hang between them, "never had anything between us until this day."

She did not acquiesce to his rebuttal. Instead, she straightened. Her spine stiffened. She might be a head shorter than he, but she stood her ground, met his gaze, then raised her brow in a coolly superior way. "I refuse to be offended by your lack of memory." She leaned forward and sniffed him. "I smell no spirits about you, but your family does have a reputation . . ." She turned away.

He had no intention of being so easily dismissed. He reached for her hand and held her captive. "What is your name?"

"Claire MacIntyre, Lady Kildare."

He frowned. "Before that."

She lifted her chin. "Claire Elliot of Edinburgh. I was the only child of the notable Scottish philosopher, historian, economist, and essayist known for his philosophical empiricism. My mother was a commoner. They both died when I was fourteen." She frowned at him. "Really, Lord Kildare, I would have thought you'd have checked on my background before asking me to be your bride."

"No more games. Tell me the truth. Why are you here?"

Her gaze moved to where his fingers held her, then moved to his face. A faint flush touched her pale cheeks, and her eyes blazed, her anger obvious.

He took a slow step toward her, looming over her as his own temper stirred. "Answer me." His nerves flicked at the soft scent of lavender, and he leaned back slightly.

She did not retreat from him, did not react in any way to his blatant intimidation other than to take a quick breath. "If you recall," she said, her voice steely, "you sent your solicitor to me with your offer of marriage."

Jules frowned. "My solicitor?"

"A Mr. James Grayson. If I recall correctly, he is located near Parliament Hall."

"Grayson had no such orders." Jules narrowed his gaze. He knew his solicitor well enough to know that he would never betray his client in such a way.

Damn, the woman was good at her deceptions. She had done her research well to discover his solicitor's name and his place of business. He studied her eyes; at such close proximity and in the dimly lit room they gleamed like burnished gold, shadowed and mysterious. Her eyes gave him no insight into her thoughts.

"Your solicitor stood as your proxy at St. Giles' Cathedral in Edinburgh. He then sent me directions to your friends so that they might escort me here, to you."

Her breathing had quickened, but she seemed otherwise at ease with her lies. The air between them all but crackled. "That cannot be."

"Oh but it is," she said, her voice smooth.

"Let us pretend for a moment that what you say is true." His own voice deepened. "Why would you accept the proposal from a total stranger, marry by proxy, then come to some unknown location to meet your new groom? What kind of woman does such a thing?"

"The kind of woman who has no other choice." Her face paled and her expression closed.

Jules remained silent. He was not sure what he had expected her to say, but it was not that. "Why did you have no other option but to marry me?"

His anger ebbed and sympathy took its place for a moment before he forced it away. He clenched his hands at his sides as memory surged. There had been another time in his life when he had simply accepted a woman at her word. He had been filled with hope and possibility at the idea of finally having a mother in his life. But that illusion had taken him down a long, dark path. A path that ultimately led to his being accused of murder.

"Life for a woman is very different than it is for a man." Claire's eyes narrowed as she noted his change in demeanor, but she did not back down. Instead, her voice lowered, her tone as provocative as it was challenging. "With no family to support me, or wealth to my name, my options were few. When Mr. Grayson approached me with your offer—" She looked away. "Let us just say it was the lesser evil to marry you."

The barb stung. "Are you certain about that?"

Her gaze returned to his. In her eyes he saw a momentary shadow.

"You cannot scare me, Lord Kildare. I know more about life and the vile places it can take a person than you ever will."

At the unexpected response, he pressed his lips together. Was she a wanton, then? A fancy woman thinking to entrap him? She looked like an angel, but a comely appearance could hide a dark soul.

Jules clenched his fists at the direction of his thoughts. He could not lose himself to his past troubles. He had to stay focused on Claire—why she was here, what she intended with him.

He would not know until he did his own investigating. But before he spent the time and energy on his so called "wife," he intended to speak with Grayson about her claims. Why would Grayson betray him, betray his creation of the "perfect" wife by finding a real woman to play the role?

As if sensing the direction of his thoughts, she said, "I am who I say I am. You will not deny me my rights as your wife, will you?"

He let a moment tick past before he answered her. "Until I have proof of our marriage, I cannot claim you to be anything but an interloper."

Her lips curved into a cynical smile. "Very well. If that is how you will play this. But be aware that I am not going anywhere while you determine the truth behind my words. In the meantime, I intend to make our guests comfortable." She turned away, heading toward the stairs.

He caught her hand and pulled her around, not harshly, as her fingers threaded with his before the touch ended. In that brief contact, an awareness arced between them, left him tingling and off balance. "And what about me, Claire? Will you act the part of wife for me?" Jules asked, attempting to sound fierce. Instead a husky timbre resonated in his voice.

Claire's posture infused with unexpected steel. Her features hardened. The weakness he had seen earlier was no longer evident, and he realized there was more to this woman than he'd first thought. "There is room in this tiny chamber for only one of us, milord," she said.

"Is that a challenge?" Ignoring all the warnings in his head, Jules reached for her hand once more, knowing as he did he was playing with fire.

She stepped out of his reach. "Think of it however you will, husband. I might be a woman who had no option but to accept what it was you or your solicitor offered on your behalf. But the marriage agreement I signed was very real. I am your wife."

Her declaration goaded awake a long-dormant devil within him, a misplaced part of himself he had managed to temper over the years to a polished sheen of civility. Slowly, his eyes never leaving hers, he moved toward her. She tensed as he crept ever closer, until he was rewarded with her faint, intoxicating fragrance.

A flicker of surprise flared in her eyes and her breath whispered across his cheek a heartbeat before he pulled her forward, crushing her petal-soft mouth beneath his. For one heady moment her mouth was pliant, and then she fought, pushing him away.

The innocence of this exchange startled him. She had no audience before which to perform. And yet the kiss felt almost real . . .

Hot color flooded her cheeks. "You may only kiss me when I allow it," she said, drawing back, her chest rising and falling with each rapid intake of breath.

"Well, then. If you are to remain here and impose on my hospitality, then you'd best get used to allowing me to kiss you frequently. For I will have some payment for my generosity."

She gasped.

He smiled, feeling once more in control of the situation. "You are not my wife. You are a creation of my own making, and one I intend to rid myself of as easily as you were created."

She frowned. "I will not make that easy."

His smile increased. "Yet another challenge, my dear?"

She delivered him a sharp, angry glance. "You cannot drive me away."

Again, that devilish side of himself reared and without hesitation he acted. He grasped her hand, spinning her around, and pulled her backside against his chest, pinning her free arm to her side.

"Consider your challenge accepted," he breathed against the back of her ear.

She struggled in his grasp, but her movements were hampered by her heavy skirts. Still, one booted foot came down on his instep, drawing a hiss of pain from him. And as quickly as the pain came and went, so too did the sudden realization of how intimately he held her. As her buttocks pressed against his loins, desire, slid down his spine. For a heartbeat he allowed the indulgence, basked in the sensation of feeling alive again, feeling lust, desire, and physical need like he had not in so many years. He might have a reputation as a reprobate thanks to his stepmother and her gossip amongst the servants, but the reality was nothing of the sort.

In that moment of relaxing his guard while his thoughts wandered, Claire pulled out of his grasp. And with a rapid intake of breath and a swish of her skirts, she disappeared down the stairs.

He stared after her, and a sensual image of Claire reclining naked upon the small, sagging bed ambushed him, flooding his mind, filling his senses. He breathed sharply. Her scent lingered in the room. His body tightened further at the sweet torture she had evoked. The woman was an intruder in his life, yet she bewitched him like no other woman before.

Even Jane.

His heart raced at the realization. How could he possibly be bewitched by such a scheming interloper as Claire Elliot, when Jane, in all her perfection, was in a room belowstairs?

One exchange with Claire and he had forgotten all about the woman he'd loved since he was twelve years old.

Jules released a heartfelt groan. For that very reason, he had to get rid of Claire.

But before he could do that, he had to summon Grayson. Perhaps his solicitor could shed some much-needed light on exactly what had transpired. That also meant he would need to hire a messenger to summon him.

Jules frowned. Hiring the cleaning women had been far more difficult than he had imagined. The two women he finally convinced to come to the manor had jumped each time he entered a room. They never made eye contact, and as soon as they were finished, they demanded their money and scurried away.

It wasn't just the cleaning women. Others in the village had retreated indoors at his approach. What other lies had his stepmother spread about him before her death?

No matter. Money could overcome their reserve if he offered enough of it. Jules's frown deepened. What little he had was going quickly. It would not be long before his funds once again ran dry and his friends became aware of his dire straits.

Once Grayson arrived and Jules learned the truth, he could send Claire and his friends away and return to this impoverished state . . . alone.

As the door to the library closed behind Jules and his new wife, a whisper of cool air entered the room. Jane shivered as she waited for the footsteps to silence in the hall. She turned to her husband. "What are we to do about Claire?"

"Nothing, at present," Nicholas replied with the steadied calm that often had a similar effect on her. Today, his steadfastness had no effect on her nerves whatsoever.

"Is Claire truly Jules's wife?" Jane asked, as a million questions raced through her mind. It felt good to finally air the suspicions she had, they all had, of Claire and her connection to Jules. They had played along with her because of her knowledge of Jules's solicitor.

"He did not denounce her." Nicholas considered for a long moment. "Only time will tell, but your plan to follow Claire to Kildare Manor was a good one. We are here to support Jules should the need arise."

"He seemed to know her," Jane said. Jules had gone along with the woman easily enough. But Jane had seen that look of hesitation when he had first seen Claire. That one look had given Jane pause, and doubt had taken root. She knew Jules better than anyone else. She knew the nuances of her friend's emotions. And the look she had seen pass between Jules and Claire a short while ago had been completely foreign to her. "However, I fear Jules could be in trouble."

"Most men are when it comes to love," Hollister said with a smile. He drew his pregnant wife against his side and wrapped an arm protectively around her.

Margaret chuckled. "Jane, dear, we will all be here to keep an eye on things. What could possibly go wrong?"

"Jules seems happy to me," David replied. "But then again, I am not very savvy in matters of the heart." He sighed. "I say we give them time alone. If there is something amiss here, the pressure of them being together will bring it out."

"I could not agree with you more," Nicholas replied.

Another whisper of cool air brushed Jane's neck and shoulders. She pulled her shawl more tightly around her shoulders, holding back the shiver that threatened as frustration dragged at her, taunted her.

Jules was married. Or at least he appeared to be married. She should be ecstatic. Yet something did not feel quite right.

Nicholas frowned at this wife. "Do you not agree, Jane?"

"I am not certain of anything at present," Jane replied. "All I know is something is not right here. I am not certain if it is Jules, this house, or Claire that has me worried, but something does."

"Very well," Nicholas said with a nod. "Perhaps we accepted Claire's word too quickly. What we need is proof." He folded his arms over his chest and met his wife's gaze. "It is time for us to find out more, a lot more, about Claire Elliot MacIntyre and what she means to our friend."

"I believe we must intrude into Jules's finances as well," Jane said with a frown. "Kildare Manor is not what it should be for an earldom that goes back to James V."

Nicholas's expression darkened. "Jules will not like our intervening."

"How can we not?" Jane worried her hands before her. "He has nothing left. With the crofters gone, there is no way for the estate to produce an income." Her gaze travelled the chamber. "I will not allow a friend of ours to live like this when we can easily afford to provide assistance."

Nicholas nodded. "I will speak to Jules and find a way to assist him without insulting him."

Jane smiled at her husband, greatly relieved. "Perhaps this whole situation with Claire is a blessing, for without her, we never would have known what kind of misfortune had befallen Jules's estate."

Nicholas did not return her smile. "Misfortune has been a part of this estate for so long, I doubt even an infusion of funds and some new furnishings can turn the place around. But we will see."

Jane straightened, ready to accept the challenge.

In a shadowed corner of an inn on the border between Kildare Manor and the village of Kildare, a dark-cloaked woman sat before the minion she'd hired to spy on the new laird.

"I am disappointed in you," she said, her voice sharp. "You have nothing to report? Surely you can get close enough to hear what they are talking about."

The man didn't answer directly. "He keeps himself surrounded by friends. It has been difficult to get close without anyone seeing me."

"When did he have time to make friends, having spent so many months in gaol?" Her anger flared. She had wanted Claire to go in, do as she'd been told, then leave her to finish the ruination of Lord Kildare. "Who are these friends?"

"They are no danger to your plans. They merely brought his bride to him. They will desert him, I've no doubt, when they see the ruin of his estate. Two of the women are pregnant. Surely their husbands will want to keep them out of harm's way by taking them back to their homes. Kildare will be alone with the girl before long."

Despite the hood that shielded her face, she stared at the man, hard. Pleasure flooded her when he flinched. "Don't come back here until you have something to report. If you disappoint me again . . ." She let the words trail off, but she knew the man understood their intent. She would threaten and she would punish those who did not do as she commanded. The twisted, lifeless body of the man's predecessor was proof of that. She might be a woman, but she did not fear soiling her hands if it achieved her goal of tormenting, then burying Jules MacIntyre. Claire would be the means by which she would gain her revenge, thanks to Jules's father. She had blackmailed James Grayson into revealing the intentions of Jules's father. But instead of a gift to his son, the father had given her a means to Jules's end when he'd found a "real" Claire to play the part of the fabricated bride. The man had meant to finally make amends to his son for a lifetime of neglect. Instead, he had provided the perfect vehicle for her own revenge.

Death would be a welcome relief when she was through with this last and final Lord Kildare.

From the back of his horse, Arthur Cabot narrowed his gaze on the wreck that was Kildare Manor. Why had the past Lord Kildare let his own estate go to ruin? The Kildares had always taken great care of the old place; he knew this as a son of one of their tenants.

Arthur could see the old farm now, across the fallow field in between two rock hedges. His parents had left the farm five years ago. After the old woman's death.

That was when things started to change. Lord Kildare had lost not only his second wife, he'd lost his younger son, and some said his will to live. He gambled with money he didn't have. And the money he did have vanished before any of the bills were paid or before he reinvested in the estate. That's when the crofters and the servants started drifting away.

Arthur rode up the weed-lined drive and dismounted in the courtyard, hesitating instead of charging forward as his directive demanded. His thoughts turned to the past, when he had left the Kildare estate at fifteen to move to town with his parents, in their effort to find a better life. And now he was back. Not as a tenant farmer's son, but on another mission. He had assumed the identity of a debt collector. Such a role was not too big a stretch. Lord Kildare owed his creditors a goodly sum.

The poor bastard.

Arthur stared at the closed doorway. He had no choice but to pressure the man into paying him something, adding a burden he was certain the new laird did not need. But his role demanded he stay close to Lord Kildare, and the woman who claimed to be his new wife.

Funny business that. Arthur had been watching the manor since Lord Kildare had arrived. So far the man's only journey had been to the village with a cartload of carpets. He had returned several hours later with women to help him clean the place.

So when had the man acquired a wife?

Arthur needed to find out more about the situation. Boldly, he rapped on the door. It took several minutes before the door slid open a crack to reveal a watery eye. "What do ye want?"

"I am here to collect upon the debts of Lord Kildare."

The door slid closed, but not before Arthur slipped his booted foot in between the door and the frame. "Now, let's not be unfriendly, my good sir. I must speak with Lord Kildare immediately."

With a heavy sigh, the old man surrendered. "Wait here," he said as he shuffled away.

Arthur waited outside the doorway, uncertain if he had been invited inside, or if the old man had truly meant him to remain standing at the doorway, staring into the faded and dilapidated house.

Several moments later, the steward returned alone. Arthur frowned. The old man was supposed to bring him the laird of the manor. The servant held out his hand. "As partial payment on whatever yer owed."

Arthur held out his hand to receive one small copper farthing. Before he could object to the sum, the massive oak door was closed tight.

One farthing.

Kildare owed a far sight more than that. It was time to turn up the pressure and make his presence known.

Claire wandered out of the house in an effort to escape not only her guests, but the man who had been so angry with her a short while ago. He did not want her here. That much was obvious. Outside, it was easier to push aside the angry look on his face, his harsh words.

She wandered across the courtyard to the back of the house, then down toward the water. Kildare Manor sat on the eastern shore of Loch Awe. From the grassy shore, she could see the rich rolling hills, covered in a blanket of heather that eased into the cold waters of the loch. The pristine reflection of the puffy clouds in the blue sky above shimmered in the steely gray water below.

The scenery was some of the prettiest she had ever seen in Scotland. Claire looked around with a sigh of pleasure until she turned back toward the manor itself. Surrounded by waist-high grass and covered in briars up to the roofline, Kildare Manor looked as neglected as it was lonely. She'd only been in the house for less than an hour, and she felt the emptiness, the grief, that had been too much a part of its history. It was as if the house mourned the loss of those who had once been so vibrant within its walls.

She knew the history of the house—the stories of Lady Kildare's mysterious death and Jules's subsequent trial for murder. Every story about the Kildares and their cursed estate had reached even the fringes of society where she existed. She also recognized the desperation and loneliness in her new husband's eyes. Those same emotions had been her constant companions since she was twelve years of age, when she'd been cast into the world with no family and no home.

But she was more fortunate than most women who had suffered her fate. Her father had left a small sum of money, and that had helped convince the neighbors to take her in and raise her alongside their own children.

But what about Jules? He'd had a family to care for him. Hadn't he? He'd had a home, and despite the neglect, Kildare Manor continued on. The place was not dead. It was merely sleeping, waiting for the right person to wake it up, to help it shed its past and begin again.

Would the newest earl be that person? Could she help him set the manor back to rights? Would he let her if she tried?

Judging by their earlier conversation, she doubted it. But even though he wanted her gone, and as soon as possible, she would do what she could in the next fortnight to set his house in order. Perhaps doing so would help her secure a way to his heart, even if temporarily.

Lost in thought, Claire picked her way through the waist-high grass at the shoreline toward a small stone building. It appeared as if it was used at one time to house boats and fishing paraphernalia, if the pile of decaying oars, rotting nets, and pocked floats were any indication. A single rowboat leaned against the side of the building. It was covered in withered leaves from a long-ago winter, caught up in spiderwebs from bow to stern.

Claire moved to the doorway and tried the latch. Locked. She moved on, rounding the other side of the small building when she discovered a rusted old scythe and a hoe. She picked up the scythe. The handle was weathered and dry and felt rough against her palm, but the blade, despite its color, looked like it might still do the job for which it had been intended.

Moving back to the grass, Claire gripped the top handle in her left hand and the central handle in her right. She held the blade close to the ground and swung at the swath of tall grass in front of her. To her delight, the blade sliced through the narrow patch of grass. She tried again, widening her stroke, but the grass only bent beneath the assault this time.

The blade was sharp enough, she knew from the first stroke. Pressing her lips together in determination, she tried again, returning to the small stroke she had made at first. Again, the grass fell to the left of the blade. A sense of accomplishment moved through her at the small path she had created. She continued scything, moving the blade from right to left, twisting her body in rhythm with each stroke.

Her arms ached at the unusual and contained movements, but she didn't care. She was doing something productive that she hoped would help her win Jules's favor.

"Stop." The harsh word hung in the air.

Her movements ceased. Her muscles tightened and her nerves leapt. Jules.

In a suspended moment, she became aware of two things. One, Jules stood behind her. Two, with the soft swoosh of the blade arrested, a loud and persistent hissing sound came from in front of her.

Before her mind could reconcile the sound, she was hauled back against Jules's chest. The scythe flew from her hands just as a brown snake with a black zigzag stripe along its back struck where she had been standing a heartbeat ago.

"A snake?" A scream wedged itself in her throat, but she held it back.

"An adder." Jules's rich baritone cut through her terror. He scooped her up in his arms and strode back toward the manor.

Claire suddenly became aware of the muscular arms that held her against an equally solid chest. Over his shoulder she looked back. The snake slithered toward them, then stopped at their retreat. The snake coiled into an S-shape once more, prepared to strike should they change their direction.

"What were you doing?" Those captivating blue eyes searched hers suspiciously.

She swallowed. "I was trying to cut the grass."

He looked unamused. "There are snakes in the grass."

"Was it poisonous?" she asked hesitantly, her heart still pounding.

"Yes." He took a deep, exaggerated breath.

"Then why did you save me?" she asked with a frown. "If it had bitten me, all your 'wife' problems would be at an end."

His heated glare sent a shiver over her flesh. "Had it struck you, you would not have died, but the next three days would have been very painful, painful enough that you might have wished you had died." He set her down and stepped back, his face blank. "You are safe now. Stay out of the grass."

She mourned the loss of his warmth. Her legs trembled beneath her, but she would never let him see such a weakness. She straightened. "Thank you."

He nodded as he turned away.

"How long have you been back at Kildare Manor?" she asked in an effort to keep him with her. Suddenly being alone seemed worse than being subjected to his anger.

"Only a few days." He stopped walking and turned around. "Why?"

She shrugged. "I merely wondered—"

"Why the place is so run down?" Though the words were edged, there was an amused gleam in his eyes that said he wasn't as angry as he sounded.

She looked askance at him. "It is not my place to judge you. I know you have suffered the loss of your father and your brother three weeks ago. I cannot imagine the pain you must be feeling."

He frowned and the light in his eyes vanished. "I had been absent from their lives for many years. As far as I was concerned, they died years ago."

"Then we have at least that in common."

His body uncoiled slightly at the words. His brow puzzled. "You mentioned you had no family." He frowned. "And yet, you received a missive from them earlier today."

She paled. "The missive was from friends who I consider family."

It was a lie, and from the look on his face he knew it but asked instead, "Then what happened to your family?"

"They all perished in the plague of 1666."

His frown deepened. "You were unaffected by the disease?"

"I developed spots, but for some reason, I was the only one to survive," she said quietly. "Whether it was a blessing or a curse, I cannot say. It was a long time ago."

His gaze fixed on hers. The compassion in his blue eyes startled her. "You've been alone all this time?"

"No," she said, hardly daring to breathe as he took two steps toward her. "I lived with a local family for a while after my parents died. The father was a painter and he taught me alongside his own children. When I was fifteen, he died, and I left their home so that I would no longer be a burden on the family."

"How long ago was that?" he asked as he moved one hand up to cup her cheek. His fingers stroked her skin, then shifted to one tendril of her hair that refused to stay coiled with the rest.

"I've been on my own for five years." She could feel his fingers twining in her hair.

He wasn't looking at her, he was staring at his hand in her hair, as if he were committing the texture and feel of it to memory. Then, his gaze returned to her face so fast it actually made her gasp. "Then my solicitor shows up and offers you marriage to me?"

She shrugged. When he put it that way, what she had done sounded desperate and conniving. "I grew weary of being alone." It was partially the truth. She had been alone for so long that she had never expected anything else. Her thoughts about Kildare Manor suddenly came back to her. She, Jules, and the house were all alone and a little desolate.

If only things were different. If they had met under different circumstances, perhaps . . . but that could never be. She came to Kildare Manor for one reason and one reason only—to save the girls.

Despite the reminder of her purpose, her heart hammered at his closeness. She could smell his warm, clean skin as he tugged her slightly closer with the end of her hair. There was no pain, only an incredible tension as she shifted forward.

He fixed his startling blue eyes on her. The raw hunger there made her cheeks warm, and a shiver slid down her spine. He leaned forward, his face just to the side of hers. His warm breath brushed her cheek in a seductive flutter.

Her breasts tightened.

Slowly, his fingers left her hair to tilt her chin up. His gaze held hers, enthralled, as he searched her face for something. "I'm telling you the truth," she said, as though the words were the answer to any question he might ask.

A half smile hovered on his lips as he brought them down to hers.

Claire moaned at the contact. This kiss was different than the last one. This one was gentle. Tender.

And it made her long for more of the same.

He left her lips to trail a blazing path down her jaw to her neck. "You are so very tempting," he whispered, as he traced the curve of her ear with his tongue. "But you are better off without me."

He pulled back and stepped away. That was when she saw Jane and Nicholas in the distance behind him.

Had he known they were there? Was that the only reason he had kissed her? Her body on fire, she watched as he left her alone once more.

Her heart lurched. She was a fool to think someone with his place in society could ever care about a common woman with no family like her.

She stared after Jules as she pushed a nonexistent lock of hair from her forehead. She tried to keep breathing as he walked away. He was all that stood between her and total devastation.

She would not fail.

Jules joined Nicholas and Jane as he fought the raging need inside him. It was raw and vicious and made him ache for all he had experienced in that one sweet kiss, but knew he could never really have, because the woman was a fraud, and he had already given the tattered remains of his heart away. That was exactly as it had to remain.

"Is Claire coming?" Nicholas asked, his gaze shifting between Jules and Claire.

She remained exactly where he had left her, a look of indecision on her face as to whether she would rather approach him, or turn back toward the snake. She was better off with the snake.

Jules had to put her out of his thoughts. "Claire will join us when she is ready."

"Perhaps I should go talk with her," Jane said.

Jules stalled her with a hand on her arm. "Leave her be."

Jane frowned, but did as he asked.

"We've found some cards and thought you might like to join us in a game of faro."

"What are the stakes?" Jules asked distractedly.

"We found some seeds to use as checks. No one need lose any money over the game." Jane paled as though she suddenly realized the cut of her words. "Oh, Jules, I did not mean—"

"Sounds well enough. Let us have at it," he interrupted, not wanting to hear her apology. He knew he had no funds. Obviously they all knew he had no funds. Why pretend otherwise?

Cards. It was the distraction he needed. As Nicholas and Jane turned back toward the manor, Jules allowed himself one last look at Claire. Their gazes met. He thought he saw a tear on her cheek, but he couldn't be certain because she turned and headed back toward the loch.

He frowned. Why was she crying? Surely not for him.

He watched until the sight of her bright copper head disappeared from view, and once again the loneliness of his life settled about him. The thought that he had contributed to her sadness twisted his insides into a tight, throbbing knot. He spun away and strode back to the house.

He had a wife.

He wanted to ignore her. He wanted to make her go away. But whether she stayed or left, he suddenly realized, nothing would be the same ever again.

Nothing.

The next morning, Claire snuggled deeper into the covers. Sleep had eluded her during the night no matter how hard she had tried to gather it to her. As a result, her head felt like a leaden weight on the pillow as she stared into the dusky gray of dawn.

She had spent the rest of the afternoon and evening away from Jules and his friends. No one had come to find her, to offer her a meal, or to even see if she had returned from the loch. Her throat tightened for a heartbeat before she shoved her sadness away. Jules and his friends had ignored her yesterday. And she had made it easy for them to do so.

Today, she would not be a passive miss. No, today she had plans. She would start her day by tackling the house. She had learned how to keep a house over the years. She would apply that knowledge here, and turn around what she could in the manor. Then she would see about winning over his friends. If they started to trust her, perhaps Jules would as well. And then, finally, she would play up to her husband. She had to find some way to win his heart.

Her eyes opened into the twilight. What was she willing to do to win his affection? Would she willingly give herself to him if it helped achieve her goal? Was she that kind of woman?

She hoped not . . . and yet . . . he was her husband. Such things were allowed, even expected between a man and his wife. Even so, self-doubt crept past her determination. What if he'd left her alone last night because he didn't find her in the least bit tempting?

He had walked away from their kiss as though it had cost him nothing at all, while she had spent the better part of the night trying to forget the feel of his warm, seductive lips on her mouth.

She sighed at the memory. If he had been so immune to her, then why save her from the snake? Why kiss her at all? She frowned. He had to find her at least somewhat appealing. She had left behind that gawkish, unrefined girl she had once been years ago. She could do nothing about the brightness of her hair, or the paleness of her skin, but she had learned proper manners and ways of holding herself that could at least accentuate her finer points. She had a small waist. And more than once men had commented on her upright posture. That was a good thing in a refined wife, was it not?

Claire closed her eyes once more, still hanging on to hope that sleep might yet come. One night of her bridegroom ignoring her would not turn her from her plans. Too much was at stake with Penelope, Anna, and Eloise. They needed her to be strong.

And as for his friends? She had seen the way Nicholas had appraised her yesterday. He, if not all of them, suspected all was not as she claimed between herself and Jules.

Claire released a groan and turned her face into her pillow, shielding herself from the faint light of dawn and the challenges awaiting her with the coming of the new day.

She had to make Jules fall in love with her. The memory of his arm curled around her waist brought heat to her cheeks. She drew in a breath, then recalled the soft scent of mint that had curled around her senses when he had drawn her close.

She would do whatever it took to make certain her girls would have the future they deserved. As their guardian, she had to see her plans with Jules through. Despite her claims yesterday, she would do anything at all to make that happen. Anything at all. Her life and her reputation did not matter. It was the three young women whose livelihood she controlled because they had no one else. That knowledge alone would steady her in her task.

As soon as morning arrived, she would begin again, and do things right this time.

The thought had barely formed when a loud explosion vibrated just outside her window. Caught between sleep and awareness, Claire twisted out of the tangle of sheets and sat up, staring into the predawn light.

Her head ached dully, and she had the uneasy feeling something disturbing had happened. What could make that kind of noise so early in the morning? The sound came again. Two, three times. Whatever the sounds were, they were coming from beneath her tower window.

"For heaven's sake," Claire cried, throwing off the covers and jumping out of bed with more energy than she truly felt after a night of little sleep. She hastened to the shutters and released the latch, then peered out into the faint light of dawn. Beneath her she could make out three dark shapes. Men.

As her eyes adjusted to the light, she saw not just any men, but Jules, David, and Nicholas. Another clatter of noise filled the peaceful morning as each man pointed a blunderbuss level with the grass and fired.

The shutters opening must have made a sound because Jules turned toward her. A satisfied smile tugged at the corners of his lips. "Did we wake you?" he called from below.

He was hunting. Beneath her window. Nothing suspicious about that. Closing her eyes for a brief moment, Claire released a long sigh. He would not make her task an easy one. "How are the pheasant this morning?" she asked, ignoring his barb.

"We've taken four already," David called up to her.

"Sounds like we will feast for supper tonight," she said, smiling at her husband with as much friendly candor as she could muster so early in the morning.

"That we will," Jules said. His gaze lost its softness and his smile faded. "'Tis a meal you will be preparing for us all."

Claire tried to keep her smile. As his wife, she was the head of his household staff. She was not much of a cook herself, but she could certainly direct others in cooking the meal. "It will be my pleasure to assist the cook in the preparation of the meal."

"We have no cook, Claire darling." The endearment was spoken so sweetly, yet the look in his eyes was anything but sincere. "I have had no time since my return to hire a proper staff. You will have to do it yourself."

Claire frowned darkly into the silvered light that surrounded her husband. She could not, absolutely would not, fold at the first challenge he threw out to her. She straightened. "Supper will be served at eight o'clock on the west terrace."

She turned her gaze toward the sky, to the pink fingers of light streaking through the morning haze. "It looks to be a warm day ahead; let us relax and enjoy ourselves and our company out in the evening breeze."

"The day has yet to begin and you are already forecasting its direction," Jules replied with a hint of annoyance.

"Oh, I can forecast a great many things, Jules MacIntyre. The weather is an easy one. The unhappy response of your female guests to your morning shooting is another, and that you will delight in the supper I prepare is yet a third."

"We will see about that," he replied with a fierce challenge in his eyes.

With a bright, artificial smile, Claire replied, "Indeed, we will." Not waiting for a response, she closed the shutters and returned to her bed. She collapsed onto the linens and pulled the pillow up over her head. Claire closed her eyes and prayed for a moment that she could actually cook something edible for Jules and his guests.

Wearily, she turned onto her back and stared at the ceiling once more. She could fret about the meal and her attempt to lure Jules to care for her, or she could get up and try to determine how to help herself.

The thought was all the encouragement Claire needed. Her heart suddenly leaping with renewed purpose, she got out of bed, dressed carefully in a lavender gown she knew made her hair look more gold than red, and left her chamber.

She also knew she should head downstairs, to the kitchen, and see to preparing some sort of meal for their guests to break their fast, but instead the silence of the house beckoned. Jules was outside with his male guests. Jane and Margaret were still abed. Now was the perfect time to explore the dark secrets of Kildare Manor. Not that she expected to find anything. Jules was far too clever for that.

But another question had burned through her thoughts in the silence of the night. Why was she here? Obviously someone was manipulating both her and Jules, but to what end?

Even in Edinburgh the stories of Jules MacIntyre poisoning his stepmother had spread through the gossip mills. The crime had supposedly happened in this very house. But if Jules had been exonerated of the crime, then who had murdered the woman?

That question filled her thoughts as Claire reached for the candlestick near the hearth and lit the wick with the last remaining coals from the fire. Perhaps she could learn more about her husband from his home. There had to be traces from his past life here that still remained, things she could use to understand him better.

Claire walked silently down the curling staircase, past the other bedchambers, to the staircase at the opposite end of the hall. The servants' staircase would provide the access she needed with a modicum of stealth as the stairwell shifted behind the wall and into a passage where only the servants usually tread.

The candle cut a pale yellow-gold swath through the darkness as she ascended the stairs. The ancient wood creaked beneath her feet. Claire flinched at each sound, but continued steadily forward. Her progress up the stairs was like entering a foreign land, revealing only a hint at a time of what lay ahead.

At the top of the stairs she came to a passage that led back to the hallway with three doors on the right and one on the left. It was the door on the left that caught her attention. Barring the entrance were several pieces of wood in a crisscross pattern. Claire reached through the wood and found the latch. She tried the handle and was surprised when the door opened easily, despite the wooden deterrent.

Obviously, the wood had been placed there with the hope of keeping others out. Claire hesitated as she bit down on her lip. Even though she was fairly certain Jules would be upset if he discovered her there, Claire gripped one of the boards at waist height and pulled until first one side of the board then the other came free. Setting the wood on the floor near the door, she bent over and peeked through the opening she had made.

Her candle illuminated only a few feet in front of her. She could see a finely tiled floor and what appeared to be a large, open chamber. If she wanted to discover more, she would have to go inside. The secrets she needed to uncover about her husband might very well be contained in this room.

Without stopping to think about what she was doing, she set the candleholder on the floor just inside the door and set to work on removing two more of the boards. In no time, she had created a hole large enough for her body to slip through.

Claire straightened and looked about her at the large, empty room, and at the layers of dust covering the floor. No one had been in this chamber for years. She held her candle before her as she stepped farther inside. Only then did she realize the room was not entirely empty.

A small table sat off to the right with one chair tucked neatly beneath it. The other chair lay on the floor, overturned. On the table was a candleholder, containing only a wax stub. Regardless, Claire held her own candle to the wick and welcomed the second sputtering light that illuminated the eerie chamber. Near the candle on the table was a single overturned teacup laying mere inches from its matching saucer.

Claire frowned into the silver-gray light. How odd that the cup and the chair remained as though something had happened in the chamber mere moments ago, when the dust proved otherwise. *Dust and a teacup.* Claire repressed a shudder. The gossip had said Jules's stepmother had died after ingesting poisoned tea Jules himself had served her.

Was this where his stepmother met her end?

"You are not allowed up here," said a biting voice from the doorway behind her.

Claire swung around at the scathing tone of Jules's voice. Her heart hammered in her chest. "I was exploring my new home."

"This is not your home." Even in the half-light she could see his face was as hard and forbidding as a granite sculpture. He did not bother to come forward but remained where he was, his shoulder propped negligently against the door frame, his arms folded across his chest, watching her.

By the cynical look in his blue eyes, she could see he was angry. "The boards across the door said, 'please, do come in?'" he drawled sarcastically.

"They piqued my curiosity."

"It was curiosity that brought you to my door, then?"

Claire's momentary shock at him discovering her trespassing gave way to her own anger. "It was your offer of marriage that brought me here," she said tightly.

"I've had enough of this charade, Claire. I did not offer you marriage, and you damn well know it."

She knew his reaction was appropriate for the situation. She had invaded his life and now this chamber, and yet she could not quell the spark of irritation that flared. She yanked the ring off her left hand. Moving toward him, she gripped his hand and placed the ring against his palm.

"Explain that," she demanded, backing a safe distance away and waiting. Her emotions veered crazily from humiliation to anger to mirth at the absurdity of this situation. She was in the wrong for violating his privacy, but how dare he challenge her honesty yet again. They were legally married. That much was true. Why they were married was her secret to keep.

"Another ploy?" he drawled cynically as he plucked the ring from his palm with his opposite hand. He brought the slim gold band with three large sapphires up to inspect it. His face paled. "Where did you get this?"

"From your solicitor as a token of your affection." A wayward chuckle bubbled up inside her. "Ha. We both know that to be decidedly untrue."

His brows drew together. "My mother's ring."

"So it would seem." Claire frowned at his odd response. All his anger had vanished. Instead, shocked surprise lingered in his voice. "When Mr. Grayson gave it to me, he said it was important to you, maybe even priceless because it was the only reminder you had of the woman who bore you."

"You have my mother's ring?"

"That was what your note to me explained."

"My note?" His gaze turned sharp, as though no longer shocked by her words.

"The one you sent with the ring." Claire took a step back, suddenly weary.

"You do not happen to have this note in your possession, do you?" He brought his gaze to hers, cynical contempt blazing in the depths of his eyes.

"Your solicitor took it back from me after sliding your ring on my finger."

"Of course he did. Why leave proof of your deception for others to dispute."

Claire felt physically ill at the thought that he might turn her away without even giving her a chance. She swallowed against the dryness in her throat. The girls. How could she protect them? How could she find them? She had tried before agreeing to this marriage, and had failed.

"This is madness. Utter madness," Claire cried. The lives of the girls were at stake. She had to turn this situation around.

"Madness has been the bane of my life for the last four years. Why would things be any different now?" he asked. The edge to his voice had lessened, and that surprised her.

"What can I do to show you how sincere I am about being a good wife to you?"

"Nothing, not until I know the truth."

"And how will you get that, if not from me?"

"I've sent for my solicitor. When he arrives we will discover the truth." Jules came closer, and suddenly his presence was threatening again. "And until then, I want you close, where I can see you, rather than operating behind my back."

Not for the first time, Claire found herself at a loss to understand him. First he wanted her to go. Now he wanted her to stay.

Holding on to her ring proved to her that he wasn't about to claim her as his bride just yet either.

Terrified her tears were going to fall, Claire tipped her head back, inspecting the ceiling. Through a haze of tears she realized she could accept his terms. For now, she would be allowed to stay and to play the part of his wife. And she intended to use that time wisely, to convince him she belonged by his side. Too much was at stake to allow for anything else.

Only two things stood in her way. The first was the enigmatic man who no longer looked at her. Instead he gazed off into the far corners of the room, his profile taut. The second was the pheasant she would have to prepare for supper.

The pheasant seemed far less of a challenge than the man.

After the midday meal of bread, cheese, and sliced apples, Claire made her way to the kitchen. Her guests had been kind about her simple luncheon, but she was certain they expected something much more hearty for supper.

Jules had made it clear she was to prepare the pheasant without help from anyone else. And although both Jane and Margaret had offered their assistance, Jules had demanded all the others walk the estate with him, leaving her with no help, which was perfectly fine with Claire. She wanted to prove to him she was capable of any task he threw her way.

Claire stood in the kitchen alone, staring down at the vacant gazes of the four dead birds Jules had left her on the wooden table. She had to pluck and roast the birds. She only knew how to cook simple foods: porridge, spitted meats, soups. Once she had successfully cooked a trout Penelope had plucked from the river. But pheasant . . .

For a moment Claire stood there, nervously rubbing the palms of her hands against her linen skirt before she gingerly touched one wing, extended it fully, then let it drop back to the table with a groan. Perhaps it would be best to simply cut off the wings, the head, and the feet. But what should she do about the rest of the feathers?

She shifted her gaze from the pheasant to a large pot near the hearth. If she dipped the birds in boiling water, would their feathers come off, or would she end up with a wet mess instead? Perhaps she should try plucking the birds.

With a gentle stroke, she brushed the bird's brownish-red chest upward, then gripped a small cluster of feathers and tugged down. They came out easily enough, but there were hundreds more. She would be plucking feathers for hours.

She offered the birds an apologetic smile. "You will be glorious by the time I am through with you. I will prevail, you will see," she said with more confidence than she felt.

Six hours later, her brow damp with perspiration, Claire finished cooking dinner. The pheasants were not as plump as she would have liked, and two of the birds that were farthest out on the spit were more black than golden brown. The carrots appeared a little undercooked, while the turnips and leeks were more like charcoal than vegetables. Regardless, she placed everything onto the serving trays and finished with a heavy sigh.

Disappointed in her culinary skills, she had no choice but to try something else if she were to win this round against Jules.

She had never used her feminine wiles to attract a man before. Tonight, she would use those attributes to the fullest in order to succeed where her meal had failed.

Before the night was through, Jules MacIntyre would not know what hit him.

Later that evening, Jules gathered with his guests in what used to be the green salon, but was now more a faded, pale beige color. Water stains streaked the walls, oddly enough lending some relief to the tedium of the unending neutrality. With no furnishings on which to sit, the six of them stood, waiting for Claire to join them.

What could be keeping her? Fin reported she had been in the kitchen since after luncheon. When he'd given her the task of cooking for his friends, he had expected her to rebel. She had not. But that was hours ago. What could be keeping her? Jules raised his chin and headed toward the door.

"I will see what is keeping Claire."

He made it as far as the hearth when she abruptly arrived. At the sight of her, his breath stilled and the room faded away.

She appeared, framed by the doorway, like a vision from above, clad in a shimmering green gown that was neither jade nor emerald, but somewhere in between. The room around her suddenly warmed from its tired beige to a brighter pale green, as though welcoming its mistress.

Claire remained in the doorway. "My apologies. Our supper is finally ready and laid out for us on the west terrace."

She had done it?

Jules peeled his gaze from her to address his other guests, then startled as he noted the satisfied smile on Jane's lips, and the appreciative gazes on Hollister's, Nicholas's, and even David's faces.

In that moment of stunned silence, he turned back to Claire and allowed his gaze to linger on the low, rounded neckline that offered a tantalizing view of her smooth, voluptuous flesh, and the long bodice emphasizing a tiny waist. The cap sleeves and full skirt needed no ornamentation other than that given by her hair. One long curl had escaped her tight chignon, which was swept back and held tight with a single emerald clip.

She was a vision of perfection, beauty, and sensuality all rolled into one, and so very different from the woman who had entered his home and his life yesterday. Before this moment he had never really considered what his "made up" Claire would look like, but he imagined she would look very similar to the stunning woman who stood before him now.

Gracefully, the real Claire came forward and slipped her hand through Jules's arm hanging loosely at his side. "If we are ready, let us escort you all to supper."

Jules shook his head to clear it. "Yes, supper," he managed dryly. He allowed himself to be swept forward for a moment before he caught himself. What was he doing? He did not need to play along with this fantasy. As soon as Grayson arrived, he would have his answers.

Jules forced himself to stop thinking of Claire. He had enough real worries to contend with. He cast a sideways look at his companion. "So you managed to cook those birds, did you?"

"I cannot be the judge of my own cooking." She would not meet his curious gaze.

"You burned everything."

She lifted her chin. "I did my best. The cooking was difficult, but not as hard as preparing the birds to cook," she said, turning her gaze to his. "I had never done that before. And from this moment forward, I will be far more grateful to those whose task it is to pluck and clean our fowl." Sincerity shone in the depths of her golden eyes, and for a second time that night he found himself drawn to her against his will by some strange magnetism she seemed to radiate.

Standing by her side, even now he felt angered and exhilarated at the same moment. Part of him felt compelled to win her approval, while another part rejoiced at the difficulty she admitted with her cooking efforts. The thought had a sobering effect on him as they continued toward the terrace and the table and chairs that had been sent up from the village only this morning.

After he had paid for all the new furnishings and restocked the larder, there was precious little money left from the sale of the carpets. And other than a few more places to sit, and a bit of food in their bellies, he was no better off than he had been five days past.

Yet even as the thoughts materialized, he knew they were untrue. He was much better off, even in his impoverished state, than he was this time last year. As a free man, even a poor one, he had so many more options than he'd had wasting away in gaol. He had to remember that, always.

Nothing would ever be as bad as that ever again. He would find a way to turn his fate, but he would do so alone. Self-preservation demanded nothing less.

He realized, looking across the table at Jane and her slightly rounded belly, that it wasn't the fact that he could not have her for his own that made him so determined to remain alone for the remainder of his days. It was that he felt he did not deserve such happiness as that which he saw in his friend's eyes.

He was unlovable.

Had not his own father proven that to him time and again over the years with his neglect, with his avoidance when Jules had caused trouble merely to get attention, and by not freeing him from gaol?

His gaze shifted back to Claire. It was better this way, for her to leave before she could discover his true nature. After tonight, he would return to his lonely and isolated state.

One last supper. He allowed himself a small smile at his unintended pun.

This would be their last meal together. In the morning Grayson should arrive. He would prove Claire's claims about their marriage untrue, and the woman before him would be on her way back to the mist from which she had come.

Perhaps then he would tell his friends the truth about creating a bride. Surely, if he would go so far as to make up a wife to get them off his back, they would stand down for at least a little while in their plans to see him happily wed. Wouldn't they?

Beneath the fading light of the day, the meal was served. The meat was dry, the vegetables burned to a crisp, except for the carrots, which were almost as crunchy as the pheasant. Despite Claire's disaster of a meal, the evening had not gone badly.

The soft sounds of the night filled the air, as did the lush fragrance of the wild lilies and roses. The golden flames from several torches danced in the lightest of breezes, and as the sun set, the brightness transformed the terrace from the ruin that it had become into a magical retreat.

After they had finished eating, Jules leaned back and observed the woman who, despite his efforts to stay focused on Jane, had stolen his attention all night.

The woman before him was not the skittish young woman he'd met yesterday. No, this Claire was seductive, alluring, confident, and, if he were honest with himself, hard to resist. Tonight her golden eyes lit up with a mixture of laughter and intelligence as those gathered had discussed the foundation of the National Library in Edinburgh, a comet in the northern sky that was visible to the naked eye, and the latest painting of the Countess of Lauderdale to be revealed by Scottish painter John Scougall.

More seriously, they talked about the latest battle at Aird's Moss between the Covenanters and the government dragoons. "They say Reverend Richard Cameron was killed, along with eight of his men," Hollister recounted as he sipped a small glass of whiskey. All the men supported the side of the Covenanters, although none of them had signed the covenant themselves.

"Twenty-eight government soldiers lost their lives," David said quietly, his voice distant as he clenched his fists on the table.

"When will the fighting end?" Jane asked, her voice tight. The pain in her eyes was tangible.

Nicholas said nothing as he stood, then positioned himself behind Jane, placing his hands on her shoulders. But Jules saw the anguish in Nicholas's eyes at the unspoken reference to her brother, who had yet to return from the conflict last year at Bothwell Bridge between the Covenanters and the government forces. Jane looked up at her husband. Their gazes locked. Something passed between them, a shared look that left Jules raw. To be so loved . . .

Nicholas pulled Jane's chair away from the table and took her hand, helping her to her feet. "Thank you for the lovely supper, Claire, but I think it is time for Jane and me to retire."

"It's the baby that makes me tired," Jane said.

Margaret and Hollister stood as well. Margaret let her hand drift to her softly extended belly. "Perhaps all of us could use some sleep after the ruckus that had us all awake before dawn." She cast Jules a look that said she'd been disturbed from her sleep by the early morning noise.

He shrugged. "Without that ruckus we would not have had this . . ." He paused, trying to find a word to describe the meal that would not hurt Claire's feelings. When nothing came to mind, he simply said, "dinner." He watched as Claire's cheeks warmed and she dropped her gaze to her hands.

David excused himself with the others, and soon Jules and Claire were very much alone on the terrace. The torchlight danced in the breeze, and silence hovered between them until he lifted the bottle of whiskey, poured a splash into two cups, and handed her one. "It's my family's own recipe."

Claire frowned at the amber liquid. "I have never had spirits before."

"Here's to the first of many firsts. Your first wifely meal cooked, your first whiskey, your first night alone with me." As his words faded into the night, he raised his cup to hers, then took a drink.

She raised her cup and took a tiny sip, and her eyes flared wide. "It's like drinking fire. Fire might actually be easier to swallow."

He grinned sympathetically and set down his cup. "It does take some getting used to."

"This is what you were raised on?" she asked, her voice raspy from the liquid.

He shook his head. "I was raised by Jane's father until my own sire felt it necessary for me to return to the family fold." He took another long sip of his whiskey, allowing the "liquid fire," as Claire had aptly called it, to numb his senses. Tonight he longed for an escape from his burdens, and to stare into Claire's warm and sensual gaze. "Now it is my turn to ask you something."

She set her cup down at arm's length, then returned her smiling gaze to his. "You may ask me three questions. That is your quota for one night."

"Why three?" he asked, chuckling.

"One is too few and four might become far too personal. So three seemed to be just right," she responded with a teasing tone and a lazy smile. "But I demand the same in return."

"Very well. Tell me, Claire, when you are not posing as someone's wife, what do you do?"

Her smile fading, she leaned back in her chair. "I am a teacher. That is how I have been able to be on my own for the past five years."

"A teacher?" He hadn't expected that, although he wasn't certain what he expected. When they'd first met, she'd said her father was a scholar, and that had led him to believe she was some spoiled aristocrat's daughter. Yet if that were true, why would she ruin herself on the altar of matrimony, especially to someone like him? "What do you teach?"

"Art mostly, but I have also taught my girls to read, to write, and to do their numbers."

He gave her a puzzled look. "You were taught those things?"

She nodded. "My father was insistent that I learn everything I could. Then when my parents died, I was fortunate to be taken in by a family who believed in educating their daughters as well as their sons and my education continued."

"Who do you teach?"

Claire fingered a locket on a chain around her neck. "I teach young women who have the desire to paint and have a need to support themselves."

Not for the first time, Jules found himself at a loss to understand her. "Why would women, especially young women, need to support themselves? Isn't that what marriage is for?"

"Marriage is not always the answer, especially when certain husbands don't believe their bond is true," she said dryly. "It is men like you who have every advantage, while women have very few, if any at all."

"Like you."

"Like me," she said softly.

"You think you have me all figured out, don't you?" he replied, watching her closely.

"No," she said with a shake of her head. "I do not know much about you. And I fear there are very few people in this life with whom you will bare your soul, or even accept as your friend."

"If that is true, then where does that leave you?"

"That is your ninth question, and I still have yet to ask even one." She pushed back from the table. "In answer to your last question, I do not see myself ever reaching your inner circle, despite our relationship."

The anguish in her voice troubled him before he tensed. "We have no relationship," he countered, suddenly disgusted with himself.

He would not fall for her helplessness again. Damnation, the woman was a master at getting under his skin.

Claire stood, staring at him with hurt in her eyes. "You have made it perfectly obvious I am unwanted, but as I have nowhere else to go, consider yourself burdened with me. That is your plight, husband, until you prove me wrong." She turned and headed back toward the manor.

He stared at his adversary with a crazy mixture of anger and regret as she disappeared from view. He should go after her. He should do the right thing and apologize. Except the "right" thing was what he had always done . . . and that had landed him in this situation in the first place. He had done the right thing by returning home from Jane's father's employ when his father had demanded. He had come home to meet his new mother full of hope and eager to do the right thing. But that hope had turned to despair when at the age of twenty-one he'd been charged with her murder. Nay, the right thing was not always the best thing to do.

Jules looked around the terrace in the sudden silence and realized the only thing he could do in these circumstances was the dishes. The remains of the supper they'd enjoyed still sat upon the table, and with no servants except Fin—who was no doubt abed by now—the only option was to take care of the mess himself.

As he gathered the plates, he tried not to think about Claire. God knew there were plenty of other things for him to worry about, but she wouldn't leave his mind.

He squeezed his eyes shut, blocking out the image of her entrance into the salon earlier this evening. He should be thinking of Jane, the only woman he had ever loved. But Claire's image was fixed firmly in his mind.

He tried to think of something else, someone else, but nothing came to him. The problem was, had always been, that there was very little inside him. Deep inside, where he should have had a soul, he felt a desperate emptiness. Ever since he was a child, he had known something was missing in him, some defect that made him unlovable. He had always blamed his shortcomings on his lack of love as a child. His mother had died when he was only three, and his father had always been too busy warring or whoring to care about his sons.

As an adult, Jules came to understand that his father's shortcomings were not the reason for his emptiness. There were others among his friends who'd had similar childhoods, such as Nicholas Kincaid, who had overcome those deficiencies to find love and happiness. Nicholas was, by all means, a self-made man whose soul was filled with generosity and goodness. While Jules's own soul was empty.

Perhaps it was best that Claire was angry with him now. She might not like his refusal to accept her word about their marriage. But on the morrow, when his solicitor arrived, he would give her what little money he had left, then send her away from Kildare Manor and himself for good. And the emptiness that had been his constant friend for the whole of his life would be his fate and no one else's.

Exactly the way it should be.

Upstairs in the tower room, Claire forced back a swell of emotion as she wearily unfastened her gown, then climbed into bed. This day had not gone at all as she had hoped. In fact, she was certain she had given Jules more cause to send her away than she had given him incentive to fall into her arms and declare his love for her.

It was her duty to manipulate his emotions, and all would be well as long as she did not blithely open her heart to him in return. For one moment tonight, when he had looked appreciatively at her, she had allowed herself a moment's pride. The warmth in Jules's gaze, ever so briefly, had told her what his words did not—that he found her attractive. And for a heartbeat she pretended that his gaze was real, that their marriage had not been forced, and that her husband truly loved her.

And then she had caught herself. As long as she kept her own emotions at bay, she could do what she had to do. If, however, she started to fall for the man she called husband, she might never be able to do what the cloaked figure demanded.

She had to do exactly as she'd been told—make him fall in love with her then walk away. Break his heart. It had seemed a simple task before she had actually met the man himself. He was much nicer than she expected him to be.

Claire drew a sharp breath at the direction of her thoughts. Such thoughts could get the girls killed. For the hundredth time in the past two weeks, Claire worried that those who abducted the girls wouldn't keep their promise not to harm them if she cooperated. That they had sent slices of fabric from their clothes meant they were near, and watching. Believing they possessed even a small measure of honesty kept her hopes alive and her purpose in place.

Despite her inner turmoil, Claire pulled the sheets up to her chin. She closed her eyes and tried to force her body into a stillness she did not feel. Thirteen days remained for her to make Jules fall in love with her. And during those same thirteen days, she would pray that the girls were safe.

Her best hope for at least the chance of winning his heart and remaining beneath Kildare Manor's roof lay with the man's solicitor. When he arrived on the morrow, Jules would have his proof that their marriage had taken place just as she had said.

Until then, she would show Jules what a good wife she could be. It was on that thought that Claire released a tired sigh and in no time at all fell into an exhausted slumber.

In the bedchamber farther down the hallway, Jane lay in bed next to her sleeping husband, mulling over the evening's events. Yesterday, upon their arrival, she had been suspicious of Claire and her motive for attaching herself to Jules. What could the woman possibly gain from marrying the impoverished laird?

Today, seeing the two of them together, Jane had determined that it was not Claire who she was suspicious of, but Jules. Upon their arrival, her friend had seemed so eager to greet his wife. Today his behavior toward Claire had been almost adversarial. Why?

Jane had no doubt that Jules was enchanted by his new wife. More than once during supper she had caught Jules leaning forward when Claire spoke, listening intently to her every word. Yet, he never touched his bride. There was no kiss upon her arrival, no lingering of his fingers as the dishes had passed from his fingers to hers. And not once did his fingers stray toward her as they sat next to each other at the table.

But Jules's lack of physicality with his wife wasn't the only thing to give Jane pause. It was also the fact that Claire was a highly educated young woman. Throughout the night, Claire had conversed with authority about academia, astrology, and art. She spoke with the men as an equal and seemed to particularly enjoy debating her own opinions with them.

Neither of those things would have given Jane pause by themselves, but together, they gave her much to contemplate because Claire was not the kind of woman Jules usually sought out. Jane approved of the change. As much as Jules needed a wife, he also needed a challenge—something to live for. Being imprisoned for a crime he did not commit had robbed him of so many things. His strength, his family, and his soul.

Jane had determined, during the last hour of staring at the ceiling, that Claire was the woman to give it all back to him. She was exactly what Jules needed in his life. Her spirit and intelligence would challenge him in ways he had never been challenged by any woman before.

And with those challenges, the two newlyweds would forge a bond—a bond that would see them through the hardships that were no doubt ahead, given the state of Kildare Manor. All that was necessary to start them on that path was time alone. Jane smiled into the darkness of her chamber. She knew exactly how to see that Claire and Jules had the entire day to themselves.

Tomorrow she, Nicholas, Hollister, Margaret, David, and even Fin would head to the village. She and Margaret would interview and select more staff for the manor while the men purchased the necessary amenities that Kildare Manor lacked. Jane knew Jules would protest their spending funds on his behalf, but once she claimed it was their wedding gift to the happy couple, he would not dare argue with her.

His beautiful wife, a day alone, a few challenges, and temptation were all the elements necessary for Jane's plan to succeed. Finally feeling as though she had come to a viable resolution to the discord between Claire and Jules, Jane drew a deep breath. By the time she exhaled fully, she was happily and deeply asleep.

The next morning, Arthur Cabot watched as the group rode away from Kildare Manor, heading for the village. Should he follow Lord Kildare's friends into the village to see what they were up to, or should he wait at the Manor and watch the laird as he had been doing for the past several days? *Keep your eye on the prize*, his own father used to say. But everyone knew Jules MacIntyre was no prize. The man had a title, but nothing else.

Arthur pressed his lips together in thought. His gut told him to stay behind. The others were not his target. His decision made, Arthur headed for the old boathouse, where he had built himself a hideout right under their noses.

Hearing the clatter of hoofbeats on the drive, Claire woke and dressed carefully in a light yellow gown that had a band of gold leaves embroidered at the hem and along the edge of the rounded neckline. The gown was simple, yet elegant, and perfect for creating a new sense of harmony between her husband and herself.

In order to succeed today, she had to take charge of her own emotions and not let them ruffle her as she had last night. Pride was one of the few comforts left to her, and she would not let Jules take that away. From this moment forward, Claire vowed she would be poised, polite, and completely unflappable, no matter how unreasonable he might become. He was testing her. And in those tests she would not fail.

Feeling quite capable of any challenge he might throw her way, she headed downstairs. "Good morning," she greeted Jules.

He stood in the hallway as though he had been waiting for her, his back to her, his posture rigid.

Claire forced a gracious smile. She would maintain her composure. "Did you sleep well?"

"No," he said bluntly. He turned around and gazed at her with those pale blue eyes. Despite the bite of his tone, it was not anger but confusion that reflected in his gaze. "Did you tell Jane and the others to leave us alone today?"

"No." Claire's smile slipped. "I heard horses. Are they gone?"

"Jane left a note, explaining they had all gone to the village to hire more servants."

"You cannot blame them for that. Kildare Manor could use—"

"I do not blame them for anything. It is you whom I blame for all this."

"Jules—"

"Drop the pretense, Claire. We are entirely alone, and so I ask, one more time, why are you here? What could you hope to gain from attaching yourself to me? It is quite obvious the estate is in ruin, and I am no prize among men." He studied her, his eyes dark with suspicion.

"Is that truly how you see yourself?" she said without thinking. "You are a peer of the realm. You have your youth, your freedom, education, and despite the state of your home, you have so much more than most people could ever hope for."

To her amazement, something close to admiration brightened his gaze for a moment and he took a step back. "You are right. With all that has happened in the past few weeks, I admit, I have lost sight of many things." His frown returned. "But that still does not explain how you came to be part of my life, Claire. I had not planned on you."

"That makes two of us, then," she agreed. She tried not to explore with her eyes the man who stood before her this morning. He was different than the man last night who had been so elegantly dressed in a dark blue velvet jacket with gold embroidery. This Jules was dressed in a simple muslin shirt hanging open at the neck, with black breeches and boots. The simplicity only accented just how incredibly powerful his body was. Unexpected warmth coiled through her and became a pulsing heat the moment she lifted her gaze to his.

He focused hungrily on her lips, and she saw raw longing in the depth of his blue eyes. His jaw flexed rigidly, as though he were fighting himself.

She pressed her lips together, realizing that despite her vow to stay utterly in control today, she wanted to lose herself and step forward to taste those well-shaped lips. The thought both scared and excited her.

He took a deep breath and ran his hand through his tawny hair. "It is just the two of us today to await Grayson's arrival." He turned toward the door. "I am going to cut some wood so we will have a fire tonight. Afterward I am going fishing so we can eat. I suggest you find something to amuse yourself."

He grasped the latch and yanked the door open. "And don't bother cleaning the house. The others will be back with women to do that by this evening."

Startled by his brusqueness, Claire watched as he shut the door behind him, once again placing a barrier between them as well as signaling her not to follow him outside. They were alone, and he would ignore her. Perfect. How many times would she fail to engage him?

Frustration sent her wandering through the nearly empty house, looking for something to do that would divert her mind from her predicament and help use her pent-up energy. She wandered from room to room until she found herself once more upstairs in front of the boarded-up chamber.

Jules had not replaced the wood slats she had removed the day before, so she once again slipped inside. She had no candle to light the chamber this time, but she remembered from her past visit that there were four small windows on the far wall. She made her way through the hazy darkness to the shutters. She unlatched the first set of shutters that opened into the room and then pushed a second set out, letting golden sunshine fill the room.

When all four windows were open, a light breeze drifted through the chamber, cleansing the once-stagnant air. Within moments, the sinister aspect of the room had vanished, leaving only a severely neglected chamber in its place.

Claire moved through the chamber until she came to the abandoned table and chairs. She righted the chair that lay against the ground and sat in it while she studied the room's crown molding, high ceiling, and empty space. The room had exquisite light and fine bones. It would make a perfect ballroom with a little renewal and care.

Jules had asked her not to clean. He had asked her to leave this room alone. Something horrible happened in this room, something that needed cleansing from Kildare Manor and from Jules's life. She knew she should leave the chamber now, stop the ideas that were brewing in her mind, but she could do neither thing as a new plan formed. She needed something to occupy her time here for the next twelve days. And she could think of no better way to amuse herself than transforming this chamber from a place of bad memories into a thing of beauty. It would be her gift to Jules when she ultimately left him.

The thought brought her out of her chair and toward the window at the farthest side of the chamber. She would have no choice but to abandon her husband twelve days from now. And she would hurt him just as she suspected everyone in his life had done.

At the window she paused, hearing the rhythmic sound of an ax splitting wood in the distance. She peered outside to see Jules bared to the waist, his bronzed back tapering to narrow hips, his arms and shoulders rippling with thick, bunched muscle as he swung the ax in a graceful arc.

Heat came to Claire's cheeks. As a painter, she had seen a man's bare arms and torso before. But somehow on Jules, they seemed so much more intimate. She was appalled with herself for looking, yet so fascinated she could not look away. Jules seemed so at ease as he swung his ax toward each waiting piece of wood and split each log with expert dexterity. His actions puzzled her because she had simply assumed he was a highly polished Scottish laird who spent his time gaming, carousing, and moving in the highest levels of society. Were his affluent friends not proof of that?

Yet today, the unpretentious and powerful Jules appeared every bit as comfortable in the wild and rugged terrain. A self-made man who needed no company but his own, and might even prefer it.

Evidently, the man had the ability to belong in whatever setting he happened to be in. He could maneuver in the highest circles of society as well as survive in his dilapidated manor house in the wilds of Scotland. For some reason, the revelation unsettled her. Who was this man—Jules MacIntyre, Lord Kildare—who she had been forced to marry? It was easier to think of him as a rogue she would hurt in the end than as an honest man who was merely making his way through this life, just as she was.

Or, she recalled yet another aspect of the man, the one who had been imprisoned for the murder of his stepmother. He had been proven innocent and released. But the woman had still died, and someone had killed her. There had been no other suspects except Jules.

His stepmother had been poisoned. Claire picked up the overturned teacup on the table. Had this truly been the murder weapon? If so, why was it still here? If Jules were guilty of the crime, would he not want all the evidence to be cleaned away, destroyed, so that no one could make any further claims?

Instead, he had left the chamber exactly as it had been. Every detail had been preserved. That fact, more than anything else, spoke to her of his true innocence. But why continue this torture? Now that he was the master of this house, why allow the memory to remain?

He had told her not to come here, that she was to leave the place alone. Claire returned the teacup to the table, exactly where it had been. Then she replaced the overturned chair she had righted earlier.

Yes, changing this room would be a gift—no, she corrected herself, an apology, for what she would eventually put him through when she succeeded in her mission. But perhaps transforming a place of horror into something beautiful would make it easier for Jules to forgive her. Or, she paused, would she leave him with yet another memory to take its place, even harder to erase?

Until she began the project, there was still time to change her mind. Meanwhile, she would record what evidence remained here in a different way. On that thought, Claire left the chamber and went downstairs to retrieve her drawing and painting satchel.

When she returned, she sat beneath one of the open windows and started to draw the scene before her in great detail. The table, the chairs, the teacup. They would all be recorded for future reference, because, with each stroke of her lead, she was more determined than ever to act upon her earlier intention. She would record the scene in case it was ever needed again, then clean this room, sweep away the old memories, and renew its purpose by giving it a fresh look.

When she had completed her drawing, she set it aside and stood. Turning once again to gaze out the open window, she saw

Jules, fully dressed this time, heading up from the loch with a large fish suspended from a line in his hand. On his journey across the weed-tangled courtyard, he stopped and turned toward the road. It was then that Claire heard what he no doubt responded to, the clatter of hoofbeats.

A single rider approached the manor at a breakneck pace. The sun had yet to reach its zenith, yet the others had been gone for several hours. Had something happened to them in the village? Claire tensed at the thought, and her heart raced as she climbed through the slats that partially blocked the doorway and hurried down the main stairs.

She met Jules outside the front door just as the horse and rider came to a stop. "Lord Kildare," the rider said. He offered Jules a bow, then hastened forward.

"Joseph," Jules acknowledged.

A sense of foreboding threaded through Claire as she recognized the young messenger as the one Jules had hired only two days ago to bring Grayson back from Edinburgh.

"Have you a message from my solicitor?" Jules asked.

"Milord." The young man was covered in dust, as though he had ridden hard and fast for some time. "I have been to see your solicitor."

"Is he following in a carriage?"

Joseph shook his head. "He cannot, milord. Not now nor ever."

"Why?" Jules asked with a scowl.

The young man paled. "He is dead."

Blood roared in Claire's ears. How could Grayson be dead? The man who had stood beside her at the wedding ceremony had been no older than herself.

She stole a glance at Jules. His face was hard, his posture rigid. "What happened?"

"Early yesterday morning, only a few moments before I arrived, a runaway carriage crushed him in the street while he was on his way to work," Joseph said gently, as if a softened voice could make a difference when the words were so cold and ugly.

A heavy silence hung over them until Jules finally asked, "Who was the driver?"

"No one knows. They did not stop after the accident." Joseph's gaze dropped to the ground. "The only witness said the conveyance was unexceptional except for the bright red fringe that hung over the doorway. The driver was dressed in dark clothing, and the only occupant was cloaked in black."

The same carriage that had reportedly taken her wards from her home. A terrifying picture of Penelope, Anna, and Eloise lying dead in the street shot through Claire's mind. She felt a scream start deep inside her, building, gathering force until it threatened to choke her. Her sweet wards could meet the same end.

She must have let a sound slip past her control because Jules turned to her. "Claire, what is it?" A deep frown furrowed his brows. "Do you know who did this?"

Tears scalded her eyes. She wanted to give in to them, to allow herself the relief of crying, but she knew she could not. If she told Jules the truth, the abductors would know and they would kill the girls regardless.

"To die in such a way . . ." She swallowed past the tightness in her throat. "No, I don't know who would do such an evil thing as to kill an innocent man."

"And the only witness to the marriage you say took place," he replied with a softer tone.

Claire's arms felt limp, and her legs went suddenly weak. She stumbled.

Jules was there beside her. His arm slid around her waist, bolstering her. They stood there for a long while, staring at each other, saying nothing until he finally broke the silence once more, saying, "Come inside."

His words snapped her back to her senses. She steadied herself and stepped away from his arm, supporting her own weight. "I am better now. I want to stay out in the sunshine. The warmth helps." Pale afternoon sunlight streamed through the tree branches overhead, creating a tangle of greenish-brown on the grass at her feet.

"I understand," he said, walking her to a large rock nearby. "Wait here for me. I won't be long."

She heard the crunch of grass beneath his feet as he moved back to the messenger. "Take your horse to the stable for a rubdown and a pail of oats. When you are done, help yourself to whatever you can find in the kitchen."

"Thank you, milord," Joseph said as he guided his horse away.

Claire closed her eyes and tipped her head back, letting the sun caress her skin and ease the chill that had settled deep inside her since the girls had been taken. She drew a steadying breath.

She knew to use another human being in such a way was wrong, yet she would do whatever she had to do to free three innocent girls. She was the only one who could rectify the situation. And if Jules got hurt along the way, then she would have to find a way to forgive herself, eventually. Because hurt him she would.

She tried not to feel sad at the thought.

The summer heat from the open door cut through the stifling, sweaty press of The Thistle and Sword at the southern edge of the village of Kildare. Across the room, a dark-cloaked figure watched as two new patrons entered the smoky tavern. At the sight of the two women, she sat up. Four men entered behind the women. Frowning, the cloaked figure stepped deeper into the shadows as she recognized the pesky servant from Kildare Manor, John Finnie. The others must be Jules's friends.

The younger of the two women made her way across the crowded room, heading toward the only open table. The regal way she held her slender, delicate body marked her as Lady Jane Kincaid. The memory of what Jane had done to save Lord Kildare from the hangman's noose made the cloaked figure clench her hands. The young laird was supposed to die, but Jane had altered that plan. Now was the time for a different plan—one of revenge, slow torture, and pain. The thought blew across her mind like an elusive breeze in the stuffy room.

The end would be worth the wait. For the end promised to be every bit as tragic as the beginning.

Jules MacIntyre deserved nothing less.

Jules returned to Claire less than a quarter hour later bearing a basket.

He had taken the time to wash and change into a clean lawn shirt and fawn breeches that didn't smell of fish or sweat. "Since the others have yet to return, I thought we might have some bread and cheese outside."

"What time is it?" she asked, coming to sit beside him on the blanket he had spread out on the one corner of the lawn that wasn't waist-high. He had trampled the weeds into submission as he'd cut several sections of logs into kindling earlier this morn.

He looked at the sun. "Most likely around midday," Jules replied, then frowned at the rest of the lawn. Perhaps it was time to tame the estate. Working outside had helped to clear his head, at least until Joseph had arrived with the news of Grayson's demise.

"When will the others return? Did they say?" Claire asked, sitting down on the blanket beside him, gazing off toward the village.

"Around four, I imagine. Do you miss them so much?"

Claire gave him a winsome smile. "No, but I am eager to move forward with the cleaning. And unless we are going to eat fish and cheese for days on end, we have no more supplies."

He looked at her with amusement. "I am very fond of fish."

"And I am very fond of cheese," she said with a chuckle.

"Then we shall be fine." Jules set a plate down, positioned the bread and cheese upon it, then turned the plate so the cheese was closer to her. "I suspect they are having a difficult time finding women who are eager to come up here to clean, no matter what Nicholas offers to pay."

Claire sliced off a corner of the cheese and popped it into her mouth, chewing thoughtfully. "Why is that?"

"They fear my reputation." He tore off a piece of bread. "The rogue of Kildare is what they call me in the village."

"Do they really?" She paused in ripping off a piece of bread. There was no fear in her eyes, but she remained so still.

He narrowed his gaze on her. "Does *that* give you pause about the man you have attached yourself to?"

"No."

There was no hesitation in her answer, and that surprised him. He searched her face, contemplating her response. "The only person who can verify your claim of a proxy wedding is now dead," he said.

An indescribable look of pain flashed across her face. "I hope that as Grayson met with such an unfortunate end, he did not suffer."

Jules ripped another section off the bread, stifling his sudden urge to reach for her hand and comfort her.

She set down the reminder of the cheese. "As for proof of our marriage, it would have been recorded in the parish records if the documents Grayson had me sign are no longer accessible."

The words brought his gaze back to hers. "I will need to go to Edinburgh to confirm that myself."

She said nothing, simply nodded in response, but that odd sadness lingered in her gaze.

This time, he could not hold back his need to comfort her. He touched her hand.

She did not pull away. A soft smile came to her lips. "I do not blame you for being angry with me. I went into this marriage fully knowing what to expect. You were not prepared for me, I realize that now."

His eyes locked onto hers, glittering yet warm and so filled with hope and vitality that he could not look away, even though he wanted to—Lord, how he wanted to. But her gaze wouldn't release him, and he had no choice but to stare. "No, I was not prepared for you."

"Why did you fabricate a wife?" she asked.

"Who told you that?"

"Grayson."

He made a small sound, a rush of breath, an aborted laugh at her bluntness. And yet it also felt good to talk openly about what he had done without the others around. Neither of them had to pretend. "I wanted to be left alone."

A frown pulled down the corners of her mouth, but did nothing to mar her features. Instead, it once again made him want to lift his hand to her cheek and stroke away the concern he saw there. "I would think after your *situation*, you would want exactly the opposite."

"Are you referring to my time in gaol?" he asked, thinly.

She nodded. "It could not have been easy."

He pulled his gaze away from the pity in her golden eyes. "It was hell on earth, and I wouldn't wish it on my worst enemy." He didn't want anyone to look at him that way, not anymore. It made him feel helpless, and he had worked hard to be anything but the victim he had once been forced to play.

"I'm sorry for that."

In her voice he heard not pity, but softness, a gentle acceptance that left him just as on edge as her pity had done. "Life is seldom what we want it to be," Jules said.

She leaned closer, and brought her hand up to cradle his cheek with an intimacy that was both gentle and sensuous. "It can be," Claire whispered.

His body stirred at the confidence in the way she held him, at the heat of her touch. This was not the meek woman he had met that first day or the prideful woman he had dined with last night. This was a different woman altogether. Since he had left her this morning, she had found a strength he hadn't anticipated. It was evident in the way she touched him, the way she looked at him—she looked not through him as others often did, but straight into his tattered soul.

He got to his feet suddenly. "I'm going fishing."

She startled, her hand remaining in the empty air. "You caught a fish for tonight's dinner already."

"We will need a second one, and maybe a third." He felt like an idiot for pulling away, yet he'd had to. It was either pull away or kiss her. And kissing her seemed like a very bad idea.

Without another word, he headed back toward the loch. Halfway there, he realized he had forgotten his fishing line. He kept on going. Perhaps he would go for a cold swim instead.

Claire stared unseeingly at the ceiling above her, the charcoal in her hand arrested midstroke. She did not understand Jules MacIntyre at all. She had just started to break through the wall he had built between them since she'd arrived, and in the next moment he was gone. How could she stop him from running away?

She dropped her charcoal into the basket of supplies she had gathered and placed it atop the scaffolding she had built. She'd created the structure from two broken ladders and a panel from an old wagon she had found in the barn. Kildare Manor might not have furnishings, servants, or stores of food, but it contained a wealth of dilapidated wood, weaponry, aging whiskey barrels, an old boat, and paint.

She had been a little shocked by the discovery of a wooden chest filled with vials of pigment and brushes, as well as various types of oil and varnish. Someone in the MacIntyre family had been a painter once, although all the evidence except for the chest was gone from the manor.

Claire's heart had soared, and her fingers had itched to create something beautiful in this big, empty house. And she'd acted on the urge, dragging the chest into the house, up the stairs, and directly into the deserted ballroom. Yet now that her initial excitement had vanished, she also realized the discovery had allowed her to forget, ever so briefly, her own important role. And it wasn't as painter to the Kildare household.

Slowly, she climbed down the scaffolding until she stood once more on the floor. A quick glance up brought a smile to her face. The design was progressing. Another few hours and she would be ready to paint. But those hours would have to come when everyone else was asleep from now on. She could not afford to lose herself to her painting during the precious daylight hours. Too much was at stake to fail.

Claire glanced down at her blackened fingers, and swallowed hard, forcing back the thick ache of memories—the shreds of fabric from the girls' dresses, the dark-hooded figures . . .

No, she would not go home a failure, regardless of how Jules responded to her. He would not drive her away, not until she knew the girls were safe.

The resolve gave her the strength she needed to leave the chamber and hurry toward her own room. It was time to toss caution to the wind. If she wanted to gain Lord Kildare's favor, she had to be willing to risk more, dare more. She had to breach that wall he had erected between them and knock it down completely. And she knew just how to accomplish that task.

If he wanted more fish for supper, than she would be the one to provide them this time. If he could fish, then so could she.

9

Thinking she could be Jules's equal, Claire headed outside toward the boathouse. It took much effort to drag the heavy wooden boat she had found there across the grassy field that seemed to go on forever until she reached the shore of the loch.

She glanced around, searching for Jules. Only an hour had passed since they'd been together earlier. When she did not see him, she took off her shoes and left them on the shore. Then, with the hem of her dress clenched tight in her fist, Claire pushed the ancient boat away from the edge of the loch. She took the last three steps on the narrow beach, two in the water, then hopped into the vessel.

Her father had taken her out in a boat several times in her youth. While he studied the fish and animal life, she had drawn the scenery. It had been one of their favorite things to do on a sunny Sunday afternoon.

The wood creaked and moaned beneath her as the boat glided over the steel-gray surface of the loch. She settled herself on the small wooden bench in the center and gripped the oars. It took several strokes to find a rhythm that sent the boat out into the loch, instead of in a circle back toward the shore.

The air around her grew a little cooler. A breeze tugged at the ends of the hair that had fallen from her chignon in her efforts to drag the boat from the boathouse to the water. The air was heavy with the scent of heather and pine. The oars gave forth a rhythmic cadence that seemed so in harmony with this setting.

Claire tipped her head back and let the sunshine warm her face. She drew a breath of clean, fresh air and relished the sensation of freedom that came to her as she glided toward the deeper waters.

She pulled the oars back inside the boat and picked up the net she had tossed in the back of the boat. Cool liquid met her fingertips and dragged down the hem of her gown as water lined the bottom of the boat. Obviously the vessel had a leak, despite the fact that she had inspected it before launching it into the loch.

A quick glance back at the shore in the distance brought a sense of unease, but she pushed the sensation away. She had come here to fish, and to prove to Jules that she was capable. And prove that point she would . . . unless she drowned herself first.

Determined to succeed, Claire turned the boat back toward the shore, then tossed the net over the edge. Several large holes were visible as the net dipped below the surface.

A leaky boat, a hole-filled net—this adventure was not turning out exactly as she had hoped. Dragging the net against the side of the boat with one hand, she reached for the oars and tried to row back to safety, but the netting hampered her movements.

The water level in the boat had risen to her ankles. She felt a pinprick of fear as the frigid water crawled up her skin, but kept rowing. The water was coming in faster now. Realizing she could row faster without the net, she dropped it, watching it for a moment as it sank down into the steel-gray depths of the loch.

Her heart constricted in her chest as the water came up to her midcalf. She had learned to swim as a child. Her father had taught her how, but it had been years since she had been in the water. She gripped the oars, rowed hard. Despite her efforts, the water flowed in, dragging the boat down, making the vessel heavy and impossible to maneuver.

Water slipped over the side. For an instant she floated as the boat slipped out from beneath her, pulling the oars from her hands. She let them go, unable to counter the deadweight. Fear threaded through her as she thrashed at the water. Regardless of her efforts, she slipped below the surface.

She felt herself falling, weightless, her arms spread and her hair escaping the tight chignon to float into her eyes. Cold water sucked at her; the boat was a colossal shadow below her as they both sank deeper into the void. Silver fish swam around her—trout. Her intention to catch a fish would have been realized had the boat not sprung a leak.

Yet now she would drown, unless she did something. She kicked, but the heavy drag of her skirt tugged her down despite her efforts. Anger warmed her, fired her blood. She would not drown. She had far too much to live for—the girls, Jules, all the paintings she had yet to paint.

She kicked fiercely at the water that surrounded her. Slowly she glided forward, broke free from the weight that dragged her down. At the surface, she drew in a breath of air, felt the bliss of warmth on her face, and something grabbed her hand. Something yanked her farther up. A man surrounded in light. Jules. His arms went around her waist. He pulled her close, his heart beat against her chest, and she drew comfort from it, from him as he swam toward the shore.

They were on the grassy shoreline. She collapsed to her side and drew a deep breath of heather-scented air.

Jules dragged her into his arms. They lay there, with his face pressed against her hair, entangled. Claire reached up and curled her fingers around his shoulder, feeling the soggy cloth of his shirt beneath her fingers, and a small smile tugged at her lips. He had come after her.

After his heartbeat slowed, he pulled back to stare into her face. "Has anyone ever told you that you are trouble?"

Her smile slipped. "Now why would you say that?"

He sat up and dusted the bank's dirt from his chest. "You sank my boat."

"I was trying to fish." Claire shoved back her dripping hair. His gaze followed her movements.

"Fishing is much easier when you are not submerged in water." His voice was light, and something reckless flickered in his expression. His gaze wandered from her face to her breasts then down to her hips. The thin, wet fabric clung to her body, molded to every curve, and revealed the dusky peak of her nipples.

The warmth of his gaze pulled her in. She shifted closer.

"I had a net," she said, in her own defense. "I just could not handle the boat and the net at the same time."

He reached up and captured a soggy tendril of her hair. He coiled it around his finger, and softly tugged her closer. "That boat was my great-grandfather's. It was over sixty years old. Whatever made you think it was seaworthy?" His voice was gentle, tender.

"I . . . I didn't think. I just wanted to catch a fish for dinner." *For you.* She swallowed roughly against a sudden tightness in her throat.

"Come closer," he challenged with a smile.

"Why . . . why should I?"

"Because you want to," he said, his voice thick.

"You don't know what I want. You don't know anything about me. Despite the fact that we are married, we are strangers."

"Yes, we are." His smile faded and he looked out at the loch.

Loneliness. There it was again, that shared emotion. She had the sudden feeling he was speaking not just about them any longer, but a constant state, and she felt an odd sense of kinship.

"You never let me ask my three questions the other night, Jules. Tell me something about you now, something no one else knows."

He frowned. "Why? So you can use that information against me?"

"No. So I can feel closer to you, even if it is just for this moment. One thing, that's all I ask."

A frown creased his forehead. He wasn't going to answer her. A heaviness descended over her in the silence that ensued until he said, "My favorite color is green. I once had a pet mouse. I named him Francis, after the saint. While in gaol, I used to imagine I was out fishing on the loch. And when my mother died, a part of me died along with her."

"Jules," she said, her voice raw.

He held up his hand, stalling her words. "I don't know what it is about you. One minute I want to strangle you. The next minute I want to kiss you."

Before she could stop herself, she touched her lips to his. He hesitated for only a moment before he responded, kissing her back, pulling her closer, letting her in. Even though she had instigated the kiss, she was unprepared for its effect. A wild, indescribable sweetness mingled his breath with hers.

With a groan, he shifted his lips to her cheek, her ear, trailing hot kisses down her neck, weaving a sensual spell, until his mouth locked on hers once more. His tongue traced a hot line between her lips, coaxing, urging them to part.

The moment she yielded, his tongue plunged into her mouth, stroking and caressing. A tingling sensation spread from her arms and legs, gathering at her core, until a strange languid heat flowed through her entire being.

She surrendered to the sensation and to the stormy splendor of his kiss. Her hands shifted restlessly over the damp fabric of his shirt. She could feel his heavily muscled shoulders and forearms beneath the sheer fabric. The sensation made her bold as her lips moved against his with increasing abandon.

When he finally pulled his mouth from hers an eternity later, their breath came in mingled gasps as the powerful, sensual force surrounding them was abandoned. Feeling almost bereft at its loss, Claire surfaced from the blissful abandon where he had taken her, and forced her heavy eyelids to open so she could look at him. He stretched out beside her on the grassy beach, his face hard and dark with passion, his blue eyes smoldering.

Lifting his hand, he tenderly brushed a copper lock of hair off her cheek, and he tried to smile, but his breathing was as ragged as hers. He fingered the locket about her neck. "You wear this always. Should I be jealous?"

99

"No," she said tenuously. "It was given to me a long time ago." He let the topic slide as Claire let her gaze drop once more to his finely chiseled mouth.

"Don't look at me that way unless you want this to progress further," he warned her in a husky, tender voice. "If you touch me again, I am not certain I will have the strength to stop."

Stunned into stillness by the harsh need in his voice, Claire met his gaze, saw the raw desire beating there. Wave after wave of heat washed over her, shimmering with sensuality. She lost herself in the scent of him, the planes of his face, the tension in his body. She took it all in and welcomed the glittering promise he offered.

Taking her silence as acceptance, his fingers came down and brushed the upper swell of her breast.

She shivered, and the muscles of her stomach contracted in response.

"If we do this," he said, his voice as heavy and sensual as his gaze, "it won't mean anything."

She arched against him. That was the old Jules talking—the man who used to be a womanizer. Now, he was a married man. "It will mean everything," she countered. It would mean the consummation of their previously unconsummated marriage, and more.

He groaned and shifted away from the intimate press of their bodies.

Instead of releasing him, Claire brushed her hand down his wet shirt, found the edge and teased it up.

His hands came down on hers. "The shirt stays on."

The muscles of his stomach were clenched and locked beneath her palms. She met his gaze as she returned her hands to his chest, stroking the hardened muscles beneath. Some of his tension eased, yet passion still burned in his eyes.

Surely it was not embarrassment that kept his body shielded to her. She had seen earlier today that he was strong and muscular when he had been cutting wood. What mysteries would she see up close that she had not seen from afar?

In that moment, a warm breeze lifted his tawny hair from his forehead and molded the material of his shirt to his chest, the same wind that caressed her cheeks. She became acutely aware of the water lapping softly against the shore, the spongy grass beneath her bare feet. The air seemed suddenly thick and hard to breathe.

"Your shirt matters not to me."

He drew a deep breath, as though he too were affected by the breeze and the moment.

The heat of his gaze was a physical thing on her flesh. "I can take you, enjoy you, then walk away."

Shock tingled through her—shock at his words that so closely mirrored what she intended to do, and shock at the desire that still flared, causing her breasts to swell, harden, and ripen beneath that gaze. He had barely touched her skin, but her body was preparing. "I would like to see you try."

His hands went to the hem of her wet gown. He tugged it up over her head, taking her chemise along with her dress, exposing her fully to the warmth of the sunshine and to his heated gaze. "That is a challenge I readily accept." He tunneled his fingers through her hair and tipped back her head. But instead of lowering his mouth to hers, he dipped farther down and touched his tongue to her nipple.

She arched her spine, welcoming the intimacy of his touch. Heat blazed through her, and she prayed the same was true for him. As much as she burned, she wanted to make certain she would become an elixir that was every bit as vital to him as the air he breathed.

He lifted his head and smiled at her. "Do you find that pleasant?"

"Very."

"And this?" His head bent, his tongue touched her other nipple, flicking it into a hardened nub.

Need flared deep inside, as did the edge of panic. Her stomach clenched. She might have wanted to control this situation, but in carnal matters she was but a novice to his master. She brought her hands up to tunnel in his hair, holding him to her. The silky feel of his hair against her fingers sent a tingle of desire to her core. Her heart was beating so fast, she was certain he could hear it, that the world, as vast and wide as it was, had now shrunk to just Jules and herself.

His hands cupped her breasts, trailed along her sides, until he reached her bare buttocks. His hands opened and closed on her, urging her into the cradle of his hips. Arousal. Stark, bold, and pulsing provocatively against her nakedness. Suddenly his clothing became a barrier to whatever awaited them both.

With trembling fingers she reached down and released the ties of his breeches. She eased the fabric over his muscular hips and thighs. He pushed his clothing aside, leaving him gloriously naked from the waist down, and fully aroused. She needed him against her, skin to skin, more than she needed to breathe.

He shifted over her, and she shivered in anticipation as he parted her thighs and moved between them. His hand fluttered across her abdomen, then rose slowly, with languid anticipation to close about her breast. Her breath caught, hitched as he kneaded, explored, and sent her heart racing.

His other hand fluttered down her side, past her waist, then slid slowly over her bottom, pressing her upward to greet him with a promise that was both explicit and seductive. Unfettered desire shone in his eyes as he caressed her breast, stroked her bottom, and filled her mouth, the heavy thrust of his tongue mimicking what he intended, and what she urgently desired.

Her senses reeled as she followed his lead into a void where only sensation existed. His hand left her breast to cup her womanhood, stroking, patting, until his fingers delved in her wet heat, stroked, then penetrated. He thrust forward, spreading her, preparing her.

Her body arched as he pressed deeper. She moaned, the sound trapped in their kiss. She pressed upward, wanting more, needing more than his fingers offered. As if in response to her unspoken plea, his fingers moved away and the blunt head of his erection took their place. He entered her, then stopped, not moving. He looked down at her, his eyes wide. "A virgin?" he asked, his voice raw with need.

"Of course," she said through a haze of lust. "What did you expect?"

"I didn't think." The pain of his restraint tugged at his features. "I should pull back . . ."

Every nerve in her body was on fire as he hovered half in, half out of her. She couldn't let him go. Not now. Their joining would mean something to him. It must. Claire brought her hips up and lunged forward.

His eyes closed and a groan of ecstasy escaped him as her tightness closed around him. "Damnation." He plunged hard and deep.

Pain flared, subsided. Fullness came, then sensation after sensation stormed through her. It was then she became aware of another sensation, an emptiness that had to be filled.

He moved slowly, back and forth, allowing her time to grow accustomed to him, but the pain on his face grew more harsh, more pinched, as though the effort to restrain himself was costing him greatly. She clutched his shoulders, desperately holding on to him to keep him inside.

She had to have all of him. It was the only thing that would take away the emptiness that grew, sharpened with each slow thrust. She wanted more. "Jules," she whispered. "Take me, all of me," she sighed as she thrust her hips upward once more.

He exploded into motion, thrusting short, hard, fast, and frantic.

An unbearable hunger grew, raged, spiraled. She thrashed her head from side to side against a pillow of grass as a desperation she had never felt before grew mercilessly out of control. "Please make it—" She didn't know what she was asking. All she knew was they were headed for something that was bigger than both of them, something she wanted to lose herself in forever.

Every stroke drew them closer. Every heartbeat melded them as one. Their breathing mingled, merged, until a dark hunger exploded, splintered into a brilliance so overwhelming it was like nothing she had ever experienced before.

"Damnation," Jules whispered as he collapsed on top of her. They lay there joined, hearts pounding, breathing ragged, for what felt like an eternity, until finally he lifted his head and brushed his lips over hers. "You are not what I expected." His voice was silken soft, as seductive as the summer breeze that whispered across their cooling flesh.

"From the Claire you created, you expected nothing at all."

"You are not the Claire I created." He looked down at her, his eyes so blue and clear she felt as if she were looking into forever. She wanted it to be forever. She wanted to continue to float on the magical plane where no one and nothing existed but them. He smiled and kissed the tip of her nose.

"Perhaps, or perhaps I am the manifestation of that wish come true. You created me for a reason. What was it?" she asked, feeling the glow of their lovemaking ebb away. She wanted it to continue. She wanted him to kiss her again, for the heat to build once more.

Instead he withdrew from her and turned onto his back, staring at the sky. "I did not think past trying to make Nicholas and Jane stop with their pleading letters, or their various attempts to introduce me to female friends of theirs. I wanted it all to stop."

"It has stopped," she said softly, then at the flicker of tension that returned to his body, she stood and held out her hand. She was not ready for their truce to end. "Come with me."

He sat up and stared at her outstretched hand. "Where?" He gripped her hand and she tugged him forward, pulling him off balance until both of them landed with a splash in the water.

The moment he reached for her, she swam away.

He laughed and swam after her. "You know how to swim?"

"Of course." She darted to the left, out of his grasp.

"Then why did you allow me to rescue you out there?" He changed course, following her.

"You seemed so determined." She waved her hand across the surface of the water, sending spray into his face.

He laughed and made a lunge for her, pulling her into his arms once more. He held her close, treading water. "You are no damsel in distress."

105

She watched the water bead onto his shirt-covered shoulders from the wet ends of his hair. A lazy smile touched his lips, making him appear much younger than his twenty-two years. Something had changed between them today, whether he wanted to acknowledge it or not. The barrier he had first erected to keep her at arm's length was no longer there. "No, Jules, I am your wife."

The moment she said the words, she regretted them. The shadows returned to his eyes. And he turned them both toward the shore. He wrapped her in his arms and carried her back to the beach, setting her on the grass. He bent down and snagged her chemise, pressing the wet garment into her hands. "We should get dressed and return to the manor." He turned away and snatched up his breeches.

"What are you doing?"

"I am getting dressed." He frowned. "Where are my boots?" He searched the area until he found the garments he had most likely discarded before coming out to rescue her from the boat.

"No, Jules. You are running away."

He tensed, not looking at her. "I'm not running."

"You are running from what we shared here, from the realization that you do care, and that you want to do it again."

He turned to face her, his features hard. "I told you I would walk away. I warned you."

She fastened the edges of her gown, straightened the wet fabric, then slipped her feet into the shoes she'd left at the shoreline. "You might walk away, but I will be there with you in your thoughts and in your mind." She moved toward him. "You are afraid. Why?"

He took a step back as he finished securing his breeches, then slammed his feet into his boots. "Leave well enough alone, wench. Leave here, leave me while you still can."

"This is where I belong."

"No one belongs here, Claire. Not even me." On those words he turned around and headed off toward the manor, alone.

Damnation, *what have I done?* Jules pounded across the open field toward the manor house. He was running, and he would keep running until he could forget what had just happened between them, until he could forget her. He could still taste the lingering sweetness of her mouth on his tongue. He could still feel her velvet softness on his fingertips.

He should have stayed away from her while the others were gone. But he'd been so confident in his ability to ignore her, or at least be his unpleasant self, to scare her, humiliate her, anything to make her go away.

But he had done no such thing. Instead, he had prepared her a meal, and talked about things he never shared with anyone. And in that talking, she had exposed his weaknesses and worn down his resolve. He had spent years practicing self-control, and he'd lost it with a kiss.

His steps slowed. He felt her presence long before she reached him—a rush of energy that made the very air stir. "Jules, do not be afraid of me."

He spun to confront her. "I am afraid of nothing, least of all you." He did not keep the steel from his voice. He wanted to scare her, to do anything that would give him back his resolve.

Her lips formed a word, then she stopped, froze, her eyes widening.

He frowned, then turned and followed her gaze to find Jane, Margaret, Nicholas, Hollister, David, Fin, and two other women staring at them. Supremely aware of the curious gazes that took in their wet clothing and disheveled appearances, Jules swallowed a curse and said, "We went fishing," as though the words would explain all, then continued on toward the house.

"Then where are the fish?" Hollister laughed in response.

"Shh," Margaret admonished, and that was all Jules heard as he moved out of earshot and hopefully out of their sight. As host, he knew it was wrong to abandon Claire, leaving her alone to face the questions his friends would no doubt press upon her, but at the moment he could do nothing else.

He was free of Claire for the moment. But he didn't feel free. Her scent was on his shirt, his skin, and he felt as if his hands were still on her body. He moved quickly toward the manor and the master's chambers. At least there he was safe from her, and there he would scrub his skin until no hint of her remained.

But the memory would remain, the memory of the way she looked, the way she felt . . . *Damnation*, he was hardening again at the thought. Coupling with her was supposed to mean nothing.

Nothing.

He drew a harsh breath as he shut the chamber door behind him. It was up to him to see that it did.

Claire felt her cheeks flame red as eight pairs of eyes inspected her. Jules's friends, his steward, and most likely the new servants they had hired, inspected her from head to toe.

"Claire," Jane said, stepping forward to take her hand. "Are you well?"

Claire smiled and nodded. "I went fishing on my own in a boat that leaked. Jules rescued me when it sank." The shortened version of what had happened brought nods of understanding from the men, but Jane and Margaret continued to study her, searching for what they did not know.

"Are you hurt?" Margaret asked.

Yes. "No," Claire replied, with a sudden shiver as the dampness of her clothes suddenly pierced her senses.

Margaret held out her arms. "Come." Claire hesitated, but Margaret stepped forward until she enfolded Claire in her arms.

Claire accepted the woman's compassion as she buried her face in Margaret's shoulder. Claire could feel her throat tighten and the warmth of tears in her eyes, but she forced them back. She had to stay strong.

Margaret stroked her hair. "Let us get you back to the manor and out of those wet clothes."

Claire nodded, allowing the older woman to support her as they walked back toward Jules's home. She felt the apprehension in the air and knew the others were watching her, waiting to see what she said or did to give them more insight into what had happened at the loch.

Deliberately she recalled the image of Jules gazing down at her after their joining, the way his eyes had filled with pleasure and wonder. That moment gave her strength and once again reminded her of her purpose. She straightened, no longer leaning on Margaret for support.

Jules had run away from her. He had said their coupling would mean nothing to him. In that he had been wrong. It meant something, to be sure. If anything, it was a sign she was making progress in her efforts to engage his affections. Yet she had to keep a rein on her own—she had to separate herself, body and mind, from the man who had awakened the most intense pleasure she had ever known.

She had to stay strong, do what must be done, then walk away without a second glance.

After washing in the basin, Claire needed something to clear her mind and help her forget the moments she had spent in Jules's arms. Her fingers reached for a paintbrush. She knew she could not risk going to the ballroom with everyone home and awake.

With a sigh, Claire sat on the sagging bed in the center of the room and tipped her head back. She smiled. Jules had purposely placed her in the most dilapidated, most frightening room in the manor. But just like the chamber on the opposite side of the house, this room had character and exceptionally good structure. A little paint, a little love, and the room would be transformed.

It wasn't until several hours later of painting a garden scene on the wall near her bed that Claire noticed the light had faded to a pinkish gray. Dusk.

Dusk. Had she been hidden away in her chamber this entire time? Claire hurriedly cleaned her brushes and her fingers, then opened the shutters to air out the room. As soon as she was certain all was concealed and the astringent fumes of turpentine and paint would blend with the usual scent of mustiness and crumbling plaster, she fled from her room and hurried down the stone stairs, anxious to join the others.

"Milady, Lady MacIntyre, Claire."

The voice pierced her distraction. She looked up to find David standing in the middle of the hallway, most likely outside his own chamber door.

"Sir David," she said. "I did not expect to see you."

He had been leaning against the wall, she realized, waiting for her. He pushed away from the wall to join her. "I simply wanted to make certain you were well after the ordeal." The intensity of his tone startled her.

"The loch?" Claire stared at him in surprise.

"Nay." David took her elbow and escorted her down the hallway toward the main stairs. "Jules told me all about it. Are you certain you are well?"

Claire stopped moving as ice infused her veins. Jules told him all about their lovemaking? Her vision blurred, and she reached out for the wall to support her. "He told you?" she whispered. Those stolen moments had been their private world, their bliss.

"Yes." Concern tightened the corners of his eyes as he studied her face. "It could not have been easy to learn of James Grayson's murder when we were all anxiously awaiting his arrival."

His murder. The horror of the man's demise reverberated through her, as did relief. David was talking about the man's unfortunate demise, not what had transpired between herself and Jules. She released a stuttering breath.

David mistook her relief for grief. His hand tightened on her elbow. "Do you need to sit down?"

Claire uttered a silent prayer for her good fortune that David had been more intrigued by poor Mr. Grayson's death than by what she and Jules had been doing down by the loch, or even by the smell of paint lingering in the hallway. "I am feeling much better than a moment ago, I assure you."

"That is well, because there are other things that need to be discussed." David's brown eyes were concerned beneath the dark swath of his brows. His expression was sincere and intense. He leaned closer, his voice lowered. "There are things you need to understand about your husband. I think you should hear them now."

They walked down the stairs. No one was around, not even the two women from the village who had come to clean. And yet, David turned toward the door leading outside. "It is best if we talk out here."

She allowed him to lead her out into the courtyard. The sky had turned a pale pink with streaks of burnished red clouds. Night would be upon them shortly, but David walked her through the knee-high grass to what looked like it had once been a rose garden. Now all that remained were tall stalks of gray and the occasional age-darkened rosehip.

Claire frowned as they walked along a cobbled path overgrown with weeds. This garden had been beautiful once. Perhaps with some love and attention it could be again. She tucked the thought away and turned to her escort. "What is so important that we had to discuss it out here?"

"Jules has been through many hardships in his life," David began as he released her arm and stood before her.

"If you are speaking of his time in gaol, I know about that already."

"'Twas Jane who saved his life, though she was unable to gain his release from gaol." David's lips thinned as he studied Claire.

"Who released him?" Claire asked.

"All his friends have wondered the same thing. We had hoped that someone was you," he asked with an arched brow.

Claire shook her head.

David's face grew solemn. "I was so certain it was you."

"It must have been horrible for him, waiting to be freed, wondering if anyone would ever come. I am grateful to whomever did release him," Claire said as a shiver trailed across the nape of her neck. "The darkness, the filth, the loss of hope, the pain . . . how had he endured all that for so long and survived?"

"Not many men would have." David hesitated as though trying to find the right words. "Jules has suffered greatly, and all of his friends mean to keep any future suffering to a minimum. That is why we are all here with him now, why we will be nearby always." His voice lowered, his expression hardened.

Claire startled. "Do you think I—"

"If you hurt him, Claire, if you hurt him at all, you will have to answer to us," David threatened.

The words surprised her, disturbed her. Regardless, she found her voice. "I will hurt him, David," she admitted. "Over the course of a lifetime, I will do something that will displease him. It's inevitable."

His gaze sharpened. "You know what I mean, not the everyday we-are-partners-in-life hurts. The kind of betrayal that leaves a person raw."

She nodded. She understood that feeling all too well. She knew what it was like to be moving along in one's life, only to find in the next heartbeat that everything you ever knew was gone.

Claire turned away from David's probing gaze. She felt as if she were falling into a deep, dark hole. She couldn't reach out, couldn't catch her breath. Her heart hammered in her chest at the knowledge that she would hurt Jules in the end. But she would be wounded as well, knowing she would never again experience the kind of passion she had shared with him earlier. They would both be raw when all of this was over. But Jules would survive with the help of his friends.

Claire's throat tightened. She would have her girls.

"Milady?" David's voice broke into her thoughts. Claire turned back around and looked up at Jules's friend, at his long, drawn face, his uncertain expression. "If my words upset you, I apologize. I simply wanted you to know we are here to support him."

"Thank you, David. I appreciate your honesty." She forced a bright smile despite the fact that her soul felt as though it was slowly being ripped in half.

Jules watched Claire enter the newly furnished green salon with David. She was laughing at something he said, and her cheeks were flushed. Her eyes sparkled, framed by tendrils of her over-bright hair that had worked their way free from her chignon to cradle her cheeks.

She seemed different—happier, definitely more relaxed, but also with a hint of sorrow in her eyes. Puzzled by the mixture, Jules watched her as David, the youngest male among them, led her to the newly acquired settee, then sat down beside her. She never stopped talking to David, who listened intently to her every word, his dark eyes unusually bright.

Something had happened between them, Jules thought, watching the couple discreetly while pretending to listen to what Jane said about all the new furniture they had purchased in the village.

Something had forged a friendship between the two of them, or was it something more? Perhaps David desired Claire . . .

She was *his* wife.

Jules frowned at the thought. When had he started to think of her as such? It was ridiculous, and yet there was no denying the tension that tightened his hands or the pulse of jealousy that warmed his blood at the way David's gaze lingered not on Claire's eyes, but on the swell of her breasts, rising above her tight bodice.

Jules's blood raced hot and furious through his veins. Before he knew what he was doing, he apologized to Jane, stood, then strode across the room.

"Claire," he demanded, feeling the harshness of his voice echo in the thrumming of his blood.

Her conversation with David ceased. Her gaze shot to his, following his every move as he came closer and held out his hand. Her brow rose in question.

"Come with me to the cellar. We must select wine for supper tonight." He knew there was very little wine left in the barrels, yet he had to do something to get her away from David.

With an apologetic smile at David, she accepted Jules's hand and rose. He could not say why it angered him that she was speaking with David, but it did. And even more infuriating was the way in which she lifted her chin, met his gaze, and his challenge.

He had wanted to ignore her, to force her out of his life as rapidly as she had come into it. Yet there was something about her that was impossible to ignore. Her innocence disarmed him. Her calm determination defeated him at every turn.

He drew a stuttering breath, trying to calm his racing heart. No one had ever affected him like this, not even Jane. With Jane, he had been attracted to her beauty, her sweetness, her compassion, but their relationship had always been one of discussion and deep thought.

He and Jane had never kissed. And if truth be told, he realized now that from the time he had been thirteen years old, he'd set Jane on a pedestal of perfection that not even she could achieve. He had turned her into an untouchable goddess, and the culmination of all his dreams.

Jules frowned. With Claire, his responses were visceral, deep, anguishing. She tempted him as he had never been tempted before. Slowly, he could feel her breaking down the barriers he had built around himself, feel her piercing through the numbness he had allowed to wrap around his heart. He had learned in gaol to distance himself from feelings. It had been the only way to maintain his sanity at the time.

Why was she trying so hard to get close to him? He had nothing to offer her except poverty, disappointment, and debt. She could never be his. It would be better for them both if he ended this charade now.

He pushed the cellar door open, lit a torch, then turned to face her. He could feel his blood pounding through his veins, but it had quickly changed from anger. He stared at her moist, full lips. With just a look he remembered their taste. He could feel her softness beneath his palms. Damnation, how he craved her.

"Before I tell the others, I wanted you to know I am leaving," he said, resisting the urge to touch her hair, her cheek.

"You're leaving?" she looked at him with such grief in her eyes he had to look away.

"Not forever," he clarified. "Since Grayson cannot come to us, I must go to Edinburgh to find the proof of our marriage. The church or the solicitor will have documents, if any truly exist. St. Giles, you said?"

"Yes." She released a soft sigh. "You won't send that young messenger back to Edinburgh?"

Jules brought his gaze back to hers. "I'll not risk Joseph's life for something that should clearly fall on my shoulders. Besides, I have business to conduct in town as well."

She moved toward him. "Jules . . ."

"We need wine for supper." He dodged her touch and went to the wine barrels lining the right side of the cellar; whiskey barrels lined the left. He reached for a wooden pitcher, made certain it didn't contain dust or debris, then opened the spigot. Nothing came out. He tipped the barrel and was rewarded for his efforts with a thin stream of pungent wine.

"I could go with you," she said, her voice quiet yet hopeful.

"No, this is something I must do alone. Look after our guests." He had meant to say his friends, but had changed his words at the last moment in order to include her in his life, at least in some small way. He shook his head, trying to clear her from his thoughts. He had to stay focused on that one task.

"When do you leave?"

"First light." He averted her gaze, fighting the urge to scoop her into his arms and carry her to his room, then spend the entire night exploring every inch of her body with his lips, his hands, and his mouth. What was it about her that made him lose his focus time and again?

He turned to leave, but before he reached the door, Claire stopped him with a gentle hand to his shoulder. He twisted toward her. Before he knew what she was doing, she kissed him on the cheek and clasped his hand.

"Be safe on your travels."

He inclined his head.

Leave. The thought pounded through his brain. Because if he didn't, he might yield to the demanding need inside him.

She released his fingers and he felt the loss of her.

At the door, he turned to look at her. Concern and sorrow reflected in her golden eyes.

Stunned, he could do nothing more than blink as he forced his feet to move in the opposite direction. He couldn't recall the last time anyone had been sad to see him go.

An hour later, ensconced in his study, Jules studied the ring Claire had said his solicitor had given her. He still couldn't make sense of how his mother's ring had resurfaced after all these years. He was positive his father had buried it with his mother. Had someone opened her grave?

Jules groaned. Nothing about Claire, their supposed marriage, or Grayson's betrayal and his death made any sense. Yet there had to be a link. What was he overlooking?

Fin appeared at the door and cleared his throat before shuffling into the chamber. "Milord, I apologize fer the interruption, but he wouldn't take no fer an answer, despite the late hour."

"What is it?" Jules asked with a frown as he returned the ring to his waistcoat. Lord, he was tired. Jules flexed his shoulders to rid himself of tension, then stood, moving toward his faithful servant. Before he could address Fin further, a young man burst into the room.

"Lord Kildare."

Jules frowned at the young, blond-haired man, instantly recognizing not his face but his purpose. He had hoped to keep the debt collectors at bay a while longer. "It's all right, Fin. You can leave us."

Fin backed out of the doorway, leaving the two of them alone. Jules waited until the door closed behind him, then said with great precision, "You're the debt collector Fin told me about. You've been living in our boathouse. I should evict you from the premises."

The man's gaze narrowed. "But you won't. I was instructed to stay close, to watch you, until your debts are paid."

"I cannot pay you . . . yet. Come back in five days, and I will have your money." Jules held up his hand as the man started to protest. "Five days or you will get nothing at all."

A flicker of irritation entered the debt collector's eyes. "Your new bride did not bring you an infusion of funds?"

"No," Jules said, his own irritation spiking. "Not all brides come with dowries. Lady Kildare's assets are a little more personal."

The man's eyes widened, but he said nothing more.

Jules had let the words slip before thinking. Even so, he realized there was some truth to what he'd said. Claire did bring certain assets into their marriage.

Assets that were getting harder and harder to forget.

The next morning, Jules set off for Edinburgh on his horse. Before he left, he made Fin promise to keep an eye on Lady Kildare and to do what he could to keep the dun collectors away. He did not need his friends or his supposed wife to be bothered by things that were clearly his responsibility.

It felt good to finally take an active role in the circumstances that had brought Claire to his door. He was determined to find the answers he needed in Edinburgh. Riding as swiftly as he could, and changing horses often, it still took two days before he arrived, late afternoon, to the city. Jules made his way to James Grayson's office, across the street from Parliament Hall.

Jules knew social dictates might require him to send a note, alerting Peter Kirkwood, Grayson's partner, of his arrival and requesting a meeting for the following day, but he did not have the luxury of time. He needed answers before anything else happened to anyone involved in his affairs.

On the third rap upon the door, an aging and stooped Peter Kirkwood answered and ushered Jules into his office. He waited until Jules had settled into the chair before his massive desk, then sat in the chair behind it and put on his spectacles.

"My condolences on the loss of your business partner," Jules said with true concern.

"Shameful business, what happened to poor Grayson. I always thought I would go first."

"Did they determine what happened?" Jules asked.

Kirkwood shrugged. "Runaway carriage, they presume."

"Whose carriage? Are there any suspects, or reasons why it might have happened?"

"None at present." Kirkwood shook his head. "Such a dreadful way to die."

"Dreadful. Indeed," Jules said with a frown.

"So, Lord Kildare, what can I do for you in Grayson's absence?" the aging solicitor asked.

"May we speak plainly, Kirkwood?"

The old man took off his glasses and leaned forward. "Of course."

"Very well." Without further pretense, Jules began, "I need to know everything Grayson did recently that relates to me. I need records, financial transactions, meeting notes, everything."

The solicitor frowned. "Is this in regard to a certain matter, Lord Kildare?"

"My marriage."

Kirkwood's eyes widened. "My felicitations, milord, I had no idea."

"Neither did I."

Kirkwood blinked. "How can that be? These things take planning, paperwork."

"Grayson supposedly took care of the details, including selecting my bride," Jules said with a frown.

Now Kirkwood looked troubled. "That doesn't seem like something Grayson would do."

"That's what I need to find out."

Kirkwood shuffled through a stack of papers. "I will need a little time to dig deeper into the paperwork, as well as Grayson's finances, if he'd made any unusual transactions of late, and if he was involved in any scheme. If a trail is there, I'll find it." The solicitor frowned. "I must confess, I was beginning to shift most of the day-to-day operations over to Grayson." Kirkwood glanced at Jules. "He was the closest thing I had to a son. I had become only a shadow around here until a few days ago."

Jules nodded. "Again, I am very sorry for your loss."

Kirkwood returned his gaze to the stacks of papers on the desk. "Come back on the morrow and I will have information for you then."

"My thanks," Jules said, standing. When the old solicitor continued to dig through the papers, with only a nod of his head, Jules took that as his cue to leave. "I will see you tomorrow at this same time. That should give us both plenty of time to investigate."

Jules left the office and stepped into the evening air. He let the slight breeze brush over him and clear his senses before he continued down the street toward the parliament buildings and the row of shops just to the south. His fingers strayed to the interior pocket of his waistcoat, and he removed the only precious item he yet possessed with any value. His mother's ruby ring.

He still had no idea how Grayson had come into possession of the ring. For a moment, he saw his mother walking with him by the loch, holding his hand. The sunlight caught the rubies, causing the red stones to sparkle. He remembered looking at his mother's hand in his, seeing the fiery stones, and feeling happy.

Shaking off memories of the past, Jules stopped in front of a jeweler's shop. He felt the weight of the ring in his hand. He did not want to sell the last remaining tie he had to the only person who had ever truly loved him, but he had no other option. The debt collectors would not wait forever, and he would rather die than go back to gaol. Distancing himself from the memories, and from what he was doing, Jules stepped inside and offered up the ring.

The jeweler was impressed with the size and clarity of the three stones. "They are exceptionally fine stones. I will give you thirty shillings Scot.""

"If they are truly fine stones, then you will pay me what they are worth," Jules replied in response to the jeweler's offer.

"I cannot," he replied with a hint of sadness. "My clientele will have a difficult time paying even the price I am paying you. I am sorry. This is my best offer."

A sort of numbness crept over Jules then, the kind of numbness that would help him do what must be done. With a nod he agreed.

The jeweler's lips pulled up in a smile as he studied the ring once more. "Since I do not keep this kind of money on hand, you will need to go to the goldsmith with me."

Forty minutes later, Jules emerged from the goldsmith with a small fortune in coins filling the black satchel he'd removed from his horse. He could pay his creditors, and he could support himself for a while longer, perhaps until the estate started to generate income again.

Perhaps.

He was ready to assume that risk, but he could not knowingly saddle anyone else with the poverty that was inevitably to continue at Kildare Manor for some time. No one deserved that kind of life, especially not a wife.

His wife. He had one last stop to make before the city shut down for the night. He proceeded down High Street toward St. Giles' Cathedral. Inside the church, he walked down the marble aisle toward the reverend, who lifted stubs of candles from the candelabras, replacing them with fresh tapers.

The scent of flowers, incense, and fresh beeswax drifted to him, enfolding him in their fragrance. As Jules made his way forward, a ray of late afternoon sunlight struck the stained glass windows, bathing the cathedral in a rainbow of colors.

Jules found himself relaxing as a sense of wonder warmed him in places he had not realized were cold. The radiance from the multicolored light filled him, lifted him up, and for the first time in a very long while he felt like his own life was not the enemy. He had come here looking for answers. He no longer feared the answers he would find. If Claire truly was his wife, then they would move forward with that knowledge.

And if she were not . . . Jules's steps faltered as he realized he hoped for the former outcome. The woman intrigued him as no other had. She was captivating, puzzling, a mystery that needed solving. Did he need marriage to solve that puzzle? Perhaps not, but at that moment it did not seem like the curse it had when she'd first arrived at Kildare Manor.

"Evening," the reverend, a man in his late sixties with white hair and keen gray eyes, greeted Jules.

Jules bowed, then stepped forward. "Pastor, I need your help."

The man smiled. "That is why I am here. How can I be of service?"

"I need to know the specifics of a certain wedding ceremony that supposedly took place here a few weeks back."

"The office has the records of ceremonies that have taken place here." The reverend gazed at him with curiosity. "Whose ceremony do you need information about?"

"Mine."

The older man's eyes widened. "Come." He motioned toward the pew at the front of the aisle. "Sit and tell me more." When they were seated he asked, "You do not recall your own marriage?"

"It was a proxy marriage."

"Ahh," the older man said, knowingly. "When did the marriage take place?"

"I am not sure precisely, but sometime earlier this month. In the last two weeks." Jules could feel the reverend's gaze on him, studying him. For a moment Jules tensed. What did he see? Could he see what his father must have always seen when he looked at Jules? Did he see the emptiness inside him? The lack of any goodness?

The reverend's gaze softened. "Your purpose here?" His voice was understanding, inviting.

Jules responded to that invitation. "To discover if the marriage truly took place."

The reverend stared at him with eyes so keen Jules had to look away. Could the man see more than Jules wished to reveal?

Jules sat taller in his chair. "I need to know the truth." He returned his gaze to the reverend a moment later.

The man nodded, his eyes shifting to somewhere behind Jules. "Let us go to the office and see what is recorded in the register. Shall we?"

Jules stood and followed the reverend out a door along the back wall of the cathedral that led down a long hallway.

As they walked the older man asked, "If you give me the names and a description of the bride and your proxy, I might be able to find the information you seek in the register sooner."

"The bride is Claire Elliot. She is in her early twenties, bright red hair, tall for a woman, intelligent." Jules startled at the last word. It wasn't really a descriptor, and yet it was. Claire was intelligent, and challenging, and frustrating all at the same time.

A smile lifted the reverend's lips. "You need say no more. I remember her well. She was nervous about the marriage."

The man remembered her. The marriage was real. He and Claire were married.

"She was nervous? Why?" Jules hadn't expected that.

The minister arched a graying brow. "She was getting married, yet her groom was nowhere in sight. I am sure there was much to be fearful of, particularly if the two of you had never met."

"We hadn't."

The reverend nodded. "You can see why she might have been a little afraid?"

Jules was spared from answering as they entered the reverend's office. The man who held all the answers moved to a cabinet along the back wall, and withdrawing a key from the folds of his robes, he opened the lock, then removed a heavy book and set it on the crude desk nearby. He flipped the weathered pages open to the back of the book and scanned the entries, running his finger down the rows of neatly printed names until his finger stopped near the bottom of the page.

Jules's muscles clenched as he waited in the silence for the words. "And Grayson? What did he look like?"

Without looking up, the minister said, "I am acquainted with Grayson. I can attest that it was he who stood next to your bride."

All the evidence pointed to the fact they had married.

"Here it is. Miss Claire Elliot and Lord Kildare, Jules MacIntyre by proxy. And it's signed by a Mr. James Grayson."

For a moment, an image flashed through his mind of a red-haired girl standing at the altar, her pale, slim hands at her sides with no one to support her as she married a total stranger. She had every right to be afraid. But suddenly he wanted to know why she had done it.

She'd said she had no choice.

She had no choice but to marry a penniless laird with a dreadful reputation and no notable estate? To any rational human, her behavior would seem mad. Yet he knew her to be quite sane.

So why had she married him?

"Is there anything else I can help you with?" the reverend asked.

Jules couldn't help himself; he laughed, an angry, self-deprecating sound. "I wouldn't know where to start."

The reverend studied him with a thoughtful gaze. "Sometimes, when we are searching for certain truths, it is best to start at the beginning."

The beginning.

It seemed like a wise place to start.

Jules returned to Kirkwood's office the next day. He already knew part of what the solicitor would tell him—that he had a wife. The knowledge that Claire somehow belonged to him filled him with as much satisfaction as it did fear.

He had no time to reflect on the thought as Kirkwood ushered him into his office. "Congratulations, milord, for you indeed are married."

Jules accepted the papers Kirkwood held out to him. The marriage documents, no doubt drawn up by Grayson, just as Claire had said. At the bottom of the document he could clearly read Claire's name, her handwriting neat and fluid, alongside his own bolder hand. Yet he had never signed these documents. Or at least he had not realized what the documents were when he'd trusted Grayson and signed the marriage papers without reading them.

Jules raked his hand through his hair. Anger at Grayson for betraying his trust mixed with sorrow over the man's death. Grayson had been more like a brother to him than a business associate. How could he have betrayed a kinship that went deeper than blood?

"Have they buried him yet?" Jules asked, once again meeting Kirkwood's curious gaze.

"Not until tomorrow."

Jules straightened, recovering his composure. "Then that is when I will pay my respects." He nodded toward the open ledger on the man's desk. "Have you uncovered anything unusual in Grayson's finances?" Jules asked as he took a seat in the chair nearest the desk.

Kirkwood did not sit behind the desk. Instead he perched on the edge, his expression dark. "Yes. It is most disturbing, too."

"Go on," Jules encouraged the solicitor when he hesitated.

"There was a rather large deposit to his account twenty-three days ago."

"How large?" Jules asked.

"Five hundred shillings Scot." Kirkwood shuffled through the notes on his desk. "Paid to him by your father."

Jules frowned. "My father? Are you certain?"

The older man nodded. "I traced the transaction back to your father's solicitor. He paid James Grayson to arrange your marriage to Claire Elliot. It appears he went to great lengths to find you a suitable bride with that first name."

"How did he accomplish that? And when? He's been dead for more than three weeks."

Kirkwood checked the papers before him. "The transaction was recorded two days before his death."

It took a second for the words to sink in, and when they did, Jules stood, no longer able to contain himself in the chair. He stood there for what felt like an eternity, breathing hard.

"Milord, are you well?" the solicitor asked.

Seven months had passed since his release from gaol. Seven months. Had his father not tormented him enough for one lifetime? Instead of coming to the gaol to release his own son, he had plotted and planned yet another horrific event.

Except Claire wasn't horrific. She was gentle, intelligent, and passionate. If he were honest, she was everything and more than what *he* had created "Claire" to be.

Jules startled at the thought. *He* had created Claire. Not his father. So how had his father implemented a plan that Jules had set into play? It made no sense . . . except, a sudden thought occurred to him. He had created his false bride five weeks ago. James Grayson knew about her two weeks before his father had paid for the marriage to take place.

Two weeks. It was enough time for Grayson to send word to his father and for his father to arrange . . . whatever he had arranged.

Why? The word thrummed through Jules's brain. He had absolutely no idea why his father would do such a thing, or even whether the man had considered his actions to be a benefit or yet another manipulation.

"Shall I get the physician?" Kirkwood asked, his face wreathed with concern.

"No." Jules shook off his thoughts. "I am well." He took another moment to collect himself, then turned back to the older man. "Did you find anything else?"

Kirkwood frowned. "Not in his financials, but when I talked with one of his friends, he said Grayson had been meeting often with someone in a black, hooded cloak down at The Doric, an inn on Market Street. I have a feeling that Grayson's meeting, your father's actions, and the hooded figure are all somehow connected."

Agreeing with Kirkwood's conclusion, Jules asked, "Who is this mysterious person?"

"That," Kirkwood said, "is what we do not know."

Jules looked at a clock on a nearby cabinet. "Then I must discover that information myself. Perhaps this cloaked person can shed some light on why my father would pay Grayson to orchestrate my marriage."

"Indeed," Kirkwood replied, still frowning.

"If you discover anything more," Jules said, heading for the door, "you know where to find me."

Kirkwood sat at his desk as Jules shut the door behind him. Jules needed to find a hackney to take him to Market Street.

That morning, Claire left her chamber determined to find Fin. With Jules gone, the steward might be more willing to answer her questions about the MacIntyre family and this house. Claire made her way through the rooms, searching, until she finally came upon Fin in the library, seated behind an overly large desk, studying the estate's ledger.

"Fin," Claire called from the doorway, not wanting to startle the aging servant.

He looked up. A warm smile came to his face. "Come in, milady. What can I do fer ye?"

"Can I ask you about the ballroom upstairs? What happened in that chamber? Why did Jules forbid me from entering?" she asked in a rush.

Fin's expression saddened. "I'm nae certain the laird wants me tae share that information with ye."

She straightened. "I am his wife. If I am ever to help him overcome his past, I must know what troubles him."

Fin's mouth quirked. "I canna argue with that." He waved her into the chamber and toward the chair opposite him.

Claire sat and then waited patiently as Fin studied her. "Ye'll nae hurt him with this knowledge?"

She shook her head even as her stomach clenched. She would never use the knowledge of what had happened in that chamber against him. "I want to help him heal and make new memories as he embraces his new life as the laird of Kildare Manor."

Tears came to the old man's eyes. "I thank ye fer that. All right, I'll tell ye. It does this old heart good tae see that Jules has finally found some comfort in this world." Fin swiped at his eyes and turned his gaze fully on her. "But ye didna hear this from me. Understand?"

Claire nodded.

"That chamber was where Agatha, his stepmother, was found dead. I was the one who found her. She was cold and gray. The only sign of what had happened tae her was the overturned teacup and the remains of the tea. The shire reeve who investigated claimed he could smell and taste poison in the liquid that remained in the cup. That Jules had purchased that very combination of herbs in the village the day before led everyone tae accuse him of murder. He was sentenced tae hang."

"He was cleared of the charges?" Claire shuddered at the thought of what Jules had been through in the recent past.

Fin nodded, but his gaze saddened. "Thanks tae Lady Jane, who testified that Jules was with her at the time of the murder. But even though he was cleared of the crime, there was an outlandish ransom tae be paid." His old eyes were haunted. "No one tried verra hard tae release him, until recently."

A lump settled in her throat as she thought about how horrible it must have been for him. "Did Jules's parents love him?"

Fin's eyes cleared. "His mother did, tae be sure. With his father, things were more complicated." The aging steward paused a moment before continuing. "I think 'twas because Jules reminded him of his dead wife that the old laird kept his son at arm's length and why it was easy fer him tae send him tae Lord Lennox. But at the end, I believe his father regretted their estrangement." Fin shook his head as though clearing the thought. "Some things just come too late."

"Do you know who killed the second Lady Kildare?" Claire asked, the bold question burning in her chest.

"Nay." The steward sighed. "I would have killed her myself when she first wheedled her way into this family if I'd known the trouble she would eventually cause. But the answer is nay. I know nothin' about her death other than that Jules dinna kill her."

"Thank you for telling me about the chamber and about Jules's past," Claire said.

Fin nodded. "His future looks much brighter now that ye have arrived."

Claire drew a shaky breath. They had no future together—bright or otherwise. All they had was the here and now. But perhaps, now that she knew the truth about the ballroom, she could find some way to exorcise the ghosts of his past.

Later that day, Claire tried to put thoughts of Jules and his suffering out of her mind as she worked in the soil. She paused in her gardening to push the escaping tendrils of her hair out of her face, then leaned on her spade and surveyed the rose garden with a sense of accomplishment. She had rid the ground of every last weed to expose the wildly overgrown stalks. Her reward for freeing them from their prison of weeds was the sweet, heady scent from open blossoms that reminded her of the summer she had spent learning how to paint roses, over and over again. She had filled twenty canvasses that summer with the wild pink, red, and orange blooms.

Claire brushed her fingers over a soft, velvet petal. And just as they had so many summers ago, the blooms caused a riot of inspiration to crowd her mind. Ideas for how and where to add roses to the ceiling in the ballroom swirled through her head in prismatic colors—a blend of orange and yellow, a light hint of pink around the edges, the stamen a mixture of brown and red, with a light touch of yellow.

The colors would fill her nights with activity and add just the right touch to the corners of the room. She would bring the outside inside and fill with light and beauty a room that had once been the site of so much anger and pain.

For the past four days she had done nothing but garden in the morning, and paint at night by the light of many lamps. She spent the hours in between with their guests who were becoming more tired every day by the advancing stage of their pregnancies. But when the women did have energy, they, too, seemed eager to transform Kildare Manor while Jules was away. Nicholas and Hollister directed the men they'd hired to clear the briars and brambles away from the manor, while David and Fin busied themselves with the grass that covered the entire estate.

Jane and Margaret were eager to share their knowledge of running an estate the size of Kildare Manor with Claire, for which she was grateful. Today they had interviewed two women who had come to the manor to apply for the position of cook.

The manor was coming back to life, as was Jules's reputation. He had said the villagers were frightened of him once. Well, something had changed in the last few days, because every day since Jules had left for Edinburgh, villagers came to the estate, asking for work. David and the others had put them to good use, inside and outside the house. Claire only hoped Jules's pride could withstand the financial assistance his friends offered him, especially without his consent.

Satisfied with her progress in the rose garden today and eager to find her paints, Claire set her gardening spade aside and headed back toward the house. No sooner had she entered through the kitchen and washed thoroughly when Margaret and Jane found her.

"There you are," Margaret said, a slow smile lighting her face. Jane was right behind her as they came into the empty space. "We've come to propose an idea to you."

Claire dried her hands on a linen towel and, with exaggerated care, folded it and placed it near the washbasin. "What manner of idea?"

"One that involves you and Jules," Margaret said with a conspiratorial gleam in her eyes. From the doorway, she waved the new cook, Mrs. Jarve, forward. The woman was herself a recipe of nationalities—part French, part English, part Scottish. She had impeccable references, but what had won her the position were the rhubarb tarts she had brought with her to the interview. The cook smiled shyly at Claire now, as she too came to stand before her.

The three of them surrounded her. Claire's nervousness rose in proportion to the glee in their eyes.

"Hear us out," Jane said, coming forward with a rustle of rose satin. "We know you and Jules married in haste with no one there to support you. I realize now it was most likely because of his financial situation that he kept things private. But we still want to celebrate with you both as is more in keeping with tradition. And now that we have a cook capable of the task"—she hesitated for a moment before continuing—"we want to prepare a wedding feast for you both when Jules returns. We will celebrate the beginning of your new life together the way it should have been celebrated in the first place."

Of all the things Claire had expected Jane to say, it had not been that.

"Oh please say yes, Claire. There is nothing like a wedding banquet with all the delicious sweetmeats and the frivolity and the guests dressed in their most colorful velvets and satins."

"It seems like a lot of work, not to mention the expense, to celebrate something that has already happened," Claire said.

"The entire event will be a gift from Nicholas and me."

"You've already spared no expense in order to repair the estate. We should wait for Jules to return before anything more is done."

Claire dipped her gaze. "I have not known Jules as long as you, but I do know he is a proud man. The changes that have been made in his absence will be difficult for him to bear."

Jane held out her hand. "Mercy, don't you worry about that. Nicholas and Hollister will take care of everything. They will enter into some sort of arrangement with Jules that will keep his dignity and his pride. But that's for the men to accomplish. Margaret and I have something to show you."

Claire stared at Jane, not moving, still unsure, so Jane grasped her hand and pulled her toward the door. "Come," Jane said.

Surrendering to her fate, Claire allowed Jane to lead her from the kitchen and through the house, up the stairs, and into the master's chamber. Claire swallowed a thick lump in her throat. This was the first time she had seen Jules's room, even though Jane and Margaret assumed she slept there. Her heart hammering as she invaded Jules's sacred domain, Claire allowed Jane to guide her toward the great bed in the center of the room. The linen hangings were tied back. On the quilted comforter lay a dress. Jane lifted the magnificent emerald gown up for Claire to admire. "Isn't it lovely?"

Claire peered at the exquisite damask silk. "It's the finest gown I have ever seen."

"Good," Jane said with a broad smile, "because I purchased this gown for you to wear tomorrow night when Jules returns from Edinburgh."

Claire shifted her gaze from Jane to Margaret, who stood near the bedpost. Margaret nodded. "We've invited several guests to attend the banquet, people who used to come to Kildare Manor over the years, but have strayed away from Jules's company."

"In order for Jules to be a successful laird, we need to relaunch him into society as a competent landowner and leader of his clan." Jane's expression grew serious. "A wedding feast gives us the perfect opportunity to celebrate both his marriage and his claim to his lairdship. Please say you will help us? Without his bride, we cannot do this."

Claire shuddered as fear gripped her. Closing her eyes for a moment, she imagined herself in that dress, greeting her husband with guests all around them. He wouldn't be able to run away with so many people expecting him to play the roles of groom and laird.

A host of questions crowded her thoughts. Could she play the role of wife and seducer? Could she be everything Jules needed her to be in front of his friends and his peers? Could she set aside her own agenda and help him be the laird his friends hoped him to become? Could she give him something that might help him in his future without her? The thought brought with it a twist of pain.

His future without her.

Despite the hurt she would cause him, he would go on. He would be the laird of the MacIntyres, and he would assume his proper place in society if she did what Jane and Margaret asked of her now.

"Yes." The word was a whisper of sound that cut through her pain.

"You'll do it?" Jane asked with a look of hope on her face.

Claire nodded and suddenly found herself hauled into Jane's embrace. "Thank you, Claire. We will make this a night to remember, just you wait and see."

"Thank you for the lovely gown." Claire was certain she would remember this night every day for the rest of her life. The memory would be steeped in sadness and pain. She would yearn for a husband she could never truly have, for all the moments of his life she would miss, and she would ache with loneliness that could never be assuaged, not because of what she did for her girls, but because she realized in that moment that she was utterly and hopelessly in love with Jules.

She drew an uneven breath, at last recognizing the truth. She loved Jules.

The words repeated, ran together, and stabbed deep. She had searched her whole life for this feeling, and only when her life had been turned upside down with threats and treachery had she found what she'd searched for all along.

Merciful heavens, it was so unfair. Visions of Jules came to her, whispering, insinuating their way into her heart, gathering the air around her until it filled her with all the joy and hope and the splendor of what was possible.

Love.

Love was a gift not to be taken for granted. It was precious and fragile, elusive.

But how could she ever indulge in her newfound feelings without sacrificing the girls? She'd never had any doubts that they would be killed if she didn't do exactly what she'd been instructed to do—to break the heart of the man she loved. She would break her own as well. Claire released her breath in a painful sigh. She moved away from Jane and Margaret's puzzled stares to the window.

Her heart was beating so quickly she could hear it in her ears. Was there a way to keep what she had suddenly found? Could she tell Jules the truth? Would he be able to help her rescue the girls? Or would the kidnappers make good on their threats to kill the girls immediately if she so much as uttered a word to her husband?

"Claire, is everything all right?" Jane asked from behind her.

She would take that risk with her own life, but not with Penelope's, Anna's, and Eloise's. Claire clasped her trembling fingers before her and turned around, suddenly finding the courage to go forward, despite the pain and anguish that pulsed through her with every thudding beat of her heart.

Claire met Jane's concerned gaze and nodded. "If we are to have a party, then we will need a room that can accommodate all of our guests." This time it was Claire who took Jane's hand and pulled her from the room, down the hall, and up the stairs until they stood before the boarded-up chamber Jules had barred her from entering on their first day together.

"The old ballroom?" Jane's eyes went wide as she pulled her hand from Claire's. "Jules has made it clear to anyone who knows him that no one is to enter that room."

"Well, I am not no one. I am his wife."

Jane smiled. "I knew I liked you."

Claire pulled on the boards she had loosened, setting them against the wall until she cleared a large enough hole to step through. "I've made a few changes to the room over the last few days." She stepped back and allowed Jane and Margaret to precede her into the chamber.

"Jules hates this room. He—" Jane broke off as Claire pushed open the shutters, allowing the golden daylight to fill the chamber. "Sweet Mary, who painted the ceiling? Jules does not have the funds to hire a painter, especially one of this caliber."

"It's beautiful," Margaret said with awe, then turned to Claire. "You did this, didn't you?"

A rush of fear and pride brought the sting of tears to her eyes. "Yes," she admitted, desperately wanting their approval.

She waited breathlessly as both women leaned their heads back and studied the beginnings of the elaborate painting she had planned. At the center of the room, Claire had painted the ceiling in perfect perspective so that the flat surface opened up into the illusion of a three-dimensional dome. After learning of the sorrow that had befallen not only Jules, but this room, she had wanted to transform it, make it appear as though it opened up into the heavens above.

"How on earth did you do that?" Jane asked, her voice tight with reverence.

"I paint," she said simply.

"You do far more than paint," Margaret said with a laugh. "How did you manage to make the ceiling look as though it had sprouted arches and pillars? It looks three stories high."

"The technique is called quadratura, and unites architecture, painting, and sculpture into one form. I taught myself how to paint this type of mural by imitating the work of the Italian painter Andrea Pozzo."

"Does Jules know you possess this talent?" Jane stared at Claire now.

She shook her head.

"Good." Jane smiled. "It will be a fabulous surprise for him." Jane's gaze shifted back to the ceiling and the compilation of angels and stars and flowers. "When you are finished here, I would love to commission you to paint something, anything at all, at Bellhaven Manor."

Margaret let out a gasp, clutched her belly, then laughed. "The baby," she said in the way of an explanation. "This one kicks like a mule." She smiled fondly at Claire. "I suspect it will be many years before Claire ventures outside of Kildare Manor. She'll be busy with her own babies before long."

Claire tried to laugh, but the words were like arrows, driving deep. She would never have babies with Jules. She wouldn't even be around long enough to finish the ceiling completely—that task would take two years or more.

"You're right, Margaret. Then let's enjoy this beautiful ceiling, show it off to our guests, and plan for the perfect wedding feast tomorrow evening upon Jules's return." Jane laughed, a cheerful sound, but to Claire it sounded like a hollow echo in an empty room.

Tomorrow they would celebrate a wedding that was real, but a marriage that had been doomed from the start.

Claire clamped her hand over her mouth to stifle an agonized moan. She would give anything to make this marriage real.

13

he Doric. The name of the inn circled in Jules's mind like a tiresome nursery rhyme as he stepped into the darkened interior of the building on Market Street. Loud voices, smoke, the smell of bodies, whiskey. And people. Too many people. The impressions came at him at once as he searched the dark interior for a hooded figure.

He hadn't expected to find the person that night. Jules frowned as he scanned the tables in the center of the room and the booths in the corners. The person he sought could be anyone, anywhere in this room. With a muttered curse, he made his way to the long wooden bar on the left-hand side of the room. He pushed his way through the crowd to the man behind the bar.

"I need some information," he shouted above the noise to the man a person's length from him. When the innkeeper paid him no heed, Jules placed a gold coin on the bar.

The innkeeper narrowed his gaze and shifted to where Jules waited. "'Bout?" He scooped up the coin.

"A patron. A person in a dark-hooded cloak who comes here often to meet with James Grayson," Jules said, lowering his voice slightly to keep the conversation between the two of them.

The innkeeper shook his head. "Ye don't want tae tangle wit' that one."

"Why?"

"She's nothin' but trouble." He said, wiping an imaginary spot on the bar with a ragged, brown towel.

"Does *she* have a name?" A female? An unsettling feeling lodged in Jules's gut.

The innkeeper looked up and searched the room. "Don't know it."

"Is she here now?" Jules persisted.

"Haven't seen her fer a week, maybe more." The innkeeper's expression turned pensive.

"She wouldn't happen to have red hair?" he asked the question that lodged in his throat.

The man shook his head. "Nay, 'tis a dark color. Maybe black or dark brown. And the woman is older, maybe in her fifties? Hard tae tell beneath that cloak."

A sense of relief washed over Jules. He hadn't realized how much he hoped the mystery person was not Claire. "Why is she trouble?"

The innkeeper remained silent.

Jules waited for an answer.

"'Cuz people she talks tae end up dead. And people who ask lots of questions tend tae end up that way as well." The innkeeper ducked his head and started scrubbing at the wood in front of him again.

"Anyone else know anything about her?" Jules pressed his luck, asking one last question.

"They are all dead." The innkeeper stopped and met Jules's gaze. "Watch yerself. Stay alert."

Jules tossed down a second coin. "Thanks for the warning, but I'll be fine."

Disappointed that his questioning hadn't brought him any answers, Jules headed out the door and continued down the cobbled street. At least he knew the hooded figure was a female, and by the innkeeper's account, deadly. As that thought formed, so too did the suspicion that the woman might be responsible for Grayson's death.

Frowning into the darkness, Jules walked back toward the main part of town, wishing now he'd thought to bring his horse rather than leave the beast stabled at the inn on Melbourne Street where he'd spent the last night.

The moon was only a sliver in the sky, and the silence of the night was palpable. Through the darkened shadows, Jules kept his pace slow and deliberate as the sound of footsteps echoed behind him. One set of footsteps was joined by a second, and then a third. Jules reached for the sword at his side only to have his hand clutch air. It was then he realized he had left his sword back at the inn with his saddle and his horse.

He quickened his pace and turned a corner. A small circle of light illuminated the street. Jules followed the source to a lantern hanging from the side of the hackney coach that waited near the curb.

Before he could take a step toward it, a hand gripped his shoulder and whipped him around. Three men stood before him, their faces twisted in a mask of hate, and death lived in their eyes. "Give us yer money."

Jules had no intention of giving them the last of what he so desperately needed, but before he could so much as respond, the men were upon him. Two gripped his arms. Jules wrenched his body left and right, forcing the men to stagger against the motion. While off balance, Jules brought his knee up and caught one man in the groin. The attacker howled and released Jules's arm.

His breath ran harsh in his throat as he shot his fist forward, connecting with the face of one of his attackers. But while his hand was extended, the third man clipped Jules on the side of the head, sending him staggering backward. He did not fall, but the blow left him dizzy and disoriented. Yet knowing he could not hesitate or he would be overpowered, Jules brought his leg up and kicked the second attacker in the gut, sending him backward like a rag doll.

The dizziness combined with the motion sent Jules to the ground. The first attacker charged, coming at Jules with a kick. He clenched his jaw as a stab of pain shot through his side. Recovering quickly, he grasped the man's foot, taking him to the ground.

They wrestled there with the cobbled street biting into his side, his back, until Jules freed his arm and with all his strength let his fist fly into the man's face. A moment later, his opponent went limp.

Jules rolled, came up instantly, his coat a-tumble, his feet planted against the cobbles. He staggered across the street to the hackney, leaving his assailants behind.

"Sweet merciful heavens, what has happened?" For a heartbeat Claire couldn't catch a breath. She hurried into the late afternoon sunshine to greet her husband as he rode his horse up the drive to Kildare Manor. His face was bruised and pale. He alighted from his horse, unfastened his saddlebag, then handed the tired animal over to Joseph, who had stayed on with them, overseeing the stable.

"I found the truth." He set down his saddlebag and waited for her to join him in the graveled courtyard. A smile crooked one corner of his mouth.

Instinctively she reached out for him, and he took both of her hands in his. She looked up into his battered face. "Did you have to beat it out of someone?"

He shook his head. "Thugs in the street tried to rob me."

Claire tightened her grip on his hands as she looked past the black-and-blue welt on the side of his cheek and beneath his right eye. "We need the physician."

"No," he said, looking at her, really looking at her as though he had never seen her before. "You are really quite lovely," he said in a husky voice, and his eyes filled with the same sense of wonder she felt.

"Thank you." Tears stung her eyes, but she didn't care. "Does that mean . . . ?"

He released one hand and brought his fingers up to brush a tear from her cheek. "I . . . I don't know anything about being a husband."

"And despite my name, I am most likely not the wife you intended."

"We could take this slow, just start out by being friends?" Despite the words, he pulled her close. His gaze moved down her body, his smile purely sensual.

Claire laughed. "We bypassed friends a long time ago," she said in a dizzying rush of excitement. In that moment all the pain and fear and grief of her lifetime melted away. He believed her. Believed in them.

A nagging truth threatened to ruin the moment, but she forced it away. She wanted this moment so badly. Just once in her life she wanted to feel as though she controlled her destiny. Today she could pretend and forget all else. Today she would indulge herself in fantasy and give herself something to remember for when she was gone. She stared up into his face, memorizing everything about him, about this moment, how it felt to be accepted.

And perhaps, if she were truly fortunate . . . to be loved.

"Are you certain you do not need a physician?" she asked as they turned to go into the house.

He shook his head, then stopped and stared at the house. His body tensed as his gaze moved along the exterior walls, now free from the brambles and grass that had engulfed the manor before he'd left. "I was only gone for five days. What in heaven's name happened to Kildare Manor?"

Silence stretched between them as Claire listened to the gentle rush of the breeze and the soft lapping of the water against the shore of the loch in the distance. He released her hand and turned to face her. "Was this your doing?" He wasn't angry, only surprised.

"All of us pitched in. The manor . . ." she hesitated trying to find the right words. "Kildare Manor has come back to life."

The tension in his body eased. He reached for her hand once more. "More than the house has changed, Claire, and hopefully for the better." The smile he offered her was filled with hope. He retrieved his saddlebag from the ground, hooked it over his shoulder, then took a step forward. She remained where she stood, suddenly feeling the weight of her lies crash around her feet.

"There is something else you should know before we go inside," she said, her voice raw.

"What is that?" She saw the uncertainty in his eyes. "Some deep dark secret you've been keeping from me?"

Her stomach plummeted.

She must have turned ghostly white, because a quick smile tugged at the corner of his mouth. "I was joking."

Claire found her voice. "The others—Jane, Nicholas, and all— have invited several people to the manor. They have planned a wedding feast and celebration of you being the new earl . . . tonight."

"Guests here?" His brows rose in surprise. "I can't remember the last time anyone came to call for any purpose other than tragedy." He fell silent a moment, then touched her chin, tilted her face, and forced her to meet his eyes. "'Tis all right, Claire. Something had to change. You were right, the house was dead, along with its keepers. Past keepers," he corrected.

She saw a transformation in his eyes from the angry laird he had been when she'd first arrived to the strong and confident man before her. He looked at her as if she truly mattered to him. Her heart sped up.

"Shall we go see what miracles you all have wrought?" They started up the walkway together, and halfway there, he reached for her hand.

Hidden amongst the trees, a hooded figure watched as Claire and Jules entered the house. The dark figure balled her fists as frustration and rage rose within her. She desperately fought to control her temper.

Jules was in love with Claire, and yet she did not leave him. Now it was time for her to break Jules's heart. Claire would pay for not following orders. There was no mistaking that look in his eyes.

Did the girl not see what she had accomplished? Or, had she changed her mind?

Claire had been warned what would happen if she didn't do precisely what the woman had laid out for her. Yet her orders were being dismissed. The woman smothered the venom rising within her. No matter. She would regain all the power and her revenge soon enough. There would be no more waiting and watching. No more bribery. No more force. Only action.

The woman stepped back into the woods, where she had tethered her horse. Swinging up into the saddle, she noted that the sky was leaden, clouds rolling, scudding with the wind. She lifted her head and smiled as a gust of moist wind touched her cheeks.

A storm was coming to Kildare Manor.

Jules smiled as he looked about his study. The swords no longer dominated the space. They still remained, but now seemed to blend into the serenity of the still-sparse chamber. His desk had been moved to the opposite side of the room so that he could look out the window onto the newly threshed field.

He'd been gone only five days, and the place looked better than he ever remembered it looking, despite his desperate lack of funds. When he had returned home, he hadn't seen anything but Claire. All else had faded from view but the voluptuous vision that had come toward him in the drive. He'd had to clamp his teeth together to keep from calling out to her. And then he'd seen the look of concern in her eyes, and his heart had raced in his chest and swelled with pride.

She was *his*.

Jules no longer tensed at the thought of a wife. His bride. His home. His new life. What had he ever done to deserve all this? A week and a half ago, he had only wanted to be left alone. Now he couldn't imagine a life without Claire. The part of himself that had been so empty before felt suddenly filled. And he realized his love for Jane had never been the all-consuming sensation Claire evoked.

With a sigh of contentment, he sat in his chair behind the big desk and awaited Fin. He'd asked one of his new servants to send the steward to him there.

Waiting for the retainer, Jules smoothed his hands across the spotless surface of the desk. They'd not only tamed the outside, they had applied fresh paint to the walls, swept out all the mice and cobwebs, and polished what furnishings still remained in the house to a shine.

"Milord." A knock at the door brought him out of his ruminations.

A young woman opened the door and curtsied. "Master Fin fer ye, milord."

"Thank you, Betsy," Jules replied, unable to keep the grin from his face. He had servants. And food in the larder. And a home, thanks to Claire, his friends, and the slightly bent, aging man before him. Jules stood and gestured Fin toward the chair he had just vacated. "Sit, please."

"Nay, lad." Fin frowned. "'Tis yer chair."

"Please, Fin, sit."

With a shrug, the older man made his way behind the desk and sat. "What happened tae ye? Yer face looks like ye've taken a hit or two. Did the debt collectors find ye?"

"Not creditors." Jules said as he waited for Fin to settle himself.

"Then who?" the retainer asked, his frown deepening.

Jules shrugged. "It matters not. I escaped in far better condition than they did."

His brow heavy with concern, Fin said, "Ye wanted tae see me?"

Jules nodded.

"I need to know about my father's last days."

Fin folded his arms over his chest and nodded.

"What do ye want tae know?"

Facing his steward, Jules paused. He didn't know where to start as one question after another filled his mind. "Why did my father never pay for my release?"

"He had not the funds fer one thing. And I think he was just as happy tae know ye were safe enough there. He mentioned tae me once that he'd made a mistake forcin' ye tae come home from the Lennoxes. He knew how much ye wanted to learn tae use a sword, and tae train as a knight. He said he thought yer brother who wanted nothing tae do with battle would be safer with ye around."

"Safe from what?" Jules asked.

Fin shrugged. "I was close tae the man, but not privy tae all his doin's."

"What about Father's behavior about six weeks ago? Was he doing anything unusual?" Jules continued.

"Not six weeks, but about a month ago. That's when he started goin' to Edinburgh. The first time he left in a hellfire hurry after receivin' a note."

"Grayson sent Father a note?" Jules asked.

Fin nodded. "Yer father was furious about somethin'. He sold off the last of the furnishings, and he and yer brother had a few heated fights."

"About what?"

"I've been not listenin' tae conversations around here fer so long, I couldna tell ye. But it was after the last argument that yer brother started drinkin'. Yer father's heart gave out a week later. Yer brother died two days after that."

As Jules listened, he tried to pull a timeline of the events together in his mind. His own discussions with Grayson had started five weeks ago. A week later, Grayson had involved Jules's father without his knowledge. A week after that his father was dead, and the following week Claire and he were married.

Jules released a ragged sigh. He may never know the truth about what had happened or why, but he could not let that stop him from what he had to do as the current laird. "Thank you, Fin, for your honesty, and for your service as well." Jules reached inside his coat to withdraw a small bag of gold coins, approximately one-third of what he had received from selling his mother's ring. He set the bag on the desk before Fin. "I am certain the estate owes you far more than this in back wages, but consider this a start toward your compensation."

Fin's tired gray eyes widened. "Where did ye get the funds?"

"I sold my mother's ring." He turned and picked up the box he had leaned against the wall. "This is for you as well."

"I had my suspicions that yer father went back into yer mother's grave fer it nae too long ago." His voice sounded pained.

Jules frowned as yet another piece to the puzzle his father had left behind was revealed. "Why would he violate Mother's grave to get the ring back?"

"He must have wanted ye tae have it somethin' fierce tae do so," Fin replied.

Jules stared at his steward a moment, trying to make sense of why his father had given Claire something so important as the ring.

Then after a moment, Jules forced his thoughts aside. He could mull things over later after he did right by Fin. Jules held the box out toward Fin, encouraging him to take it.

Fin stared suspiciously at the box, which was tied with a string. "What is it?"

Jules laughed. "Open it and find out."

His lips pressed together in concentration, Fin pulled the string free, then lifted the lid to reveal a new gray suit, shirt, and shoes. Startled gray eyes searched Jules's. "Milord? New clothes?"

"Yes, Fin. And when you change into them, promise me you will burn the others."

"Thank ye, milord." The steward smiled. "Thank ye, fer comin' back here and fer facin' what yer father and yer brother could not."

A flicker of unease moved through Jules once more at the reminder, but he forced the thought away. He didn't want to worry about that now. For the first time in years he felt eager and hopeful. He had every intention of enjoying the sensations while they lasted.

On that thought, he left the study and Fin in search of Nicholas. Another third of the funds he had received would go to his friend as partial payment for all he had spent on Jules's behalf. The last third would go to that rapscallion from the village, Arthur Cabot, so that the young man would stop following Jules around.

Jules had been given a second chance at life, and he would find a way to pay for all his debts, including settling the one debt that annoyed him the most—the debt he owed to the mysterious person who had released him from gaol.

He did not want to be indebted to anyone ever again.

The last rays of the setting sun broke through the gathering clouds and came through the windows of the ballroom, bathing the room in golden light. It was as if the sunlight had battled the storm that was building outside to glory in the celebration.

The sweet melody of harpsichord, violin, and flute wove through the crowded ballroom. Jules's gaze moved over the chamber. Never in his life had this many people been at Kildare Manor at one time, especially in this room.

He used to hate this room. Yet now, thanks to his friends, and especially Claire and her talent with a paintbrush, the chamber had been transformed from a place of horrific memories to a place where hope existed. It was more than just fresh paint and a cleaned floor that had transformed this room and his life as of late. It was Claire.

Jules swallowed to ease the tightness from his throat. It was Claire, not Jane, who filled his thoughts. Not two weeks ago he had cursed God for the terrible unfairness of his life for having taken Jane and everything else that had ever mattered away from him. Yet now, he could see the bigger picture, the divine plan that He had put into place. God was always fair and just and good, in his own time.

Jules smiled at the thought that that time was now. He turned toward the doorway of the ballroom as a stillness came over the room. "My God," Jules breathed as Claire appeared in the doorway.

She was dressed in an emerald-green gown with elegant wide skirts and long, full sleeves that were fashionably cut to reveal a gold chemise beneath. The golden light caressed the silky texture of her loose red hair and played on the smoothness of her breasts revealed by the low cut of her bodice.

Her color was high, her step bold as she entered the chamber. And Jules had never seen her look so beautiful, or more compelling.

"Merciful heavens," David murmured beside Jules. "She is a woman any man would find hard to ignore."

Jules did not intend to ignore her this night, if ever again. He caught her gaze, and she returned it as though he were the only other person in the room. She came forward, as regal as a queen, as alluring as a goddess, as defiant as a warrior going into battle. Yet he could still see a hint of uncertainty in her eyes.

That uncertainty moved him like nothing else ever had. This woman was as rare as they came—honest, true, and innocent. His body hardened, the blood rushing to a part of him that always responded to her nearness.

She stopped before him and smiled. Her hand came up to

flutter across the swelling at his cheek and what remained of his black eye. "Does it pain you much?"

"I hardly notice."

"I am glad to hear that," she replied tenderly as she held out her hand. "Would you care to escort me to our wedding feast, my husband?"

She was asking for more than an escort.

He knew this moment of decision would come since he had returned home a few hours ago. He fully understood the consequences of what would happen if he let her into his heart tonight. He knew what was at risk if he gave in.

He looked down at the hand she extended. So strong, so small, so capable, and so very talented.

And yet, her fingers trembled.

Without further hesitation, he closed his fingers around hers. "My lady," he said, loud enough for those gathered close to hear. He held her hand as they moved toward the tables that had been set up at the far end of the room. "You are beautiful tonight," he said close to her ear.

"You are stunning yourself," she said with a smile of appreciation at the creamy white shirt he wore beneath the MacIntyre tartan. He had dressed for her tonight, and for the first time in a very long while he was actually proud of his family's heritage, proud of the MacIntyre name—a name he had passed on to her through their marriage.

He stopped in the center of the chamber and studied her face. "You, milady, have not been entirely honest with me."

She stiffened, then paled. "What . . . what do you mean?"

"I'm no fool, Claire," he said gently. "I knew you were up to something in this chamber the first time I found you here." He tipped his head back and stared up at the ceiling, at the incredible painting she had begun. "Why did you not tell me then that you wished to paint?"

She forced a laugh. "You wanted nothing to do with me when I first arrived. Had I asked you then, you would have said no. I could not risk that. I had to do something to this chamber to rid it of all the painful memories."

"You were right." For the first time in years Jules did not feel the anger, resentment, or even the fear that usually came to him whenever he thought about this room, his stepmother, her murder, or his incarceration. He remained silent a moment then said, "However, when you told me about your work as an artist, you seriously understated your talents."

She shrugged. "I learned long ago that most people do not believe a woman can paint."

"I would say they are wrong."

"You would be one of the few," she said softly.

He smiled then. "Tonight, no one can argue with what they see."

Again she shrugged. "I have already heard two people say they believe I had help from a painter in the village. A man."

"Did you?"

Her eyes narrowed. "No."

Jules squeezed her hand and started walking again toward the head table at the front of the room. "Then who cares what they say. We know the truth."

Instead of his support making her happy, that ever-present sadness came back into her eyes. Regardless, she forced a smile. "Thank you for saying that. I don't know what I would have done had you made me stop painting."

"You can paint every wall in this old house, and when you are done here, I will buy you more walls to paint." They reached the head table and Jules pulled out a chair for her to sit beside him. Jane and Nicholas were seated to his left. David was seated on Claire's right, then Margaret and Hollister.

The rest of their guests had found their seats at long tables that ran perpendicular to the head table. Space for dancing remained in the back of the room for when the banquet ended. Jules marveled at the feast Claire and the new cook, Mrs. Jarve, had been able to pull together in such a short period of time. Roast venison and turnips, boiled capon, salmon, shrimp, sausages, quince pie, frangipane, and custard tarts were served by the new servants Jane and Margaret had hired in the village.

Jane. Jules watched as she talked, her features animated, with the husband at her side. She laughed and Nicholas brought his arm up to curl around her shoulders, drawing her closer to him. For once, the act of affection did not bother him. Instead, Jules smiled and turned back to Claire.

He was entranced by her expressive golden eyes, the smoothness of her skin, her scent, the way she held her chin just slightly to the left when she was uneasy or uncertain. Was she uncertain about him? His change of heart? Every aspect of his life had changed in the past few days.

Because of Claire.

Music and laughter filled the chamber—both things Jules had never expected to feel in this house again, much less in this very room.

When they had eaten, Jules pushed away from the table and held out his hand to Claire this time. "Dance with me, Claire."

She stood then hesitated. "I'm not certain that is wise."

He frowned. "Why not? Everyone here is expecting us to celebrate our nuptials."

Her face grew pensive. "Have you ever wanted something so badly—something that was within your grasp—and yet you were afraid to reach out and take it?"

He knew the feeling well. "What is it you want, Claire?" He reached up to brush a wisp of hair away from her cheek. Her hair was softer tonight, less severe than it had been when she'd first arrived. And he liked it.

"You."

His heart stilled even as the noise of the room rushed around him. His fingers pressed reflexively against her back, pulling her closer. "What did you say?" he asked in a strained voice. He'd heard her, but he needed to hear those words again.

She smiled, and the unrestrained pleasure in her face lit her eyes. "I want you, Jules. Only you."

Claire stared into Jules's eyes, watching them darken with desire. The music swirled around the two of them, filling her with triumphant exhilaration. A light breeze came in through the open windows and touched her cheeks as though the very wind was celebrating this moment. That wind brought with it the scents of earth and mist that were part of Kildare Manor, part of the man holding her in his arms.

"They have accepted you, you know," Jules whispered next to her ear. A shiver raced across her flesh as the warmth of his breath ignited her sensitive skin.

The crowd moved aside for them as they danced, watching them with approving eyes. As Lady Kildare, she had won their hearts tonight. She would be a part of their lives, Jules's life. And she wanted that reality to go on forever.

Before the thought had fully formed, the crowd parted yet again as the refrain of the song came to an end. Jules placed his hand at the center of her back to guide her not back to the table, but toward the door. "I thank you for your efforts tonight, but I would rather be alone with you right now than anywhere else in the world."

She turned to look at him when she saw something familiar out of the corner of her eye. A familiar face. A dark head of hair. *Penelope.*

Claire gasped. *Her ward.*

Penelope stood at the edge of the crowd wearing a dusty-pink gown that was far more mature than her sixteen years should have allowed.

Jules stopped his progress forward. He gazed at her curiously. "What is it, Claire?"

Claire darted forward. She had to get to Penelope. But the crowd shifted as a new melody began, and Penelope disappeared from view. A heartbeat later, the bodies before her shifted, revealing her young charge once more. Her gaze connected with Claire's. In her frightened blue eyes Claire saw a plea for help before the young woman stepped back into the crowd and was lost.

With an anguished cry, Claire hurried through the dancers to the spot where Penelope had stood moments before.

She was gone.

Claire searched the crowd frantically and found no sight of the girl. She breathed a desperate sigh. Had it been her own imagination that tortured her now? Had she wanted this whole nightmare of kidnapping, blackmail, and lies to end so badly that she had conjured the sight of Penelope in this very room?

Jules joined Claire at her side. His hand went to her waist, pulling her against him. "What is it?"

"I thought I saw someone I knew," she said, her words raw. *Come back, Penelope. Come back. Oh sweet heavens, I'm so sorry you are caught in all of this . . .*

Claire staggered, suddenly feeling hollow and lifeless and sad. Then she felt herself being swept up into Jules's arms. He pulled her against his chest, and she wrapped her arms around his neck, indulging herself in the scent of him, the feel of him. He was a safe harbor in a storm that suddenly didn't make sense.

Penelope.

Curious eyes watched them, and a few suggestive comments were tossed their way as they left the chamber. Instead of heading toward the tower bedroom, they went the other way. "My chamber?" she asked.

"You no longer sleep there, Claire. From this night on, you will sleep in my bed, next to me."

Claire tried with every fiber of her being to ignore the haunting memory of Penelope's face. No matter how hard she tried, the effect of seeing the young woman's face, or imagining that she had, left a heaviness inside her.

"You have nothing to say about these new arrangements?" he asked teasingly.

"I hope to not be saying anything before long," she replied and was rewarded with a grin.

He stopped outside his bedchamber door and pressed the latch open with his elbow. Slipping inside, they moved to the huge bed in the center of the room, where Jules set her down on the sheets that had been sprinkled with pink rose petals.

The memory of Penelope's face slid through Claire's mind, and she thrust it away. "Your doing?" Claire picked up a delicate petal and brought it to her nose, inhaling the heady, sweet scent. She looked up at him, then her breath hitched at the spark flaring in his blue eyes.

"Most likely 'twas Jane. I hear I have you to thank for finding the roses amongst all the weeds." Jules sat on the bed beside her and, slowly, he removed the pins from her hair, allowing the length to fall to her shoulders and down her back.

"Your hair is glorious. You should leave it loose about your shoulders, not tied back and hidden from sight," he said, coiling a long strand around his finger and bringing the length to his lips.

Claire watched as he intimately caressed her hair. An enveloping warmth burned at her core until she grew breathless just watching him. The sensation heightened as he traced his fingers up her arm, exploring her as though for the first time. Then his fingers vanished and his lips took their place, until he nestled into the curve of her exposed neck.

"You're trembling," he said in the gentlest of voices.

"I know," she admitted with a nervous tremor in her voice. "I'm not sure why."

His lips left her neck to work their way up her jawline to her ear, leaving a trail of heat behind. "Don't you?" His fingers slipped around her back and started plucking one by one the small pearls that fastened her dress. "It's because unlike the last time we were together, this time it will mean something."

She stiffened. "You—"

"Were right. It meant something even then." He captured her lips in a hard, insistent kiss and did not stop until the tension in her body vanished and she was breathless with anticipation despite the disjointed emotions that were tumbling through her. He eased the silken fabric away from her shoulders, leaving her sheer chemise behind. Slowly, he eased her dress down her ribs, across her hips, and onto the floor. Her shoes and stockings joined her dress, until she was clad in only her thin chemise.

He eased off the bed and gathered her gown, then set it on a nearby chair before he released his belt. The fabric of his tartan tumbled to the floor. She expected him to come to her wearing his shirt. Instead, he removed it, leaving him gloriously naked and aroused before her.

His body was perfect, and she wondered for a heartbeat why he had left the garment on the first time they had made love. But the thought vanished a moment later as he moved toward her. Golden candlelight bathed his flesh in a shimmering light as he strode back to her, confident and strong, then settled on the bed beside her.

Slowly, he eased the edge of her chemise up her legs, over her thighs, her chest, and finally over her head. The fabric caressed her skin, leaving her tingling and wanting as she lay bare before him. Desire reflected in his eyes, pounded in her heart, and filled the room with need. He put his hand on her arm, his thumb stroking soothingly.

Moments ticked by as he looked into her face. His eyes, dark with a promise she could not read, held hers, until he bent his head and his lips found hers once more. A deep-seated ache burned through her at the feel of warm, strong hands sliding over her bare arms, across her stomach, to her hip. Instinctively, she turned into his caress, her body on fire with need.

Closing her eyes, she breathed in the fresh, masculine scent that was only his. She ran her hands through the silk of his tawny hair, delighting in the way the waves curled around her fingers. His hands ran possessively over her breast, cupping its fullness, then teasing her nipple to taut awareness. He brought his mouth down and grazed the sensitive bud while his hands moved to the other. She moaned as he increased the pressure.

Her hands slipped across his back, exploring his flesh, when she suddenly stopped. The ripple of scarred flesh greeted her fingertips. Her chest tightened as she ran her hands up and down the multiple lacerations that marked his back. "Who did this to you?"

This time there was no shame, no apology, no fear in his eyes. "My jailers. They were convinced they could whip the evil out of me."

"There is no evil in you," her voice was ragged at the thought of what he had suffered.

"I used to believe there was." He shrugged. "I still do to some extent."

"I understand, but know that to me you are perfect, Jules." His name fell from her lips in a breathless whisper of longing. She stared into his eyes, hoping he saw the truth. Proving her point, she slid her hands over the rigid muscles of his chest, watching as his muscles coiled and flexed beneath her touch. She brushed her fingers against his nipples, then brought her tongue down to flick the sensitive bud as he had done and was rewarded by a sharp intake of breath from him. His hands stilled against her back as she continued sliding her hands lower until she stroked the length of his arousal, felt it pulse beneath her touch.

His hands splayed against her back as he held her to him, then shifted her beneath him, his rigid shaft poised at her entrance. Their gazes met. Across the few inches of heated shadows between them, their gazes held as she slid her arms up around his shoulders and Jules eased into her tight passage until he filled her with heat and strength. She welcomed his warmth, his weight, as he slowly drew back with agonizing slowness and controlled intent before he surged slowly forward again.

The friction was exquisite and intense as sensation after sensation rippled through her. Claire felt something wild and primitive building inside her as his slow caress continued. This time between them was different, though just as pleasurable; this time was more intense and all-consuming.

His rhythmic thrusts accelerated their tempo as he drove into her again and again, sending pleasure streaking through her in endless waves. She arched into him, in a fevered need to take him with her into that sweet abyss. Ecstasy overtook her, and she cried out her joy. At the sound, he released a groan and gave in to his own release. With earth-shattering glory, they climaxed together and tumbled headlong into the abyss.

After a time, they floated back to reality in each other's arms. When some of their strength returned, Jules moved onto his side, taking her with him. Her hair spilled over his chest in a red, silken waterfall. He lifted a hand to smooth it back from her face and gazed into her eyes. "Even after all my searching, I have no idea why, exactly, you came into my life. But I am thankful. You belong here with me."

Despite the satiation flowing through her limbs, Claire tensed and wished with everything inside her for a future together. Tears came to her eyes at the thought of what she had to do. He would never forgive her.

She would never forgive herself.

"Claire, why are you crying?"

She offered him a tremulous smile. "Because I am happy." The image of Penelope came to her once more. She let her tears fall. After tonight, she would never be happy again.

With a heartbreaking smile, Jules rolled her onto her back and devoured her with his mouth, claimed her with his hands, and then his body. Claire let him ease her sorrow as she gathered up every touch, every kiss, every caress, in the hopes they would get her through the rest of her days—days that would be dark and alone.

I've never seen Jules look so happy," Jane said as she watched her friend carry his new wife out of the ballroom, away from their guests.

Beside her, Nicholas looked on with a dark frown. "I only hope she doesn't crush his soul."

Jane startled at her husband's uncharitable words. It was so unlike Nicholas. "Why would you say such a thing?"

His expression softened as he looked down at her. "Men who have lost everything, then find what they were missing, fall harder and faster when it is taken away."

Jane froze as her gaze moved past her husband to the vacant doorway. "She won't . . . will she?"

"It's hard to tell." Hollister stepped forward, joining the discussion with Margaret on his arm. "We know so little about Claire. What ever became of our inquiries?"

David joined their little group near the back of the room. "Claire is what she says she is, a teacher. She rents a tiny painting studio on Leith Road. She has three wards, all of whom are child prodigies, much like herself, who were orphaned early in life. Claire took them in and not only teaches them, but she is for all intents and purposes their mother."

The information startled Jane. "Then where are those girls now if Claire is here?"

"And why didn't she say anything about them to Jules? She—" Margaret broke off with a gasp. Her hand went to her distended abdomen. "Sometimes I believe this little one is a musician in the making. Whenever I am around music the baby dances inside of me."

"Margaret, are you feeling well?" David asked her, his face pale with concern.

"Yes," she said with a light laugh. "The kicking only hurts for a moment."

"You are certain?" David insisted.

"Why do you ask, David?" Hollister brought his hand down to cover Margaret's abdomen protectively.

David bent down and moved the edge of Margaret's skirt out of the way to reveal a palm-sized circle of blood on the wooden floor.

Margaret gasped and leapt back, revealing two more drops of blood. "It is not me, I promise," she said, reassuring the man at her side.

Hollister pulled her into his arms. "I'll not take that chance. We are going to our room to lie down. I will send for the physician."

"Sweetheart, there is really no need."

David dipped his finger into the red droplets before him. "There is no harm in rousing the physician, because if this is not your blood, then it most definitely is someone else's." He stood and moved past the droplets near Margaret's feet, following the trail of blood.

A shiver moved through Jane. Someone was hurt.

"Hollister, take Jane and Margaret with you to our chambers while I help David," Nicholas said, with a fierce look in his eyes. "Keep them safe."

Hollister didn't hesitate. He gathered both women and escorted them from the room, but not before Jane saw David and her husband following the trail of blood across the floor.

The blood was fresh. David followed the trail, all his senses on alert. Images swam in his head of the pretty dark-haired girl with the striking blue eyes he had seen earlier that night, peering through the crowd, her face pale as she watched Claire and Jules dance. He didn't know why, but something inside him had connected with the girl.

He knew that look—hopelessness mixed with fear and anger. David clenched his fists, forcing that image from his mind. There was no reason in a room full of people that the person they were looking for was the one he could not clear from his thoughts. The trail led to the far corner of the ballroom, behind where the head table resided before it was taken away to make more room for dancing and mingling. But there was nothing there, only a group of people talking.

That was when David heard a gasp of pain coming from behind one of the new tapestries that had been hung only this morning—a wedding gift from Lord and Lady Davison. He stopped before the finely woven depiction of Adam and Eve in the Garden of Eden, lifted the bulging edge, and froze.

"Merciful heavens," Nicholas ground out beside him.

It was her. The dark-haired girl. Blood covered the front of her dusty-pink gown. She clutched her hand in the fabric of her dress as she slumped against the floor.

David knelt down beside her. Gently, he lifted her face and forced down an expletive at her bloodied lip and swollen cheek.

She turned her pale blue gaze on him. "Help me," she whispered. "Don't let her find me."

A chill shot through him at the terror in her eyes, in her voice. "My God, who did this to you?" That chill turned to rage.

"Don't just stand there staring at her," Nicholas's voice pierced his dark emotions. "Let's get her out of here."

David appraised her quickly, looking for the best way to lift her in his arms. Her hand was hurt, bleeding. He slipped his arm beneath her legs and another around her shoulders and lifted her slight form against his chest. She cried out in pain as David got to his feet, jostling her hand in the process. "We will keep you safe," he promised, his voice thick.

She tried to lift her head as they shepherded her from the chamber without notice, then down the stairs and to a bedchamber near his own. "You're safe." He repeated the words over and over. A chant he hoped was the truth.

Claire stirred from her slumber before dawn. Jules curled against her back. His arm kept her close while his hand cupped her breast possessively, claiming her as his even in his sleep. The closeness they had forged last night lingered deep inside her as she lay there for several long moments. She allowed the silence of the morning to wrap around her.

Satisfaction warmed her and brought a smile to her lips, until she remembered that everything they had shared last night was a lie. Everything about their life together, except their actual marriage, was a dream that could not continue.

In the silence of the morning, she heard rain as it pattered against the window. A flash of light followed by a roll of thunder confirmed that a summer storm had come in over the night, perfectly reflecting Claire's somber mood.

Slowly, gently, she slipped out of Jules's embrace until she stood beside the bed. She had intended to reach for her dressing gown, then realized the only clothing she had in this chamber was from last night. She slipped her chemise over her head then moved to pick up her gown when her gaze snagged on a small, wooden box tied with a pretty red bow near the door.

Claire set her gown aside and moved toward what appeared to be a present. She knelt beside the package. A note had been tied to the bow and read, *For my darling Claire*. He had called her his darling once before, but only in anger . . . She glanced back at the bed, to Jules lying there, relaxed and at ease. How had he managed such a feat while she had been lying curled in the warmth of his arms all night?

Curious, and a little nervous to see what he had left for her, she slid the bow off the box and lifted the wooden lid. A note lay inside.

Penelope can no longer paint.

Claire frowned. What did it mean? She removed the note, then gasped. She felt a sudden cold sickness in the pit of her stomach. Her fingers trembled as she stared at the contents.

A bloody, severed index finger lay inside the box on a bed of dusty-pink fabric. It took only a heartbeat for Claire to remember the familiar face she had seen amongst the crowd.

Penelope.

Claire couldn't breathe. Her heartbeat pounded in her ears. Did this all mean Penelope was here, that it was real? Claire drew in a shattered breath and reached for the door latch. She had to find Penelope before something worse happened to her charge.

She grabbed the gown she had thrust aside, slipped it over her head, fastening it quickly before hurrying from the room. She stopped in the hallway. Where would she look? Tears came to her eyes, and she let them fall to her cheeks. Why was this happening? She was doing everything they had asked. She would give Jules up to keep her girls safe, exactly as they had demanded.

And they had harmed Penelope anyway.

"Claire," Jules called from behind her. "What is wrong?"

When she didn't respond, he grasped her shoulders and turned her around. Her gaze fixed on his face as agony tore through her. She couldn't tell him. They made her promise not to tell him anything. She stiffened suddenly. They'd also promised not to hurt the girls.

His eyes darkened with concern as they searched hers. "Are you hurt?"

She shook her head and held out the box, her decision made. He would hate her when he found out what she had done, but right now she needed his help if she was to get Penelope away from her tormentors.

Jules's eyes flared as he stared at the contents. He grasped Claire's hands, searching for a missing finger.

"It's not mine."

He frowned. "Then whose?"

"One of my wards," her voice was raw. It hurt to speak.

"Your what?" His face contorted. "I don't understand."

"I have three wards." She reached for her locket and flicked it open, showing him the miniature of the three girls inside. "Penelope is here, somewhere. I saw her tonight, in the ballroom. The glance of her face was so quick I had assumed it was only my imagination." A sob broke free. "They promised not to hurt her."

"They who?"

"The people who threatened me." She stared into his face, memorizing his features one last time before she pulled free from his grasp and backed away. Her blood ran icy cold.

"Who threatened you?" Jules spoke haltingly.

"I don't know. All I know is . . ." Pain tore through Claire. She wanted to heap explanations and apologies on him, to make him understand why, but she knew it wouldn't help. "They forced me to marry you, to come here."

He watched her closely, his face a hardened mask.

She swallowed roughly and continued. "They wanted me to make you fall in love with me, then to leave abruptly."

He went so still it was frightening.

"Say something, please."

He stared at her, his face pale. "You used me?"

Claire flinched at the word. "Yes, I won't deny it, but it was only because of the girls."

She had hurt him. More than she realized she would. She wanted to tell him she was sorry, but the words were little and useless in the face of reality. So she stood there, staring at him, waiting.

"Christ, I feel like a puppet," he said closing his eyes.

"I had no choice," she said hoarsely.

His eyes opened to reveal his anger. The heat of his gaze forced her to step back. "Who gave you the right to manipulate me, my friends, everyone who came here last night to celebrate our union?"

"I didn't only take, Jules. I gave you myself in return. I gave you what you wanted—a wife."

He laughed. The sound stark, cold. "That's right. You gave me your body. I would say it wasn't a fair trade, Claire. I lost even more than I already had on that bargain."

The words cut deep. She deserved his anger and his bitterness. She turned. "I need to find Penelope. She has to be here somewhere."

"Now who is running away?" Jules reached for her, clamping her shoulder. He turned her around. "Let's finish this."

"No." She took a step back, out of his reach. "We do not have to pretend any longer. And I refuse to hurt you any more than I already have."

"Claire—" His contemptuous gaze raked her. "If that is your real name . . ."

"It is. That was no lie."

"Why?" She could hear the rawness in his voice, the need to understand.

Tears glittered on her eyelashes, threatening to spill over onto her cheeks. "I love you, Jules. That wasn't supposed to happen, but it did. I fell in love with you, everything about you. And for a moment I considered sacrificing the lives of the girls to continue our life together. But I couldn't do it. I could not sacrifice the lives of others to maintain the happiness I felt in your arms." She paused as tears fell onto her cheeks. She forced the words she had to say past the tightness in her throat. "Last night was a gift I will treasure forever."

"Last night was a mistake."

She flinched at the hatred in the voice she loved and drew a sharp breath. "I will always think otherwise. Now, I must go find Penelope, Anna, and Eloise before it is too late." Claire turned away only to see David at the end of the hall. How much of their conversation had he heard?

"If you are looking for Penelope," he said, "she is in this chamber."

"Alive?" she asked, her heart hammering wildly.

David nodded and motioned toward the door. "The physician has been to see her. He had no choice but to cauterize her finger to stop the loss of blood."

The smell of blood and burnt flesh reached out to her even before she entered the chamber. Claire swayed at the thought of losing a finger. Penelope had to be devastated by its loss—a loss that was all Claire's fault. If she had only done as she had been instructed . . .

Claire forced the thought away. There would be time enough for guilt later. Penelope was alive, and where there was life, there was hope.

Striding through the doorway, Claire crossed the room, then sat on the bed next to her young charge. The flickering candlelight revealed Penelope, asleep. Her face was calm, her body at ease.

Behind her, she sensed Jules had entered the room, but she did not turn to confirm the sensation. "Laudanum?" she asked David.

He nodded.

"Penelope," she whispered. "Do you hear me? It's Claire."

There was not the slightest response on her face.

She had not really expected a reaction, but it made her feel better talking to the girl. Her gaze travelled down Penelope's arm to her hand, and the clean bandage that concealed her missing finger. Claire reached out and put a hand on Penelope's arm and stroked the length from her shoulder to her elbow. Merciful saints, her skin was cold.

Jules strode forward then stopped at the bedside across from her. "What are you doing?"

She lifted her gaze to his ice-blue eyes, met them with a boldness she did not feel. "I must wake her."

"She is ill." The words were sharp.

"She is the only one who can tell me where Anna and Eloise are. They are in every bit as much danger as Penelope herself."

Jules's hands opened and closed at his sides as his gaze shifted to the girl on the bed. "Why didn't you tell me you had a family?"

A family. She had never really thought of the girls as such before, but he was right. They were her family, her only family. And she would do anything for them. Even lie. "I could not risk losing them. I have no idea who is threatening me, or why, and I had no resources to battle whoever threatened the girls. My only choice was to cooperate."

"You could have trusted me."

She shook her head sadly. "The risk was too great." She returned her gaze to her charge. "They only cut off Penelope's finger. But that they cut off the one she valued most means they do not want to murder the girls, they want to torture them, torture me."

"There is more to this than that." Jules's gaze narrowed. "Why force you to marry me? How do I figure in to all of this? Unless—" He paused. His eyes darkened. "Unless this is some sort of plot against me. But who would want revenge against me?" His accusing gaze connected with hers.

"I have no knowledge of revenge or anything else. I simply did what I was told to do in order to keep the girls safe. And even that did not guarantee their safety." Claire's gaze returned to Penelope.

"Whomever it was harmed her." His voice softened. "They did not kill her. It was a warning."

"A warning we should heed." Claire shook Penelope's shoulder. "Penelope, if you can hear me, please open your eyes. I need to talk to you for Anna and Eloise's sake."

The young girl stirred. Her eyelids fluttered. "C-Claire?"

"Dearest, I am here." Her voice broke with emotion.

Familiar blue eyes stared up at Claire. "The woman . . ."

"We need to know who she is, and where Anna and Eloise are hidden."

"Don't know her name," Penelope whispered. "The girls are . . . in Edinburgh."

Claire straightened. "Then that's where I must go."

"Not alone, you won't," Jules replied with an edge in his voice.

Penelope turned her head toward Jules. "Your husband . . ."

Despite the words, Jules's face miraculously softened. "Shh. You must rest. We need you to help us find the others." He looked almost boyish as he smiled down at Penelope. Claire's heart constricted at the sight, and a twinge of envy moved through her. He might never smile at her like that again.

Claire forced the thought away. "We need to let her rest if we are to leave for Edinburgh at first light."

His smile vanished, but he did not look at her. "We will leave when I say we will leave." Jules's voice was harsh.

Claire forced back the threat of tears. It was difficult to believe that only last night they had lain contently in each other's arms. In one moment, everything in her life had changed. She had touched true happiness only to have it ripped away.

Well, she would not stand by and whimper or cry. Her change in circumstances might not be as bad as it seemed. Jules had not cast her out of his life, not entirely. He would go to Edinburgh with her and search for the girls, along with whomever had threatened them.

They both needed answers, answers that would either heal the divide between them or cast them apart forever.

Claire knew which alternative she preferred.

She had no idea about Jules.

Last night's storm had cleared, leaving the sky a pale blue and streaked with thin wisps of clouds. Jules stood in the courtyard of Kildare Manor with David, preparing the horse for the long journey ahead. With only two horses and four riders, the travel would be slow, slower than Jules preferred. But they would have more maneuverability if they rode the horses rather than travelled by carriage. Claire would ride with him. Penelope would double with David.

"I wish we could go with you," Jane said. She and Margaret and their husbands were staying behind because of their pregnancies. Jane handed a saddlebag filled with provisions to David.

David offered Jane a smile. "You and Margaret are safer here with your husbands, despite the fact that the mysterious woman could still be nearby, or she could have partners who might act in our absence. If the intention is to hurt Jules, then there is no more vulnerable person than you."

Nicholas appeared in the courtyard and handed a final saddle-bag to Jules before moving to his wife's side. "Hollister and I will make certain Jane and Margaret are safe."

The arrival of Claire and Penelope cut any further discussion short. Jules was surprised to see both women were dressed in serviceable gowns. He was not certain what he had expected, but then again, Claire was not a frivolous woman. She carried no baggage, nor did Penelope. But the biggest surprise of all was the peach muslin splint Claire had devised for Penelope to rest her injured hand during their journey. The rustling of the horse might cause her pain, but the sling would help keep the movement to a minimum.

Jules turned away from Claire before she could see the look of admiration in his eyes. He refused to give her even that much. "Thank you," Jules said, extending his hand to Nicholas. "Be well."

"Godspeed," Nicholas said in response.

Jules bent to kiss Jane on the cheek. "Take care of yourself and that baby."

"I will," she said, moving into Nicholas's arms.

Jules turned away with jerky movements to stand beside Claire. With his hands on her waist he lifted her onto the horse, then mounted behind her. Instant awareness shot through him. The scent of lavender teased his nose, as did the flowing tendrils of her hair that brushed against his chest. His body clenched. Why had he ever encouraged her to wear her hair loose?

He had a sudden memory of her hair spilled across his chest after their lovemaking last night, the color of burnished copper in the pale candlelight. An aching sense of loss coiled in his chest. He looked down to see his hands clenched on the reins, and felt the horse prance beneath the pressure. Impatiently, he relaxed his grip.

They had a long journey ahead of them, and they needed to get under way. The rough travel ahead would at least help him keep his mind off the woman in his arms.

"You are very grim," David said as they rode away from Kildare Manor. "You've spoken barely a word since earlier this morning."

"There wasn't anything to say." Jules glanced back at his home. Instead of the aging gray stone, he saw Claire, her chin tipped up in pride as she presented the roasted pheasant he'd challenged her to prepare, heard the sound of her laughter as they danced in the ballroom she had transformed into an artistic wonder, recalled the sleek curves of her naked body as she swam in the loch. How would he ever go back to Kildare Manor and not be haunted by her every moment of every day?

He silently groaned at the memories and spurred the horse into a faster gait.

David matched his pace.

"Thank you, Jules," Claire said, breaking the silence that had fallen between the two of them.

"For what?"

"Helping me find the girls." Why he had decided to help her, she could only guess, but she was grateful for his assistance.

Jules inclined his head but didn't speak, and Claire knew better than to push him. He was still angry with her, and who could blame him? She hadn't trusted him enough to tell him the truth. And now he would make her pay for that decision.

The hours passed as they rode. Claire looked at the scenery until it all ran together in a blur of rolling hills covered in green shrubs and purple heather. Tired of the monotony, she dropped her gaze to Jules's hands as they held the reins. His hands were large and strong, well shaped and masculine. They were the hands of a warrior. The hands of a man who was not afraid to fight for what he wanted.

The thought cheered her as much as it frightened her. Would he fight for the one part of their time together that had not been a lie? Would he fight for their marriage?

Without thinking, she reached out and touched the third finger of his hand, where a wedding ring should have been. She'd never given him a ring, and he had taken hers away from her. At her touch, he pulled his hand away.

"What are you up to now?" he asked suspiciously.

"Believe it or not, I still enjoy touching you. That hasn't changed no matter what else has between us." Claire clutched her hands together and twisted them in the fabric of her dress to keep from touching him again.

"There is nothing between us that my solicitor cannot change," he said, his tone severe.

She went still. "Meaning what?"

"I'm starting divorce proceedings."

David eased his horse back from the two of them, giving them at least the semblance of privacy.

"You're what?" she breathed as the world around her swayed.

Jules must have felt her movement, because in spite of his words, his arm tightened around her, keeping her from falling off the horse. Her eyes filled with tears. Until that moment, she had hoped that somehow, someway, she might be able to reach past his anger and start anew. No matter the anger and vehemence in his voice now, they had shared something special, something worth trying to rebuild.

And God help her, she would find a way to make that happen. He would not abandon her yet, not until they found the girls. Claire sent up a silent prayer that they would find the girls alive and well, and that somehow in the next several days she would find a way through the ice encasing his heart.

As silence once again settled between them, David kicked his horse abreast of theirs. He held a sleeping Penelope in his arms.

"How does she fare?" Claire asked, grateful for the distraction.

"She is still weary from the trauma and the laudanum the doctor gave her last night," David replied.

"That might be for the best. At least the journey will be bearable as she sleeps." Claire noted the protective way David held Penelope in his arms.

"Why did they cut off her finger?" he asked, his tone perplexed. "The threat was that they would kill her. I am glad they did not, mind you."

"To a painter, losing a finger is certain death, especially a female painter," Claire replied.

"How so?" David asked.

"With no other way to support herself, her prospects for survival grow slim." At David's darkened expression, Claire added, "I will not let her fall victim to that."

His brows furrowed as his gaze shifted between herself and Jules. "But how will you—"

"I will find a way. I always have," she said with a tilt of her chin.

David nodded. "We are on the right path. I can tell from the broken branches and displaced earth that three riders have been through here since last night. The storm last night would have slowed down their progress, but they have had a head start on us."

"Then we had best make up for some of that lost time," Jules said, kicking his horse into a faster gait. The pace forced their conversation to end. They rode hard for the rest of the day, stopping just once to rest the horses and eat by a brook in a glen.

Only when orange and red fell in silken threads through the twilight sky did they stop. Instead of lodging at an inn, Jules prepared a campsite. It wasn't until he had created an overhang made from tree boughs and ferns, laid a fire, cooked the meal, and watered the horses did he finally speak to her again. "It's late." He stopped in front of her as she sat near the fire with Penelope's head in her lap. "You should settle Penelope into her blankets, then do the same. I will keep watch."

"No," Claire said. Penelope's eyes opened at her forceful tone. "You are exhausting yourself. We can all take turns keeping watch."

"I'll take the first shift," David volunteered.

Claire nodded her thanks. "If we change positions every two hours, we will all be able to get at least a little sleep. Those who we seek are ahead of us on this journey. There is no imminent danger to us until we catch up with them."

"You are wrong." Penelope lifted her head from Claire's lap and sat up. Penelope was marble-pale in the moonlight, her thin body swaying slightly. It was the first time she had spoken since last night. "These people are ruthless. They could be anywhere."

Claire reached up and pulled the blanket that had slipped from Penelope's shoulders around her once more. Penelope did not look away from the fire as she said haltingly, "Especially the woman. She took everything from me when she cut off my finger."

"A female? Could she be the one the innkeeper warned me about?" Jules asked.

As Jules became lost in his own thoughts, Claire turned back to Penelope. "No," Claire said fiercely. "That woman took your finger, but nothing else. You will heal in mind and body. "

Penelope looked away, but not before Claire saw the fear in her eyes.

Silence hovered over the campsite as Claire's thoughts tumbled through her brain. What kind of vile creatures were they chasing? Creatures who kidnapped young women, then tortured and manipulated them for their own gain? Claire stood, no longer able to contain her emotions without movement. "David, thank you for taking the first shift. I will take the second, so Jules can have a chance to rest."

She moved to grab one of the blankets piled near the fire when Jules gripped her shoulders and forced her to meet his gaze. "This isn't a game, Claire. This is real. The threat is real. If you've forgotten that, look at Penelope's hand. How will you defend this campsite? With your paintbrush?"

The words hit her like a blow. She flinched. He was still mad at her deception, but she would not bow to his anger. Not this time. "Do not underestimate me, Jules. I am stronger than you know." She shook off his touch and set her blanket near Penelope's. "I blame myself for what happened to Penelope, but I will not let anything like that happen again."

His face softened. "Do not blame yourself. You did not make them do such despicable things."

She was raw and hurting, and wanted so desperately to go to Jules and find comfort in his arms. But she could not. She wasn't welcome there any longer. Instead, she would have to live with the ache, the regret, and the sorrow.

She turned away, knelt on the ground, then settled herself beneath the blanket. "Wake me in two hours, David. My paintbrush and I will find a way to keep you all safe. A woman can do anything if she is strong enough."

It was on that thought that Claire closed her eyes. She had to be strong enough to find the girls, and when they were safe, she had to find the strength to reach for what she truly wanted.

Jules.

Annoyed that she had shut him out, Jules grabbed a blanket and settled it on the ground next to Claire's. He'd be damned if he would let her take watch alone. Did she not realize the danger? He reached up to touch the still-bruised flesh around his eye. These people, whomever they were, would not make finding the girls easy, nor would they give them up without a fight.

He lay down on his side, facing Claire. In the firelight, he could see that her eyes were firmly shut. She wasn't asleep, not yet. He looked down at her hands on the outside of the blanket. Such small hands, fine-boned, graceful, and delicate. In that moment, he regretted his words about her paintbrush. He was angry, and without thinking the words had slipped free. He started to reach for her. The need to touch her was great. Then he stopped, letting his hand fall to the blanket a few inches from her hand.

He was hurting. He wanted desperately to pull her to him and—

Damnation, he couldn't stand much more of this. He forced his hands to unclasp and release the wool blanket captured in his clasp.

Claire suddenly shifted onto her side, away from him.

His anger returned. How dare she try to calmly dismiss him from her life? Didn't she realize she belonged . . . He blocked the thought before it could become fully formed. Again he clenched and unclenched his hands at his side.

Claire blocking him out should have been a relief. If she kept herself separate from him, it would be easier to obtain the dissolution of their marriage.

Yet, her behavior only fired his blood for more of the passion they had shared, and with fear for what she would do on her own. Jules settled against the hard dirt beneath his back and stared at the stars, glittering like diamonds overhead. Even the beauty of the night sky did not calm the turmoil inside him.

He was ready to rid himself of his wife, wasn't he?

17

Hidden by the darkness and the trees, a cloaked figure looked down upon the small campsite. She drew a silent breath as she contemplated the situation.

Her plans for Kildare and his wife had been foiled by her own impulsive behavior. She'd intended to strike at the manor, while they were all on familiar territory and where they might have relaxed their guard. Yet, her own anger had forced her to react, and in the heat of her emotions, she'd destroyed the young girl's hand, alerting them to her presence.

Instead of disappointment, anticipation burned through her body. This current situation was better than what she had planned. She smiled into the darkness as she watched the orange glow of the campfire. She would follow them to Edinburgh. She knew they were headed to the other girls. And when they'd figured out the

191

trap she had set, she would strike them all. No longer could she be satisfied with punishing only Kildare.

They all deserved to suffer for what he'd done to her. She yearned to finally have her justice. She'd plotted and planned for years. Eagerness churned inside her. Too many years she'd been fantasizing about this moment. With it so close, it was hard to maintain control.

Her stomach clenched. And for a heartbeat she considered just killing them all now. Until reason returned. She drew a slow, steadying breath. It would be better to wait. She must not be impatient. Her thirst for revenge would be whetted more fully if she took the time to anticipate and enjoy the hunt that was about to ensue.

The time for revenge was almost at hand.

"Claire. Wake up."

It was Jules's voice, but it no longer held the anger and irritation it had held the night before.

Morning. Claire opened her eyes to the morning light. She sat up. Jules was beside her. His face looked softer than it had as well. "Why didn't you wake me earlier?"

His gaze ran over her tumbled hair and flushed cheeks, and a flare of desire came into his eyes. He stood and backed away. "You were sleeping so peacefully, David and I decided to let you sleep."

She frowned, stood, and smoothed the wrinkles from her gown. "That wasn't the arrangement."

He turned away. "There are oats in the pot over the fire for breakfast. While David and I break camp, please see that you and Penelope have something to eat. We have another long day of riding ahead of us."

Claire didn't argue as she was suddenly eager to be on their way. By dusk they would be in Edinburgh. Perhaps by nightfall, the girls would be safe. And life could go on as it had for years. The thought left her empty inside, but she forced the sensation away. There would be time enough after this was over to deal with the loneliness.

She gathered the blankets she and Penelope had used and rolled them the way Jules had before they'd left. Penelope's cheeks held more color today despite the lines of sorrow Claire saw in the young woman's face. Relief lightened Claire's mood. All would be well, eventually. Penelope would adjust to the loss of her finger, and she would find a way to go on.

Silently, Claire moved to the fire and dished up oats for herself and her ward. When they had finished eating, Claire gathered the blankets she and Penelope had used and rolled them the way Jules had before they'd left. After handing the blankets to Jules, Claire started toward Penelope to help her up on the waiting horse. David beat her to Penelope's side, lifting her onto the horse. A heartbeat later, he cradled the young woman in his arms. Claire bit back a smile as a tiny, sparkling ray of hope tightened her chest.

Perhaps things really would be all right in the end.

"May I help you up?" Jules asked. He reached out his hand to her.

"Yes, please," she replied brightly as she was lifted, then she settled in front of him on the horse. He took the reins and led them farther into the forest. "We are keeping to the trees?"

She felt him nod behind her. "It is safer that way."

"Are you worried that we are being followed?" She shifted her body to gaze behind her, into his face.

He tightened his arms around her. "I will not be at ease until we reach our destination."

Claire fell silent as the horse picked its way through the dense forest. It felt strange to be riding across the same terrain she had crossed less than a fortnight ago. It seemed a lifetime since she had married a total stranger.

"You're very quiet," Jules commented. "Are you weary of travel already?"

"No," she said, swallowing to ease the sudden tightness in her throat. "I was thinking about all that has happened since I left Edinburgh. I am no longer the same person."

"Much has happened to you." His hands tightened with violence on the reins.

"To you as well." She could feel the tension in his body, and gazed at him with aching tenderness.

At the look, he straightened his shoulders and deliberately loosened his grip on the reins. "We were both caught in someone else's game." His gaze shifted to her face.

For a moment she forgot to breathe at the tenderness in his eyes, then the look vanished. He glanced away and kicked the horse into a faster pace. David matched his speed. They galloped across the countryside, each step bringing them closer to their goal.

The summer sky had begun to soften, blurring at the edges in dusky shades of red and gold as they arrived on the outskirts of Edinburgh. "We are here." Claire breathed a sigh of relief.

Jules reined his horse to a stop, waiting for David and Penelope to come alongside them. Penelope had remained quiet during the journey, but at their arrival her features brightened.

"Where do we start looking for the girls?" David asked.

"A wise man once told me the best place to start is at the beginning." Jules turned to Penelope. "Where were you when you were taken?"

"At Claire's—I mean, Lady Kildare's studio," the young woman corrected herself.

Jules turned to Claire. "Where is your studio located?"

"On Leith Road, close to the coaching inn at Shrubhill."

Jules nodded and kicked his horse forward. "Then let us proceed there before it grows dark."

They rode through the busy street in silence. Until they came upon Gallow Lee. Claire could not help the shudder that moved through her.

"What is it?" Jules asked.

Claire's gaze stayed fixed on the spot of land where several executions had taken place over the years—from witches, to murderers, to, more recently, Covenanters—who were either strangled then burned or decapitated then buried at the base of the gallows. "This place has a gruesome history, and I cannot help but feel the pain and misery of those executed here each time I pass by."

Jules pulled her closer and reached up to smooth the hair at her temple. "The ghosts of the past cannot hurt you." His voice was gentle, as it had once been after they had lain in each other's arms. He must have sensed the direction of her thoughts, because he pulled his hand away and kicked the horse into a faster pace until they passed the gallows.

The sun had started its descent in the evening sky by the time they reached her studio. David took the horses across the street to the coaching inn, while Jules, Penelope, and Claire entered the building.

Inside the small space, the scents of turpentine, linseed oil, and paint lingered. The smell of home.

Claire lit the sconces, and golden light illuminated the paint-spattered floor and the half-finished canvases that lined one wall and the completed ones on the other. The walls of the studio were painted with stone pillars covered in ivy and flowers that coiled together, reaching toward the sky. From behind a mass of clouds populated with cherubim and seraphim, the sun struggled to break free.

So many images, so many colors . . . they warmed the small chamber and made it appear much larger than it was. Smiling, Claire turned to Jules. "Welcome to my home," she said.

Her smile died a moment later at the odd look on Jules's face. "You live here?"

"Upstairs. There are two bedchambers and a small kitchen. We can stay here for the night. Penelope and I will share one room. You and David can have the other."

Jules nodded and took the saddlebags up the small stairway at the back of the room while Claire led Penelope to a chair. "Dearest, I know this will be difficult for you," she said when both David and Jules had rejoined them. "You need to tell us exactly what happened the day you were taken. I was upstairs gathering supplies . . ." Claire started the conversation, hoping it might help Penelope remember the rest.

Penelope nodded. "We were setting up our easels." Her gaze moved to the back of the room where three easels still remained. "The door opened, and we thought for some reason it was you. Only it wasn't." She shivered at the memory. "Instead, three men entered the room. They came at us fast. Anna screamed. I remember that frightened sound even now." She closed her eyes and continued. "Eloise didn't make things easy for them. She bit the man who grabbed her on the hand. He yowled and grasped her by the hair. She kicked him and he slapped her across the face, hard, sending her to the floor. I thought he had killed her. Until I heard her crying." Penelope's voice shook with anguish.

Claire pressed her hand to her mouth to hold back a gasp of horror. She felt heavy inside, so weighed down with tears that she tried not to shed. Then Jules's hand tightened on hers. Claire brought her gaze to his. In his eyes she saw sympathy, but not the look of connection they had had back at Kildare Manor. He would give her support, but not himself, she realized. A sob died in her throat as she forced her own hurt aside.

Penelope opened her eyes. "They tied us up and forced us to drink something bitter." She shuddered again. "That is when the world went dark."

David moved to kneel in front of the chair. He took Penelope's small hands in his own. "Do you remember anything about where they took you?"

She shook her head. "I woke up in a small room. It was dark and musty."

"That's good," David said. "Tell us about the scent."

Penelope's brows drew together in concentration. "During the day it smelled like sulfur and rotting flesh. At night it was cold and I could feel . . . this will sound as though I am mad . . . but I felt surrounded by a tragic sea of souls."

"What about when your captors took you out of there to transport you to Argyll?" David asked.

Penelope paled. "It was night, but I thought I saw dark stone—headstones perhaps?"

David turned to Jules, his eyes wide. "Could it be they are hidden in a kirkyard somewhere?"

"Perhaps," Jules replied with a scowl. "But which one? There are many."

"St. Giles', Greyfriars, Canongate, St. Cuthbert's . . . it could take us a week to explore them all." Claire pulled away from the warmth of Jules's hands and knelt beside Penelope. "Do you remember anything else? Noises, smells, anything at all that might help us narrow our search?"

She stared off and to the right, as though searching her memory. "A wall. I believe we passed through Flodden Wall." She released a long sigh. "I would know the place if I saw it."

"Greyfriars. Flodden Wall is closest to that kirkyard."

"Let us go," Claire said, standing.

Jules glanced at her face, and through the muted light met her gaze. "The cemetery at night can be a dangerous place."

David frowned. "I am not afraid of ghosts."

"It is not the ghosts that concern me," he replied, as a tick came to his jaw. "Whomever planned this whole charade is clever. We need to progress slowly, make certain we are not walking into a trap."

"Usually, I would agree with you." David's brow furrowed. "But I think we need to strike now, before they know we are here."

"You could be right," Jules agreed.

Claire could see the indecision on his face, felt his tension as though it were a palpable thing. He turned to her. The look on his face chilled her. "Is there any way I could get you and Penelope to remain here while David and I scout the area?"

"No," she said, despite the fact that she had an ominous feeling about what would happen that night.

He nodded. "Then gather cloaks and as many lanterns as you have. David and I will need a little time to prepare."

Claire did as he asked. With Penelope's help she found four cloaks and three lanterns. They returned to the studio in time to watch Jules secure his scabbard and sword at his side and drop a dagger into each of his boots. A shiver went down her spine at the blatant reminder of the dangers the night could hold.

"Ready?" Jules asked.

With her heart hammering in her chest, Claire nodded. She lit the lanterns, handing one to David, then one to Jules. On a fortifying breath, she took Penelope's cool hand in her own, and together they stepped into the night.

18

In the shadows near the coaching inn, the woman drew her hood closer to her face, shielding her identity from the four little lambs who walked right past her. They paid her no heed. And while that was the goal, rage coiled her fingers around the fabric she held.

Patience.

At the reminder, she eased her grip. Soon she would have her revenge on Jules MacIntyre for always failing to see what was right in front of him, for refusing to take what she had offered.

Paradise denied would soon bring only desperation and pain. Her hand crept down to her side, to the belt that carried the means to her revenge—a whip, a dagger, and a third weapon that just passed her by.

Penelope.

She was the oldest of the three girls she had kidnapped, and the one who would eventually remember all that she had wanted her to. The girl would lead them into her trap, into the darkness, from which there would be no return.

Flickering lantern light curled golden fingers around the headstones as Jules led the way through Greyfriars kirkyard. The heat from the day had cooled, but because of the rain a few nights ago, mist hovered just above the ground, giving the cemetery an even more surrealistic feel. They should have waited until daylight. Yet if anything happened to those girls because they had waited . . . They were doing the right thing, exploring the graveyard at night.

"Do you recognize anything?" Jules held his lantern toward Penelope, casting both the young woman and Claire in a circle of yellow-gold light.

Penelope's face was pale and taut. "Not yet."

They continued on, winding their way toward the gated area that had been vacated only eight months before by the Covenanters who had been captured and held as prisoners after the Battle at Bothwell Bridge. David had been part of that battle, as had Jane's brother and father. Neither of Jane's relatives had returned.

At the gates, they paused, and Jules felt David's tension shred the silence. "Do you want to go inside?" Jules asked, softly.

David nodded and pushed the gates open with a whining creak of sound. Noiselessly, they followed him inside. The large grassy area was lined with stones on either side, most likely monuments dedicated to those who had passed over to the other side of life years before, or the entrances to mausoleums that housed the generations of families from Edinburgh. But there was something else that lingered in the open space as well, something that had no form or substance. It was a feeling of pain and suffering, of violence and brutality.

Something horrific had happened here to the men who had once been prisoners of the Scottish government. Jules could feel his heart hammer in his chest in response to that anguish. Did the others feel it as well?

David's face was pale as he walked through the area, his lantern lighting the dark stone, illuminating the carved figures of heavenly angels and grotesque skulls and skeletons, along with the faces of those who were buried within the graves.

David knelt beside a particularly gruesome representation of a skeleton with long hair and a crown upon its head. Beneath it was a long line of hash marks etched into the stone, as though one of the prisoners was keeping a tally of how many days they had been detained behind the bars.

Jules stood beside his friend. He counted one hundred and fifty-three marks. He closed his eyes against the agony that clenched his heart. He knew what that kind of confinement could do to a person. He fisted his hands at his side, trying to control the rage and the fear.

An unexpected touch made him jump. Claire stood beside him. She worked her fingers into his grip until he relaxed, and she enveloped his hand with her own.

"So much pain," she whispered.

Whether she referred to the pain of the souls who had suffered here, or his own suffering, he wasn't certain.

Push her away, his pride demanded. But he could not. Instead, he gripped her hand in return and stared at her, ached all the way to his bones for the comfort she was giving to him, the darkness she helped keep at bay.

"Dear God," David's voice cut through the moment.

"What is it?" Jules asked without taking his gaze from Claire.

"The one who carved these notches—he signed his name below." David's voice was strained, uncertain. "It can't be . . ."

"Who?" Jules asked, pulling his gaze from Claire.

"Jacob Lennox." The words pierced the silence. "Jane's brother. He was here."

"At least for a hundred and fifty-three days," Jules said dully. "Come. We can do nothing for Jacob at present, but we can still help the girls." He released Claire's hand, snapping himself back to the present. "We must continue our search."

Jules turned back to the open field. "Where's Penelope?" Tension brought a tick to his jaw as he searched the shadows for some sign of the young woman. That was when he saw the lantern she had been holding in the distance, turned on its side and sputtering to stay lit. Outside the ring of light lay a dark figure.

Claire gasped beside him, and he knew she had seen Penelope's body as well.

They bolted across the open field. "Penelope." Claire knelt, cradling the girl's still body, rocking her back and forth in an agony of sympathy.

Penelope shuddered. Her eyes fluttered open.

"Is it your hand?" Claire smoothed Penelope's hair back from her face.

Penelope shook her head, then groaned.

"You are safe now. I'm here," Claire soothed.

"What happened?" David asked, kneeling down beside the two women.

"Looks like she fainted," Jules replied.

The young woman looked about her as though trying to remember where she was. She raised a trembling finger and pointed to the mausoleum in front of her. "This is the one," she whispered. "This is where they brought me out before we headed to Kildare Manor."

Jules studied the square edifice with two pillars that flanked the doorway and the arch that connected the two, forming an opening. The place looked like no one had disturbed it in the last hundred years, until he held his lantern over the gravel that covered the front entrance to reveal an impression left behind from the gate. It had been recently opened. A thousand emotions tore through Jules—fear, anger, but most of all, relief that they had found where the girls were being held.

He bent down beside Claire. "I beg you to stay here with Penelope while David and I go inside."

She opened her mouth to speak, but he pressed his finger against it.

A frisson of sensation tingled along his finger at the intimate touch. "Just this once, do as I ask?"

Her eyes went wide as though she'd felt it too—that odd sensation. She nodded.

Jules stood, then reached inside his boot and set a dagger on the ground next to her. "Just in case," he said, then he and David disappeared through the gate of the mausoleum.

Claire moved Penelope into a sitting position, then palmed the dagger and stood. She offered her other hand to the young woman. "Can you stand?"

"I think so." Penelope struggled to her feet.

"What happened?" Claire asked, looking around them in the hazy light. She swallowed. Why had she never noticed before that moss growing on the sides of stone looked like rivulets of blood in the darkness?

Penelope reached for her head and rubbed the back of it gingerly. "I think something hit me." She pulled her fingers away to reveal a smear of blood.

"You are certain your hand is okay?" Claire asked.

Penelope looked down at her bandaged finger. The pristine white linen fairly glowed beneath the silver moonlight. "Not my hand. Something else."

"Something or someone?" Either way, they were not alone. Whoever hit Penelope could very well be waiting for David and Jules inside that tomb.

She knew Jules would not be happy with her if she followed them inside, but she couldn't simply wait outside either if she could do something to alert them to the danger ahead. "Come on, Penelope, we are going after them." She didn't wait for an answer but pulled Penelope along with her into the gated opening. "We have to hurry," she said breathlessly.

She showed her lantern into the dark mausoleum ahead. For a moment she couldn't see anything in the fetid darkness until her eyes adjusted to the low light. In the inky darkness, she saw two sarcophagi positioned in the center of the chamber. And beyond that another chamber.

"I don't like this place," Penelope whispered.

"I know. We will be out of here soon, and you can put the memories behind you," Claire said in her most reassuring voice.

Penelope nodded as they stepped into a broad hall-like ante-chamber. Claire held up the lantern. There were three openings in the chamber, tunnels, apparently, that led in different directions.

"Do you remember which one of these you came through?" Claire asked as she studied the tunnels uncertainly. Which way had the men gone?

"I don't remember." Penelope's gaze shifted from one tunnel to the next.

"That's all right," Claire reassured her. "We will follow each one until it takes us to the men or the girls. With any luck, both." She moved toward the opening on the far left. She came to steps and proceeded down them, following the tunnel as it veered to the right. Except for the light from the lantern, they were in total darkness. They went on, inching their way forward as the walls grew narrower and the roof lower.

"Do you remember any of this?" Claire asked.

"I think I do," Penelope said, in a stronger voice.

Encouraged by the information, Claire pushed forward, probing the darkness with the light from the lantern. She came to a step, then another, and put her hand against the wall to help guide her way. How deep into the earth did this tunnel go? Perhaps she had chosen the wrong opening to explore. Common sense told her to turn around and go back.

Then she heard a noise. It was low, rumbling, like the sound of voices. She signaled Penelope to be silent and set the lantern down. It would not do for the light to give them away. Scarcely daring to breathe, she crept forward. In one hand she gripped Penelope's injured hand. In the other she clutched the dagger.

"Are you afraid?" Penelope whispered.

Claire swallowed. "Of course, but fear cannot stop us. We must press on and find the girls." *And Jules*. She sent up a silent prayer that nothing would happen to Jules or to David.

In the inky light, Claire crept toward the sound. Suddenly, without warning, the floor slanted sharply down. Claire cried out, slipping and sliding into the void. The last thing she heard was Penelope's scream. Then her vision went black.

A woman's scream echoed through the tunnel. Sheer terror tore through Jules.

"Penelope." David breathed beside him.

They both started running, lanterns swinging, painting the black walls with a kaleidoscope of orange and yellow. The sound of their footsteps echoed through the tunnel, matching the beat of Jules's heart. Why did the sound of Penelope's voice come from below them when the girls were aboveground? Unless . . .

Jules clamped back a moment's fear. They had taken one of the tunnels, and not the one in the middle like he and David had.

They rounded a curve in the tunnel and entered a chamber carved into the stone. Bright light spilled through the open space, revealing three people in hooded cloaks with their backs turned.

Jules drew his sword, poised to strike, when the hooded figure in the middle turned around. "Welcome, Lord Kildare." Beady eyes peered out from beneath the hood. "If you know what is good for you, you'll put that weapon down."

A female voice.

The two hooded figures on either side of her turned to reveal Claire and Penelope both tied and bound, on their knees, with a knife at each of their throats. Penelope's blue eyes glittered with tears. Claire's golden eyes sparked with defiance.

"Look what dropped into my lair?" the woman said, stepping toward Claire, stroking the side of her face with the back of her hand.

Claire pulled away despite the danger. "Leave me. Find the girls."

"You'll never find them, at least not before it's too late." The cloaked figure turned her hand around and dug her nails into the side of Claire's face, leaving three long, bloodied scratches.

Jules took a deep breath as he fought the fury building inside. He and David could easily take the three of them if it weren't for the women. He had no doubt that if either of them made a move, Claire and Penelope would be killed. Jules set down his sword, and David followed his lead.

The woman lunged forward and grabbed both weapons, hurling them behind her. A sinister laugh erupted from her. "I have been waiting for this moment for the last six years."

"Who are you?" Jules demanded. Six years ago he had been summoned home from his position as Lord Lennox's squire by his father.

"You actually have no idea, do you?" The woman came closer. "Oh, this is delicious—better than I could ever have hoped for."

Her voice sounded familiar, but such a thing would be impossible. His mind was playing tricks on him. "Reveal yourself."

"Not before I reveal my purpose."

"Revenge?" Jules ground out. "What else could this be?"

The woman came to a stop just out of his reach. If only he could grab her and the dagger in his boot before they slit Claire's throat. He shifted his weight to the balls of his feet, ready to strike.

The hooded figure must have seen his subtle movement because she took a step back. "But is that revenge against you? David? Claire?"

"Without knowing who you are, it makes it hard to tell," David growled, earning a glare from those beady eyes.

"Would you like to know?" The woman's voice changed; became less strained, as though she had been modulating it before to hide something. A shiver raced down his back. He recognized that voice—the new one. He could only stare as the woman reached up and gripped the edges of her hood. Slowly, she slid the dark wool back to reveal a head of darker hair streaked with gray and an age-lined face.

A familiar face.

"You." Jules's voice remained steady and did not betray the shock tearing his gut.

"Me." She smiled, the look sinister.

He remembered that smile—the one that always marked her as a little bit mad. "You are supposed to be dead, stepmother."

"Your stepmother?" Claire whispered.

Jules's heart hammered against his ribs as he tethered his shock and his rage. He had spent sixteen months and twenty-seven days in gaol for a murder he had never committed. Undeniable proof now stood before him as his brain scrambled back to the past. "You staged your own death, Agatha. Why?"

"You refused to give me the one thing I wanted. The thing I longed for most in this world. You made me suffer, and I wanted your death." An angry flush touched her cheeks. "But you didn't die. So now it is my turn to make you suffer as I have through the years."

She reached beneath her cloak and pulled out a coiled length of rope. She held it out to David. "Form a loop in the rope and slide it around your wrists."

David didn't move.

"If you do not do as I say . . ." she let the words trail off as she looked at the man who held Penelope, "the young one dies."

Penelope whimpered.

David took the rope, formed a loop, and slid it over his wrists.

"Good." She nodded to the man holding Penelope. He forced her away as he reached to grab David. He tightened the noose around David's arms, then twisted it around his torso, tying it in a knot behind his back.

"That should keep you subdued for a while," the lackey said.

"Don't do this, please let him go," Penelope sobbed.

"Shut her up," Agatha demanded.

The lackey gripped a sword.

David, despite his bindings, hurled himself forward, taking the man down before he could strike. The man's head hit the stone wall with a sickening thud, and he went limp. The sword clattered to the floor.

Agatha started toward the sword.

"You are a coward, Agatha." Jules lashed out with the only weapon he had available. He had to keep Agatha distracted while David struggled to his feet. "You're a spineless coward who has to kidnap little girls in order to feel powerful."

Agatha's face turned red as her focus returned to Jules. "Watch what you say."

"If you wanted revenge," Jules continued as David's hands edged down to his boot and the dagger hidden inside, "you should have come after me. Instead you went after children. That is as spineless as they come."

Agatha's eyes sparked. "Bastard!"

Yes, get mad at me, leave the others alone. "What did I do to you, Agatha? Was it that I refused your perverted advances?"

"I offered you a world of pleasure."

"You were married to my father."

"He wasn't enough for me. Neither was your brother." Jules startled at the revelation before he could catch his response.

"You didn't know?" She laughed. "He wouldn't touch me at first, but good old Kildare whiskey weakened his resolve." Her features turned hard again. "But you were never one for the spirits, so I found something else that would bring you to heel."

"Your vile plans won't work, Agatha."

"They already have. You should thank your father," she said with a villainous smile that made Jules's blood run cold. "He came to see Grayson and begged him to reveal your whereabouts. He had discovered the truth about my death, and feared for your safety once you were released from gaol seven months ago. However, Grayson knew the rift between you and your father went deep. Your solicitor's strong sense of loyalty to you went on for months. But your father's pleas wore Grayson down, eventually. I'll give the man credit for holding out as long as he did."

Jules stiffened as though struck by a sword. "Why should I believe anything you say?"

"I have no reason to lie, not now when I am about to get everything I ever wanted from you."

"And what did you want?"

"To watch you suffer as I suffered. You gave me the means to my revenge when you created Claire. All I had to do was wait your father out and blackmail your solicitor. Both were easy enough to do. Your father wrestled the truth behind your false bride out of Grayson, and that was when I took over. I let your father find you a bride, then I stole her away. I forced her to play the game my way."

Agatha turned to Claire. "You always had a soft spot for a damsel in distress. I figured she would be an easy way to seize your attention and your heart. Her little wards were an added bonus, and the perfect blackmail to use against her if she failed to cooperate."

"Where are the girls?" Claire demanded, fighting against the ropes at her wrists.

"Close and yet so far away," she said, smiling confidently. "You should be less worried about the girls and more worried about yourself." Agatha turned back to Jules. "I can see why your father chose this one. She has courage. That courage will make her more interesting to try and break."

"She means nothing to me," Jules said, his tone sharp.

Claire froze.

"You don't fool me, Jules," Agatha said through narrowed eyes. "I watched you from afar for days. You gave her things you refused to give me."

"I will not deny that I enjoyed the pleasure she brought me, but that was all we had between us. She means nothing to me. Nothing." His voice was sharp.

Doubt flickered across Agatha's face. "Why would you use her like that? It's very unlike you."

"She's a beautiful woman. I gave in to temptation." Jules shrugged. "As you said, my father chose well."

Claire's face paled.

Jules tore his gaze from the hurt in Claire's eyes and narrowed his gaze on the woman before him. "You are a fool, Agatha. You only saw what you wanted to see. You are a fool and a coward."

She spat at him. "Chain him up!" she shouted at the man who held Claire. The cloaked figure startled, then came forward and, with trembling fingers, gripped Jules's right wrist, securing it to the wall.

For a heartbeat Jules fought the assault until he caught a glimpse of the desolation on Claire's face. Her pain was almost unbearable. He closed himself off to it, focusing on the madwoman who wanted revenge. He had to make her think he wanted nothing to do with Claire. It was the only way to keep her safe.

The lackey pressed Jules backward against the stone and secured his left wrist in the all-to-familiar restraints that were fixed to the stone. His feet were next, until he was securely detained.

"Do you remember what it felt like, to be helplessly chained to a wall?"

He remained silent, fighting the desolation and panic he had lived with every day of his incarceration.

"No? Well, perhaps I should remind you of more than just the loss of your freedom. How about this?" She withdrew a whip from beneath her cloak, uncoiled it, and sent it flying across the space that separated them.

Pain bit into his chest as the lash reached its target. He bit back a groan, forcing himself not to react. "Why?" he asked, grateful his voice remained strong, not revealing the terror that threatened to swamp him. He had to stay in control.

"Eventually, you will beg for that which you once denied."

"Never."

She gave him a demented smiled as she sent the whip singing through the air once more, but in the opposite direction.

Claire!

Claire cried out at the biting sting of the leather as it connected with her shoulder. The lash tore her gown, leaving her shoulder and the welt beneath exposed.

With a growl of fury, Jules threw his body toward Agatha, desperate to be freed.

"Oh, yes," Agatha said with a note of glee in her tone. "You will beg me for just about anything before I am through." Murder burned in her gaze.

Jules fought against his restraints, like a wild animal caught in a trap. "You are right," Jules bit out. "I will do whatever you ask, just leave the others alone."

Out of the corner of his eye, Jules saw that David had almost sliced through his bindings. "You want me to touch you, Agatha, I will, but only when we are alone." He would touch her all right. He would gladly wring her neck and willingly go back to gaol for her murder if only to protect the woman he lo—

Jules blocked off the thought. He could not lose himself to his emotions. Their survival meant playing along and convincing the madwoman before him that what he professed was the truth.

Agatha lifted the whip once more, and a thrill of fear clutched at Jules. "I am yours, Agatha. All you have to do is release them."

Indecision clouded her eyes even as a maniacal smile tugged at her lips. She hesitated, searched Jules's expression, and must have liked what he reflected back to her. "Very well—" Agatha's words ended abruptly when David sent the second lackey flying backward. David gripped Agatha about the neck, dragging her back against the wall.

Agatha's eyes bulged from her head as she attempted to break free of David's strong grasp. She struggled to breathe. Her fingers left David's arm to disappear beneath her cloak.

"Watch out!" Jules warned a second too late as she brought a dagger up and slashed David's forearm.

He grimaced, but held tight.

"You . . . will . . . pay . . . for this." Again, Agatha brought the dagger up, this time aiming for David's neck, but instead of striking out, she howled—the sound a mixture of rage, fury, and frustration. The animalistic sound echoed through the chamber as Penelope plunged David's dagger into the woman's side once more.

"The first was for my finger. The second for Anna. And this is for Eloise." Penelope struck a third time. She pulled her hand back, her once-pristine bandage now covered in blood.

"That's enough, Penelope," David said forcefully, jarring the young woman out of her vengeful stupor.

Penelope's eyes went wide and her face paled with horror. She dropped the dagger at her feet. "What have I done?"

David released his grasp on Agatha. He snagged the blade from her hand a moment before the injured madwoman wilted to the floor. "You've served justice, where justice was due, Penelope. Nothing more."

Claire took advantage of the chaos. She gained her feet and in the same moment she swung her bound arms at the head of the lackey behind her.

He staggered backward but did not fall. When Claire moved to hit him again, he forced his hood back, revealing his face.

Jules recognized the debt collector instantly. "Arthur Cabot?"

"Stop," Arthur said, putting up his arms in a defensive stance. "It is my duty to follow you in an effort to recover what you owe your creditors. I have been pursuing you since your return to Argyll. Just as she has," he explained.

The explanation did nothing to stop Claire. She swung at Arthur again, knocking him in the gut.

He groaned at the impact, but did not fight back. "I know where the girls are," he said.

Claire froze.

"I followed her here to the cemetery and into the mausoleum. They took the tunnel on the right. At the end of it, while they were occupied, I peered into a chamber similar to this one and witnessed them putting two young women into a sarcophagus."

Claire fell to her knees. She cried out as if in pain.

"No, no," Arthur exclaimed. "They put them in there alive."

Claire drew in a harsh breath. "They are alive?"

Arthur nodded.

"You'll never . . . get to them . . . in time," Agatha said between gasping breaths.

Jules let loose a growl. He pulled at the manacles as hard as he could. "Get me down from here."

David was at his side a moment later, pounding the tip of his dagger against the lock.

Arthur held out a key. "This might be quicker."

"How did you come to be here then? Dressed as you are?" David asked while he accepted the key.

"I unfortunately made a noise while I was observing. One of

Agatha's henchmen came to investigate. I knocked him out, took his cloak, and assumed his role in her schemes."

Jules was freed a moment later. "Show us where the girls are."

Arthur grabbed one of the lanterns and headed out of the chamber. David retrieved his sword and a second lantern, then helped Penelope to her feet. "Are you coming?" he asked Jules with a frown when neither he nor Claire moved to follow.

"Right behind you," Jules said. "Claire." He waved her toward the doorway.

She looked back at the woman on the ground, at the blood seeping from her wounds. "What about her?" she asked haltingly.

"We will leave her here and send the authorities back to get her."

"If she dies . . . Penelope . . ." Claire broke off.

Jules shook his head. "Penelope is the victim, not this woman."

"She's not a woman, she's a monster," Claire said, her tone flat. "I knew it the moment she took the girls, then tried to manipulate me . . ."

"You are not to blame here either, Claire." He held out his hand.

She moved past it, out of the chamber, leaving him alone with Agatha. Jules stared at the chamber that had been alive with Claire's presence a moment before and wondered how or if they could move forward from here.

Jules reached for the remaining lantern.

"Don't leave me . . . in darkness." Agatha stretched out her hand, an appeal for mercy, despite all she had done.

A cold, blessed numbness settled inside him where his heart

should have been. "From experience, I know you can survive in darkness far longer than it will take the authorities to arrive."

She scowled. "You'll pay . . . for this."

"I already have."

A howl of rage followed him down the passageway as Jules made his way to the others.

Claire hardly dared to hope as they raced down the tunnel. The girls were alive? Her stomach knotted in panic. Her heart pounded in her ears. They had to be alive. There was no other outcome that she would allow herself to imagine.

They would be well. Unharmed. Whole. The wish filled her thoughts and echoed in her steps as she held back a sob and ran faster. She was dimly aware of Jules behind her.

She reached the main part of the cavern and turned toward the left, heading down the right tunnel, where Arthur had said he'd seen the girls.

It wasn't too late. It couldn't be.

They were alive.

She held on to the thought as she ran into the glow of the light ahead. Inside the chamber, similar to the one they just left, sat a large sarcophagus. David was on one side of the lid, while Arthur and Penelope were on the other, straining to shift the heavy stone off its base.

"We've only moved it the slightest bit," David informed her as she joined them in the center.

Claire pushed against the solid limestone with all her might. Still it refused to budge.

"Let me help," Jules said beside her, joining her in the effort. The five of them strained and pushed, until finally the lid shifted, scraping along the limestone base with a grinding whine. Slowly, it inched back, revealing more and more of the darkness inside, until finally half of the grave was exposed.

Claire swallowed and gazed dully into the darkened space. No sound came from within. There was nothing but stillness in the chamber. Beside her Jules bent, he reached inside the deep stone tomb.

Her heart thundered in her ears.

"I see them," Jules said, the sound muffled by the heavy stone. He straightened and motioned for David to join him. One more time he delved into the dark tomb and came back with first a blonde-haired girl, then a brunette. *Anna and Eloise.*

They were both limp and pale as the men set them on the floor. And yet . . .

"They are breathing, Claire. Both of them," Jules said, his face grim in the light of the lanterns.

Claire could feel tears of profound thankfulness running down her cheeks. The girls were alive. She knelt beside fourteen-year-old Anna and smoothed a finger across her cheek. "Anna? Can you hear me?" She reached for thirteen-year-old Eloise and smoothed the young girl's hair back from her face. "You are safe now. I'm here."

When neither girl responded, she turned to look at Jules. "Why are they like this?"

They both turned to Arthur. "I did not see what they did to the girls, only where they put them before the henchman came looking for me."

"They might have been drugged," Jules offered, his voice rough. "Agatha did always like her potions."

"Or they could have shut down to protect themselves from the terror of being closed off in total darkness in a tomb with its original occupant," David offered.

Claire shuddered. "How could she be so cruel?"

At Jules's stark look, Claire wanted to go to him, to comfort him. It must have been terrible living with such an evil woman during his youth. A mother was supposed to provide love and support to her children, not stage her own death and send her child, even a stepchild, to suffer in his own private hell.

Fighting her instincts, Claire turned back to the girls. She balled her fists at her sides with the effort it cost her to hold back her sympathies. What was once between her and Jules was over. He had said so himself. She would not make a fool of herself and press her unwanted emotions upon him. "We have to get them out of here. Perhaps the fresh air outside will bring them around."

Jules bent and picked up Anna, while David drew Eloise into his arms. Claire put her arm around Penelope's shoulders, and they all made their way back to the moonlit night. They walked in silence through the streets of Edinburgh until they returned to Claire's studio.

In the mausoleum, Agatha heard a scurrying sound and panic flared. Rats. Creatures of darkness. They were coming to get her.

She tried to pull herself upright, then screamed in agony at the effort. Sweat broke out on her forehead. Her breathing came in short, sharp gasps. Blood flowed from the wound in her side, teasing the rats with the promise of a meal. They wouldn't care that she was still alive. They would crawl in her hair and gnaw at her flesh, until they finished what Jules had started.

She heard scurrying again.

"Murdoch?" she called to the lifeless man beside her. "Wake up, you miserable toad. Get me out of here."

At his silence, Agatha dug her fingers into the rock floor, inching herself forward. She had to move, had to drag herself to safety before the rats came any closer, or before the authorities arrived.

Her work was not yet done.

Again, she dragged her body across the cold rock floor. The movement made her dizzy with pain, and yet she continued, anger and pain fueling her movements.

She heard the rats scurrying again, closer this time. Exhaustion overtook her movements, and she lay against the floor, breathing hard. If she didn't move, she would die here in the darkness. The creatures, they would devour her, and that would be the end of her revenge.

Inch by inch she made her way down the tunnel, toward the light. She had to get to the light. The creatures would not follow her there.

The light would see her through. Then and only then would Jules, Claire, David, and Penelope be vanquished from this earth forever.

Upstairs in Claire's studio, Jules looked on as his wife bathed both the girls, who had woken from their stupor on the way back to her home. The physician had been to see them and pronounced them both well.

And the authorities had been sent to the tomb after Agatha, only to report that the woman had vanished, leaving just a trail of blood behind. They had followed the path out of the kirkyard, but then the trail had disappeared.

Jules hoped it meant the woman had perished, but he knew better than to trust that she was gone without cold, hard evidence. Agatha was like a phoenix, always rising from the ashes. She would continue her revenge if she could.

And Claire would remain a target unless he set her free.

She was his wife.

Only three days ago he had told her that wasn't enough to keep them together. He regretted those words but knew they were the right ones if he wanted to keep her safe. The only way to minimize the threat to Claire and her wards was to stay away from them, away from her.

He could leave David behind to protect Claire and her girls. He doubted he would have to do much convincing in that area. David seemed particularly fond of Penelope. Jules went to speak with David.

He had to let Claire go.

The next morning, Claire found herself dressing with particular care in a gold gown trimmed at the neck and sleeves with sage-green lace. She was not dressing for Jules, she assured herself, even though she knew she was. If this was to be their good-bye, then she wanted to at least be remembered well.

When she came into the studio, she saw that Jules, too, had taken pains with his attire. He wore a crisp white shirt beneath his MacIntyre tartan. She stopped at the stairs to admire his beauty and his strength. She would paint him like that—paint this final memory of him in his full splendor. She curled her fingers at her side, fighting the urge to grab a brush and begin that task. Instead, she committed him to memory.

At her approach, he met her gaze. "Good morning."

"Good morning," she replied, coming fully into the chamber.

They were silent again and she didn't know how to break the charged stillness in the room. Jules was different this morning. The easy rapport that they had developed over time at Kildare Manor was gone and all that remained was the tingling awareness of each other's presence.

The silence between them lengthened.

"How are the girls?" he asked finally.

"Better. They are even talking again. I think David was correct in his assumption. The shock of the kidnapping and their subsequent torture was too much for them, and they both shut down." She walked about her studio, from easel to easel, until she stopped in front of a canvas bearing a landscape. She'd started the oil painting the day before Jules's unfortunate solicitor had approached her about marrying Lord Kildare.

At the thought of the solicitor she turned to Jules. "I was just thinking about James Grayson." She paused. "Do you think Agatha had him killed?"

"Most likely she drove the carriage," Jules replied solemnly.

Claire shivered. "She could be out there."

"She's not after you."

Claire frowned. "How do you know that? How does anyone know what goes on in a disturbed mind like hers?"

"We don't, thank goodness." He moved to stand beside her. "We know nothing except that she is injured and—"

"Injured animals are the most dangerous of all. They have nothing to lose."

"She's not after you and the girls anymore, Claire. She wants me to suffer. Me."

Claire could not argue with that. "How will you protect yourself?"

"That's what I want to talk with you about. It is time to say goodbye." He took her hand and lifted it to his lips and kissed it. "It is time for us to stop hurting each other, and quit while we are ahead."

She gazed at him wordlessly as he turned her hand over and lingeringly pressed his warm lips to her palm.

Intimate. Warm. Tender.

And final.

He was saying good-bye. Forever.

"Jules, I don't want us to—"

"There is no us."

He dropped her hand. "Good-bye, Claire. I wish you well."

He didn't wait for her to respond but turned toward the door. A heartbeat later he was gone.

Claire couldn't breathe. He was the best thing that had ever happened to her, and now he was gone. She squeezed her eyes shut, clenching her fist in her skirt. She had known when all this began that she risked everything, including her heart. And at first she had tried to protect herself, to keep herself from falling in love. But the moment he had looked at her by the loch with both pain and desire in his eyes, she had done it anyway.

Now there was no going back, no way to fall out of love with him. He had made it perfectly clear he did not want her.

It was time to return to her old life. She fingered the edge of the oil painting next to her. She had to convince herself it was what she wanted, even though she knew it was not.

She turned away from the painting and grabbed an already-prepared canvas and her charcoals. She set to work on the initial lines of the painting, letting her fingers guide her instead of her brain. She drew a sweep of a shoulder. A powerful arm. Soon a shape emerged. The shape of a man. It was the image of Jules standing in her studio, looking powerful and unforgettable.

Her fingers stilled. How could she do it? How did one forget a man like Jules MacIntyre?

She picked up the canvas and threw it across the studio. It was pointless to torture herself. It was over between them. He would soon petition for a divorce. She would be alone again with her painting and her girls. The thought made her chest tight and brought tears to her eyes.

She was a fool to fall in love with him. And yet, despite it all, she loved him still.

He was gone. It was what he wanted.

She could still hear the sound of the door closing in her mind. And she wondered if she would ever forget that sound or the feeling of emptiness that followed.

On the seedier side of town, Agatha lay in a narrow bed while a sawbones she had bribed out of his bed with gold coins cauterized her wounds with a hot knife. The pain should have knocked her senseless; instead she gathered it around her heart, allowed it to fuel her need for revenge against Jules and his little bride.

A glow of warmth that had nothing to do with the scalding blade in her wounds settled over Agatha. Comforted her. She should be angry that fortune had robbed her of the chance to kill Jules, but that was not the case. Now her precious stepson knew he was hunted, and every last moment of his life would take on a new importance. He would most likely hold those he loved closest to him, protecting them from harm. And she would be there watching and waiting.

When the end was finally near, and she took every last loved one from him, as she had his brother, it would be in a dazzling explosion of pain and grief, sorrow and panic.

It was that thought that soothed Agatha's pain and frustration and caused her to smile in pure joy as the scent of burning flesh filled the chamber and her spirit was once again restored.

20

One week after he'd returned home, Jules said good-bye to Jane, Nicholas, Margaret, and Hollister. Since he had safely returned to Kildare Manor, his friends were eager to return to their own homes to await the births of their children.

Alone in the suddenly empty halls of Kildare Manor, Jules tried to purge Claire from his mind and tear her from his heart. He knew he was losing the battle when he found himself upstairs in the room he once hated for so long. Suddenly it seemed to be his favorite chamber in the house. He would stop in the center of the ballroom and lose himself in Claire's painting for hours on end.

Claire stood in her studio, staring into empty space. *Jules*. She closed her eyes and pushed the thought away, just as she had done every day since he'd left her behind a week ago. She had tried cleaning her studio at first in an effort to forget him. She'd scrubbed every splatter of dried paint from the wood floor. She'd walked through the streets of Edinburgh with the girls. But every time she saw something beautiful, something inspiring, she wondered what Jules would think if he looked at it with her. How he would respond?

And she always ended each day right where she stood now. In her studio. In front of the half-drawn image of Jules she had started when he had left. A frisson of excitement shivered along her skin as she gazed at the image. Her fingers curled at her sides, and before she could stop herself, she grabbed her palette and her paints and set to work. Perhaps if she put him on the canvas, she would be free of him in her mind.

Or at least that was the hope as she lost herself in painting.

Two weeks later, Jules found himself sitting alone in the drawing room. He gazed into the flames in the hearth, trying to concentrate on an estate ledger, but it was Claire he saw in his mind and not the columns of profit and cost.

Even so, the estate was beginning to recover. His tenant farmers had returned and were preparing the soil for a crop of winter wheat. The estate was starting to repair itself.

If only his heart would do the same.

Claire finished her painting of Jules a week later, and still he continued to haunt her.

She spent her days with the girls, teaching them new techniques in painting. Recovered from their ordeal, Anna and Eloise had finally returned to their usual behaviors. The younger girls had even started to laugh again, as they did now, filling the studio with their high-spirited voices while they painted a still life Claire had set out for them of a candlestick, a book, and two apples.

Penelope had not recovered as quickly. Her once-cheerful face now held an ever-present sadness, and her lovely blue eyes seemed haunted. Penelope sat in a chair before her easel, her brush in her uninjured hand, arrested above the canvas. She could learn to paint left-handed if she tried.

But instead of trying, the girl had been withdrawn and without spirit since the events at Kildare Manor. Claire could feel tears of sympathy burn in her eyes, but she blinked them angrily away. They could not change what had happened, only how they responded to it. If only she could get Penelope to respond.

She had tried to be consoling. She had tried to inspire her. She had been firm, and she had simply held Penelope in her arms and let her cry. But nothing seemed to change that look of desolation in her eyes, nothing except David. Only when he was near did she brighten.

Claire walked slowly across the studio and lifted her cloak from a hook on the wall. She nodded to the guard David had hired. "I will return shortly." To the girls she said, "Keep painting. I have a short errand I must attend to."

The younger girls nodded. Penelope simply stared at the blank canvas with a dull and hopeless look in her eyes.

The August air was crisp, yet the sun shone overhead as Claire hurried down her street, past the coaching inn, and into the heart of Edinburgh. She was on her way to David. Perhaps he had an idea of how to return the vivaciousness to Penelope's spirit.

As she headed toward the rooms David had let a few blocks away, she passed by the storefronts. The sound of the shopkeepers and tradesmen hawking their wares filled the late-morning air with a cacophony of noise mixed with the jangling harnesses of the carriages and the steady beat of horse hooves on the cobbled streets.

Darting through the crowd, Claire slipped closer to the buildings to avoid a cart filled with cabbages when she passed by a jeweler's shop. At first she walked right past, but something familiar caught her eye. She stopped, retracing her steps until she stood before the window, staring at a gold and ruby ring that could only have come from one source.

Jules's mother's ring.

Had he sold it?

Surprised and a little unsure, she went inside the shop.

"May I help you?" an older man asked, coming around a small desk in the corner of the shop.

Claire pointed toward the window display. "The gold and ruby ring in the window, did you purchase it recently?"

The old man nodded as he reached for the ring, holding it between two fingers. "That I did. A fine purchase, if I do say so myself. They don't cut the rubies like that anymore." He pulled out a pair of fragile glasses from his pocket and, setting them on his nose, scrutinized the ring through the lenses. "Everyone wants sparkle. But the rich color is far more valuable. Are you looking to purchase this ring for yourself?"

Claire laughed. "I might be, if I could know a bit of its history. Can I ask from whom you purchased such a fine piece of art?"

The old man looked at her over the rim of his lenses. "Came from a young laird who appeared a little down on his luck."

"I see," she said, trying to appear uninterested in the piece even as a shiver rippled across her flesh. "How much are you asking for the ring?"

"Sixty shillings Scot."

Claire tried not to react to the outrageous sum. She frowned and turned away from the ring. To show how much she wanted that particular ring would only increase the cost. She had to make him think otherwise. "What else do you have to show me? I want something with rubies."

The shopkeeper's smile slipped as he looked about his cluttered shop. "Hmmm."

"Well, if you have nothing else," she said in a calm and even voice as she turned toward the door.

"Wait," he called. "The ring is all I have with rubies. If you would just take another look. It is an exquisite ring."

Claire sighed. "I had my heart set on a pair of earrings to wear to the Davisons' ball this Saturday . . ." She strung the words out, hoping the shopkeeper would bargain with her. She had nothing to lose.

"Forty shillings Scot."

"Thirty."

He released an audible sigh. "All right, my dear. You drive a hard bargain, but I agree. Thirty shillings Scot."

Claire nodded. "Hold the ring for me. I will return on the morrow with the funds."

He agreed, and Claire left the shop before she either cried out her delight, or swooned. She had a feeling the latter was far more likely. Once outside, she leaned against the first wall she came to, and pressed trembling fingers against the cool stone.

She had found Jules's mother's ring—the only link she would ever have to Jules or his family. Once she saw the ring in the window, she knew she had to do anything and everything to possess it.

Her breath caught. And she had made it her own. Now all she had to do was figure out some way to get the funds by the next day, or all her efforts would be for naught.

When the initial exhilaration of bargaining for what she wanted so desperately wore off, she realized she had the answer to her problem already. The lie she had concocted about Lady Davison was not entirely false. The woman had asked her to attend a ball at her winter home in Argyll the following year, after Claire painted a ceiling for her that would make her the envy of her friends.

Claire had met the woman in the ballroom of Kildare Manor, at the party Jules's friends had planned. Perhaps it was time for Claire to agree to hire out her talents. Lady Davison had said she would agree to any terms. Would she be willing to advance Claire her fee before she had even started, and allow the girls to come along with her?

There was only one way to find out.

At the thought of heading to Argyll, Claire began to feel light-headed. Lady Davison lived within walking distance of Kildare Manor. If Claire went to Argyll, she would be close to Jules.

She drew a deep breath, forcing herself to be calm. Jules would never have to know she was there. She could paint the ceiling and be away from Argyll long before Lady Davison's ball.

Her decision made, Claire headed toward Amberly Place, Lady Davison's Edinburgh home, where the woman was fortunately in residence.

Across the street, Agatha slipped from the apothecary shop. Her hand closed around the small bottle of poison the young girl had created for her. It was a pity that Agatha had had to dispose of the girl, forcing her to drink her own concoction. Agatha had to be certain the poison was not only lethal, but fast.

The time to strike was coming nearer. She had to be prepared for when the opportunity presented itself.

It would eventually arrive, and the bottle in her hand would serve her purposes well.

Three weeks later, out of need to find some connection to the woman he missed so desperately, Jules climbed the stairs to the tower room, hoping and praying that the room still smelled like her. He entered the chamber and froze at the sight before him.

Everywhere he looked, the ceiling, the walls, even the floor, had been painted to resemble a garden in springtime. She'd painted the ruins of an ancient Greek temple that was surrounded in lush ivy and a riot of flowers. Beneath the shade of a willow tree was a fountain that looked so real Jules could swear he heard the soft trickle of water.

And to the side of the fountain, resting in a bed of violets, were two figures, their bodies entwined. He moved closer, and recognition flared. His heart stopped.

She'd painted the two of them as they had been by the loch. Their bodies glistened with drops of water, their skin vibrant and alive beneath the sun's light. The lines of their nude bodies were obscured by a sheer white cloth, yet the very covering only made what the viewer did not see more explicit. The very portrayal was as realistic as it was exotic and sensual.

His entire body burned. He groaned at the painful loss that filled him. How would he ever forget her, when she had made Kildare Manor such a part of herself? Everywhere he went, he was reminded of her, from the tower to the stable, the loch and the kitchen. There was no safe place in his own house where memories did not consume him.

He often wondered how she fared. If the girls had fully recovered from their ordeal. He wished he knew where she was, what she was doing, and if she missed him as much as he missed her. Wearily, he lay down on the small bed in the center of the chamber and looked up at the clouds she had painted on the ceiling. He tried to close his eyes, but as was usual these past three weeks, he could not sleep. He never slept anymore, not unless he had exhausted himself in the fields with his tenants, or he imbibed the family whiskey.

Quite often he lay awake as he did now, wanting her with a passion that transcended all reason. They had to stay separated. It was for her own good. Until Agatha could be found and locked away for the rest of her life, Claire would have to remain a stranger to him.

"Why are we in Argyll?" Penelope asked from the bottom of the ladder Claire stood on. She was painting the first quadrant of the ballroom ceiling in Lady Davison's country home.

"We are on a grand adventure as far as Anna and Eloise are concerned," Claire answered as she applied a final swoop of gray to a mass of blue-gray clouds.

"That's not what I mean," Penelope said, "and you know it."

"What *do* you mean?" Claire asked with a frown as she stepped down the ladder. She needed to clean her palette and brushes, then start on the cherubim and seraphim. She was making excellent progress on the ceiling. At this rate, she and the girls could be back in Edinburgh before the end of the year.

"Why are we in Argyll, so close to Lord Kildare, without going to see him?"

Claire smiled sadly. "He's not part of our lives any longer. But we wish him well with his." She poured turpentine on a rag and wiped the gray off the wooden board in her hand.

"But you are still married to him," the young woman cried.

"Yes."

"Don't you think he misses you?" Penelope asked.

Claire shook her head and drew a stilted breath. "No. I hurt him too badly. He will never trust me again. Besides, he can't miss something he never loved."

"He loved you," Penelope said, her voice choked with sorrow. She stepped toward Claire and, ignoring the palette and the odorous cloth, wrapped her in a supportive hug.

"Not enough." Claire turned out of Penelope's arms, grateful for once that the mention of his name did not bring an agony of pain. She'd grown numb over the last month. That numbness helped her now as she moved to her paints and refilled her palette with white and brown, and just a hint of red, yellow, and green, to create the flesh tones she needed.

The two words echoed in her mind as she blended the paint.

Not enough.

The following morning, Fin entered the drawing room, where Jules was standing, staring at empty space. "Milord," Fin interrupted.

Jules turned toward the door, expecting to have to reassure his worried steward, when he saw an unexpected sight. "Peter Kirkwood?"

"Good morning, milord," the older man said, making a small bow before coming into the room.

Jules frowned as anticipation edged with worry. "What brings you to Kildare Manor?" Jules waved him toward a seat on the settee.

"A startling discovery I felt you should know," he replied, settling into the cushions. His voice was quiet and even, but there was an undercurrent to his words.

Jules remained standing as the unknown tightened his chest and made it hard to breathe. "Is it Claire?" he blurted out, needing to put words to the fear that was always there, taunting him. Had leaving her alone with David been the appropriate action?

"Nay, milord. I have uncovered new information about your father's last days."

The revelation startled Jules. "Go on."

Kirkwood leaned forward. "I could not leave things the way we did in Edinburgh. I decided to take things upon myself to dig deeper, to understand your father's motives for bribing Grayson to do something that was so beyond his character."

Jules raised a brow. "What did you discover?"

"In Grayson's notes, I discovered that your father did not pay the ransom to release you from gaol, but that he paid the warden to keep you incarcerated."

Jules strode across the chamber, no longer able to stand still. He paced back and forth. "He kept me in? Why? Did he hate me that much?"

He had not realized he had spoken aloud until Kirkwood answered. "I think it is quite the opposite. I went to the warden and spoke with him. He said your father was worried the last time he went to the gaol to make a payment. He had no idea you had been released the week before. The news brought him to his knees, the warden said. When he asked Lord Kildare what was wrong, he said he could not let her get to you. Do his words mean anything to you?'

"Yes, they mean everything." What Agatha had told him was true.

"There's more." Kirkwood interrupted. "From the financial trail your father left behind, it appears that he sold everything in the manor a few weeks after that encounter, and that was the money he used to pay Grayson to arrange your marriage to a Miss Claire Elliot."

Jules stopped his pacing as a realization he could no longer avoid crashed over him. His father had cared, at least in the end, what happened to him. "It still doesn't make sense as to why he did what he did."

"From what I could discover, he seemed determined to find you a bride. I talked with several carriage drivers who said they escorted your father around town as he sought out women with the name Claire who were single, available, and somewhat down on their own luck."

"He chose my bride?" Jules echoed his previous sentiment, still not quite believing the words.

Kirkwood nodded. "It appears your father's last act upon this earth was to make certain his younger son would have a future, and if I might add my own sentiment, a reason to live."

A reason to live.

Jules smiled. He wasn't certain if it was because of the proof of a father's love, or knowing that his father had chosen a woman for him based entirely upon her name, or both.

Claire had given him a reason to live. She had helped him settle into his role as laird. Such a thing would have been unbearable without her. She was his life, his heart, his soul. And he suddenly wondered why he'd felt it necessary to keep her at arm's length, because without her he was barely alive.

At Jules's continued silence, Kirkwood rose. "I hope the information is reassuring, if not somewhat inspiring."

Jules nodded. "Inspiring, yes."

The older man nodded. "I will continue to investigate and let you know if I discover anything further."

His enthusiastic tone made Jules smile all the more. "You seem to enjoy these forays into investigation."

Kirkwood nodded. "After a lifetime of papers and law, your queries have lent some spice to my rather mundane existence, milord."

"Thank you, Kirkwood," Jules said with a nod of his head. "Your efforts have been extraordinary."

Now it was up to him to do something with that information.

Later that afternoon, Jules finally found the nerve to walk the short distance from the manor house to the family crypt where his father, mother, and brother were buried.

Jules entered the chamber. He held his lantern in front of him. The light cast leaping shadows on the pinkish-gray marble walls and shimmered off the effigies of his kin. His mother's grave was dusty. With his hand he cleaned it off, revealing the image of the woman he remembered—a heart-shaped face, high cheekbones, and kind eyes. Even set in stone, her eyes still held that softness he had once felt gaze upon him in life.

Beside her was the image of his father. His father's likeness stared up at him. His face had held an expression of pride and a warmth Jules never witnessed again after his mother's death. Had death brought him the peace he had searched for all those years? Jules hoped so. As he continued to study his father's features, other questions crowded his thoughts. Had his father truly loved him? Had he kept Jules in gaol as a means of protecting him from the monster who had latched herself to their family? Had his father really known Agatha was still alive?

Jules's thumb caressed his father's brow. "For whatever happened between us, for all the unspoken words, and the words that were spoken in anger, I apologize. I had no idea what kind of monster had entered our lives. I should have talked to you. I should have trusted you. I should have done so many things. For that, and for your untimely death, I apologize."

His own spirit lightened at the admission of his own failings. His father might never hear the words, but at least Jules knew he had finally said them.

He would never know the truth about his father's actions or inaction toward the end of his life, but he wanted to believe that the man had actually loved him and tried to protect him instead of shutting him out and leaving him in that hellhole for dead.

Jules slid his gaze to the right, to the effigy next to his father's. The heavy lid sat slightly askew, as though it had been moved then shifted back into place. She'd tricked them all, staging her own death and then having assistance in her resurrection from her tomb and this crypt.

For a heartbeat he wondered if that kind of evil could ever die. She was still out there, still a threat. She had robbed him of his freedom for over a year, and now she was robbing him of his happiness.

It was then that the realization hit him. That was exactly what Agatha wanted. She wanted him to be miserable without Claire. She had ruined the lives of his father and brother, and now he was allowing her to do the same to him. Jules's eyes ached with unshed tears while his chest filled with hope. He had turned his own home into a prison, instead of rotting away in one.

But what was he to do about it? He returned his gaze to the images of his mother and father. "What do I do?" he asked, not really expecting an answer, but hoping that one would be provided all the same.

Encouraged and defeated at the same time, Jules returned to the manor, where he prowled the hallways and paced the drawing room, searching for an answer. It wasn't until late afternoon that an answer was provided in the form of another visitor.

"Milord." Fin cleared his throat as he entered the drawing room, stopping Jules's trek across the newly restored carpet for the hundredth time. "There is someone to see you."

Jules's heart hammered with a mixture of hope and dread as Fin stepped back and Penelope entered the room.

She bowed. "Lord Kildare."

"Penelope, what a surprise," Jules said coming forward and taking her uninjured hand in his. "How did you get here?"

"'Tis only a short walk from where I am staying."

"The exercise agrees with you. You look well." Color had returned to her cheeks. She wore a pink glove on her injured hand that matched the color of her dress.

She blushed and pulled her hand from his. "'Tis the country air."

He studied her face, then lower, his gaze moving to her missing finger. "Does it still pain you?" he asked.

She shrugged and looked away. "At times. Sometimes I feel as though my finger is still there, even though I know it is not. I feel sensations. I know it sounds strange . . ." Her voice trailed off.

"Not at all," Jules said, bringing his gaze back to hers. "I have heard it said from others who lost limbs in battle. The phenomenon is quite normal."

Penelope gripped her hand, held it gently against her chest. "I was not in a battle."

"Yes," he said tenderly, "you were. A battle of the worst kind because it doesn't make sense at all what happened to you."

She gave him a partial smile. "Thank you for saying so. I often wonder if this is just punishment for some horrible sin I commit—"

"You did nothing wrong. Do you hear me?" Jules interrupted, his anger rising that the young woman even considered that she was at fault for Agatha's maniacal actions. "You were innocent. And I hope you will realize that someday soon."

"I am trying."

"Good," he said softly, then regarded her curiously. "Might I ask what brings you to Argyll? And more particularly, my house?"

She laughed. "Yes, it must seem rather strange that I show up out of the blue. But in reality I have been here for two weeks."

He frowned. "Two weeks? Who? Where?"

"All of us," she said, emphasizing the first word, "are staying at Lady Davison's while Claire works on a commissioned ceiling."

"Claire is here?" Just the sound of her name brought a tightness to his chest and an image of her to his mind—her wide golden eyes staring up at him, the wind tugging at the loose strands of her copper hair. He missed her with every fiber of his being.

"She's made mistakes," Penelope said. "But then, everyone makes mistakes. If we are not making mistakes, then we aren't really living, wouldn't you say?" She looked up at him expectantly.

The thought haunted him, tormented him, surprised him. "I can only agree."

"Then wouldn't you say if someone made a mistake, like Claire perhaps, that they might deserve a second chance at making things right?"

With an effort he ignored the leap of hope that flared to life inside him. It was unfair to put her in that kind of danger. She deserved someone who could give her a normal life. She deserved someone who would not bring death and pain into every day of their lives. Not someone like him.

At his silence Penelope continued. "She hasn't been the same since you left. She never smiles. Her paintings are all in grays and greens. She never sleeps. She hardly eats. She's slowly killing herself."

"She would be in danger if I went anywhere near her." He was surprised to hear how hoarse his voice was, how rough.

"She's in danger now of slowly fading away."

She never smiles? It was her smile that had made him ache for all the things he never knew he wanted. All his life he had wanted someone to look at him and see not an empty shell but the person he had always wanted to be. When he was younger, he'd thought that person was Jane. But Jane never looked at him the way Claire did.

Claire.

He thought of how it felt to lie in her arms, to have her press her cheek against his chest, to hear her heart beat next to his own. When Claire looked at him, she saw him for who he really was. When she kissed him with a light, breezy touch, she stamped his soul more deeply than their lovemaking had. With Claire, his loneliness fell away, replaced by a sense of wonder. His heart swelled at the memories.

Agatha.

The reminder of the ever-present danger did not have the power it usually held over him. Yes, the woman was still a threat. She would come for him, for them. It was only a matter of time.

But would it be better to spend that time apart and miserable, or together, trying to recapture something that had changed them both?

His heart seemed to stop for a moment, then picked up speed. He knew which option he preferred.

"Where is Claire?"

Jules entered the Davisons' ballroom silently. His gaze immediately went to Claire. She stood on a ladder, her head tilted back, facing the ceiling, a paintbrush in her hand.

He said nothing, made no sound, and yet she stopped as if sensing a presence and looked toward the door. He started toward her, all the while trying to discern the expression on her face. Did she look happy to see him?

In the long, lonely nights without her at his side, he had rehearsed so many speeches—all the things he'd longed to say. Yet not one word he had practiced came to him now as he watched her slowly descend the ladder.

Left without a place to start, he took the only course available to him and tipped his head back to study the painting she was creating on the ceiling of Brightwood Hall. It was of the heavens parting to reveal a burst of bright light, surrounded by a host of angels.

"An interesting scene for a ballroom," he replied, not knowing what else to say to his wife.

"It's what Lady Davison wanted," she said with a shrug. "I do not always have the freedom to choose what I paint."

The sound of her voice was like music to his ears. Had anything ever sounded so sweet? "You can paint whatever you like at Kildare Manor."

He looked back at her, saw the shock on her face, and knew he had to proceed now or lose the moment. "You look well," he said coming close enough to her to take the paintbrush from her hands. He set it on the closest wrung of the ladder behind her, then took her hands in his. The scent of paint and turpentine did not hide the fragrance he had come to know and love—the scent of lavender that always reminded him of her.

"I have been better," she said nervously, her expression one of fear mixed with hope. "And you?"

He gently clutched her hands, praying the subtle pressure communicated what he was finding difficult to say. "Fine, if you take into account that I have been half dead for the past three and a half weeks."

It took her a moment to comprehend what he was saying, and when she did, tears filled her eyes.

"I've been working hard at the manor. The tenants are back, and with what money I had left from selling my mother's ring, I was able to purchase seed for the crops. If we can just hold on until next fall, our finances will be much better. I hope that you will take that into consideration when I ask you to come home with me."

Tears shimmered in her glorious golden eyes, as did joy and relief. One tear broke free to roll down her cheek. "The money never mattered to me. It still doesn't. As I got to know the laird of Kildare Manor, I wanted a different outcome from the one I'd been sent to obtain."

His breath caught as he dared to hope. "What was that?"

"You. True love. A real family." She dropped one of his hands and reached inside the bodice of her gown to pull out a gold chain that held her locket as well as another object. On that chain dangled his mother's ring.

"How? Where?"

"I saw it in a store window in Edinburgh, and I realized what you had done in order to keep the estate afloat. I know how much this ring meant to you, as the only reminder you had of your mother. And as the only reminder I had of you, I bought it back."

He frowned as he reached out and fingered the metal that still possessed the warmth of Claire's body. "How did you get the money to buy it back?"

Releasing his other hand, she slipped the chain over her head and placed the ring, the locket, and chain in his hand. "I hired myself out as a painter, and since I did not intend to ever go back to Edinburgh, I moved us out of my studio."

With a raw ache in his voice he said, "That studio was your livelihood, your life."

She shook her head. "Something else took its place not too long ago as the center of my world."

He hid a smile as he unhooked the chain and slipped the ring off. The rubies caught the light, sparkled as though they had suddenly come back to life. He took her left hand in his. "I know I have no right to ask you this, not after everything I put you through, but you would make me the happiest man in the world if you would take a second chance with me. You as you. Me as me. No secrets. No ulterior motives. What do you think?"

Tears spilled onto her cheeks. She nodded. "It is an honor to meet you, Lord Kildare," she said, her voice rough with tears.

"This question is long overdue, but Claire Elliot MacIntyre, it would mean the world to me if you would wear this ring as a sign of my love and be my wife."

"I already am your wife."

"Then let me marry you again, and be by your side as we take our vows. No proxy. Only me. Will you do it, Claire?"

"Yes, Jules, I will marry you again and live the rest of my days in your company because without you, the sun does not shine."

Moved by her tears, Jules slipped the ring on her finger and pulled her against his chest. He did not feel so empty anymore. Nay, his soul felt full to overflowing with love and joy.

"I will need a lifetime to make up for all the pain I've caused you," Jules spoke the words in his heart. "I am so sorry for my hurtful words the last time we were together. I did not mean—"

She kissed him, cutting off his words. "Don't torture yourself," she said several moments later. "We hurt each other. And that is in the past. Second chances mean a fresh start. There are no ghosts of the past to haunt us any longer. It's just you and me and the girls—" She pulled back suddenly as her eyes filled with concern. "The girls. I cannot abandon them."

He smiled and cupped her face between his palms, wiping her tears away with his thumbs. "The girls are already on their way back to our home," he whispered, his voice raw with his own unshed tears. "I do not want just a wife, Claire, I want a family. That includes the girls."

Fresh tears glistened in her eyes. "How did you know we were here?"

"Penelope."

"Remind me to thank her later," Claire said as she valiantly tried to hold back her tears.

"Much later," Jules said with a smile as he gathered Claire to him. He bent to kiss her.

"Can I ask you something?" she asked, stalling his movements.

His eyes widened as he stopped midway to her lips. "Now?"

She nodded as determination flared in her golden eyes.

He released a frustrated sigh. "Anything for you, my dear. What would you like to know?"

She hesitated for a heartbeat then said, "I want to know what happened between you and Agatha, but only if it will not hurt you to disclose that secret."

"I have no secrets where you are concerned. Not anymore." Jules threaded his fingers through hers. "Agatha demanded my father bring me home from the Lennoxes. She did so under the pretense that she wanted us all to be a family." He could feel his lips twist into a bitter smile. "She did not want a family."

Claire looked at him, her brow furrowed. "What did she want?"

"Agatha came to my bed two days after I returned. I turned her away. She came again the next night, and I did the same. She begged, she pleaded, she teased. She knew exactly what she was doing to me, the torment she caused. She kept at it every night for weeks, months, then years." He shook his head at the unpleasant memory. "I would not cuckold my father."

"No one around you knew the truth?"

He shrugged. "No one saw what Agatha did not want them to see, but the servants all knew I was angry with her. They could see my hatred, and that only fed into the lies she told them about me."

"That must have been very hard for a young man to be so alone with such a big secret weighing on him," she said with sympathy instead of the repulsion he had feared.

"One day I told Agatha I'd had enough. The torment would stop or I would go to my father and tell him what she was." He could feel one corner of his lips lift in a twisted smile. "She wasn't pleased."

"What did she do?"

"The next day she was found dead. I know now she'd arranged everything to look like I'd poisoned her. She played upon the anger I felt for her and pitted the servants against me. Without proof otherwise, I was convicted of murder and sentenced to hang. But Jane changed that outcome."

She shivered and held his hand more tightly. "How?"

"Because I could no longer look at my father without wanting to harm myself, I left Kildare Manor that night. I rode all night to reach Bellhaven Castle, Jane's home. She testified that I could have been nowhere near my own home when the murder took place."

"Then why did they charge you at all?" Claire asked.

"Because shortly before I left for Bellhaven, I had purchased poison. I had intended to kill her. For that, I was sentenced to time in gaol until someone could pay my ransom. I deserved what punishment I was dealt, because if I had stayed at Kildare Manor that night, I would have killed her."

"Thinking of something and doing it are two very different things." Claire looked at him in astonishment. "Your father brought that woman into your household and let her hurt you. If anyone is to blame, besides that monster who pretended to be your mother, it was your father for closing his eyes to what was before him."

He nodded his agreement. "I came to that same conclusion this morning. And despite it all, I forgave my father. Just like the two of us, he made mistakes. If I was ever going to move forward with my life, I had to let go of the anger I felt toward him, and even toward Agatha."

His brow furrowed as he held Claire's hands. "You're trembling."

"I'm not as forgiving, I fear. I don't like what that woman did to you." Her voice was raw. "She hurt you. She can hurt you still."

He shook his head. "No, Claire, she can't, because I won't let her, and neither will you." With his thumbs, he rubbed her palms until her trembling stopped and another emotion fired in her eyes. He pulled Claire to him and bent his head. He stopped just before their lips met, waited a heartbeat so that she could sense his hunger. "That game with Agatha is over, and we've won. She cannot steal what we have found again this day. True happiness has no end."

He closed the gap between them, pressing soft kisses to her lips, kisses that hinted at the passion he held in check, kisses filled with promise for the future. He teased her lips until he felt her relax in his arms, until her nerves were as taut as his own, and until she was as desperate to return to the paradise only the two of them could enter.

Her eyes on his, she drew back, caught his hand in her own, and led him from the room. She led him up the stairs to the bedchamber she occupied at Brightwood Hall. "I cannot wait until we return to Kildare Manor," she said, her voice rough with passion.

He shut the door and pulled her into his arms. The place did not matter. She was all that mattered. "Neither can I." Light from the late afternoon sun shone through the window, illuminating the chamber in hues of pale gold.

She met his gaze in the pale light, and he felt rather than saw her desire flare. He took a moment to savor the sensation. Raising both hands, he framed her face, tipped it up to his. He looked down for one long moment, searching those lovely eyes, then bent his head to kiss her.

Claire knew the moment his lips touched hers that this was a new beginning. While Jules deepened his kiss, his hands moved to the ties of her paint-splattered dress, and slowly he slipped the garment from her shoulders, down her hips, until finally it pooled about her ankles.

Time seemed to slow as he lifted her in his arms and carried her the short distance to the bed. Gently, he set her there, then bent to remove his boots. He dispensed with his waistcoat and breeches, setting them aside, then, as if the slowness of his other motions cost him his restraint, he yanked at his shirt, loosening his cuffs as he slipped beside her on the bed in his full naked glory. He reached for her, wrapped her in his arms, and instead of acting on his passion, he simply held her. "I promise you, Claire," he whispered against her ear, "no one will ever hurt you again, especially me."

She pressed her cheek to his, and drew in the scent of mint and man. She closed her eyes, savoring the sensation of his body as it warmed her own. "That is not something you can promise and keep." She pulled back and looked into his eyes. "We will hurt each other. It is part of trusting each other with our lives. We'll make mistakes, but we'll learn from them."

"Ever the wise one." A hint of a smile came to his lips. "Then let me promise that if I do hurt you, I will make it up to you with my lips." He kissed her temple, her cheek, the tip of her nose, until finally he kissed her lips. The kiss was gentle, patient, as though he waited for a response. When she gave it to him, he coaxed her into more until her body melted against his. He kissed her longingly. Hungrily. Yet his hunger was restrained as he let her taste his wanting. Holding back, he gave to her without taking.

When the tide of her longing matched his own, he broke the kiss, his voice rough with need as he whispered, "With my heart." His gaze never leaving hers, he brought his hand down to cover her chest above her heart where that organ fluttered beneath his touch. "And with my body."

Jules wove what he felt for her into each gentle caress as his hands sculpted to her back, her hips, her thighs. He let her feel his need of her in each slow kiss, each press of his hand against her heated flesh. He continued his assault with a slow, steady stroke, creating his own masterpiece with her as his muse.

Their lovemaking before had been passionate and intense, and a part of her grew restless, waiting for the fulfillment of the promise he created with each tender touch. She reached for him, trying to caress him in return, but he pressed her back into the pillows, evading her touch, gently anchoring her wrists with one hand above her head.

With his free hand he stroked from the hollow of her throat, over her breasts, along the flat of her stomach, to her woman's core, branding her with an unspoken promise. He touched her with reverent possession, as if he still couldn't quite believe she was his.

She tried to shift into him. He held her back. "Don't," he whispered with passion thickening his voice. "I want to be the one who brings you pleasure, pleasure so intense that it is close to pain. I want you to feel in my arms the way you feel when you're painting."

"You bring me that kind of pleasure every day that you weave your hand with mine." Merciful heavens, he was beautiful. The candlelight bathed him in a golden glow, delineating each feature of his face, the tough, sinewy grace of his chest and shoulders.

"Tonight, I want to make you feel as if we are the only two people in the world."

"We are," she breathed and pressed back against the linen.

"Yes, we are," he echoed, and she felt the brush of his fingers as they traced the underside of her breast, the side, the top. Moving slowly, smoothly, he palmed the fullness, then traced her nipple with his thumb. Flames leapt with each movement against her heated skin, desire flared, and yet he continued to explore first one breast, then the other, with infinite deliberation. It felt as though he were discovering her anew, claiming her for the first time.

Or making amends for all that they'd been through. With every caress of his hands, with every sweep of his fingers, with every inch of his thorough exploration, he left no doubt about his feelings. He laid his heart bare before her. Her breath caught at the realization.

"Jules . . ." His name was part prayer, part plea. "I love you," she whispered.

He found her lips and covered them with his. She arched into him, inviting his touch. He was her valiant warrior, her husband, her laird. He loved her, she knew, even if he failed to say the words.

He made her ache. He teased her senses, and took slow, unhurried possession of her body.

Her heart sang, and her body thrummed when he finally released her wrists. He moved over her and gently parted her thighs. He entered her slowly, carefully, until he filled her entirely. Her nails dug into the linen beneath her. His very slowness and deliberateness were unbearably erotic and sensual. He used his knowledge of her body to arouse and sustain her pleasure. He roused her to a frenzy of passion and then gave her an equally fiery release.

But he never allowed himself that final climax of passion, never permitted himself to lose control. The realization fueled her with a new purpose. The time for penance was over. She no longer cared about his purpose—only her own, and that was to make him relinquish that control and give himself over to her.

Jules tried to surface from the sensual plane she had driven him to with the softness of her body enveloping him. Having held himself back for too long, now he craved her touch, longed for it like she was rain and he a square of parched land.

She slid her hands over his chest, down his sides, and around him to cup his buttocks, to urge him forward. He drove inside her, deeper, thrusting to her core with swift and powerful strokes. She moaned her pleasure as she continued her silken caress across his hands, up his arms, to his shoulders, and through his hair. He leaned his head back as she worked her way back down his chest, and lower, stroking his skin as well as his soul.

She was raw passion and need, a bright flame he would never be able to live without. Opening his senses, he drank her in, soaked up every drop of pleasure until his hunger overflowed. She made no move to guide or direct; she simply urged him on with her legs around his thighs.

The hunger between them built, their bodies clenched, desire coiled tighter and tighter driving them both to that plane of total abandon. He could feel his ecstasy mounting, tried to hold back until they crested that peak together.

She cried out as she reached that pinnacle and fell into the void. Feeling her contract around him sent him reeling along with her as they fractured into bliss and floated.

In perfect sync, cocooned in golden glory, they drifted back to the here and now. Spent, he slumped upon her, then shifted to the side, taking her with him. They lay there entwined as he listened to her heart racing, matching his own.

The room was silent except for the sound of their breathing. Her arms slid around him, and she held him possessively, protectively, as though she never wanted to let him go.

He reached up and gently brushed back the hair from her temple, feeling closer to her at this moment than he had ever thought possible, and yet he still had one more thing he longed to give her—something he had denied her before. "Claire?"

"Hmmm," she nearly purred.

He pulled back and studied her eyes, then leaned closer, gently framed her face with one hand. He lowered his head and brushed her lips with his. "Your name really is Claire, isn't it?"

"Yes." She brought her hand up and laid it over his.

He smiled slowly, as his chest swelled with emotion. He kissed her again—a longer kiss, one that stirred the flames between them once more. "Good," he said against her lips. "Because suddenly it is the only name I desire."

She grinned, and his heart felt achingly full.

"That settles it. Three days from now we will be married again."

"Three days?"

"Two."

She laughed. "I believe we can arrange the entire affair in two days."

"If only it could be tomorrow." He pressed another, more urgent kiss to her lips.

"Jules," she said his name in a breath that was part sigh, part moan. And then, there was no talking at all.

23

Two days later, the morning dawned cold and bright and clear. Kildare Manor had been decorated with a sea of purple heather and white roses. The wedding was to be a small affair with Claire and Jules, the girls, David, and their servants.

Jane and Nicholas had sent word they would not be attending, as Jane had gone into labor the night before. Margaret and Hollister were staying behind with their one-month-old daughter to help Jane through her trial.

Upstairs in her chamber, Claire donned her wedding dress. She had not had a special outfit to wear for their marriage the first time. She had worn her gray gown before the minister, and despite the ceremony that had been very real, she had not felt like a bride. Not like now.

Claire sighed as she ran her hands down the lovely dress she wore. The garment was not new, but it was the perfect dress for today. Jules had brought her a chest two days before that contained his mother's wedding gown and veil. The pale blue gown with short puffed sleeves and a straight neckline had been well preserved. A seamstress had been hired to alter the fit, and it suited Claire's taste to perfection.

She stood in the center of the bedchamber, admiring the exquisite brocade gown that was covered in an intricate pattern of silver thread and tiny seed pearls, feeling very much like a bride. All that remained was for one of the new maids to come and help her with her veil.

As if Claire's thoughts had conjured her, Marie slipped into the room, her back turned and her arms full of the silky veil. A second servant followed behind her, a man dressed in stiff black and white.

A new footman? Claire frowned. She had yet to meet all the new staff. As soon as the wedding was behind them, she intended to get to know them all.

Marie turned around, although it wasn't Marie. "Good morning, Claire."

"Agatha," Claire whispered. Claire had no time to say or do anything more as blinding pain crashed through her left temple.

Belowstairs and outside on the formal terrace, off the east side of the manor, Jules waited for his bride. He nervously smoothed the pleats of his tartan. He had dressed in his family's colors today as a symbol of not only passing on his name, but also sharing with Claire the responsibility of the MacIntyre clan.

"Don't worry," David said beside him on his left. "It is fashionable for the bride to make the guests wait. She'll be here and everything will be perfect."

Jules tried to smile as his fingers fumbled with his sporran. Patience was never one of his virtues. Jules forced his idle hands behind his back. His heart raced in anticipation. His gaze fixed on the terrace doors.

A light breeze blew across the terrace and ruffled Penelope's, Anna's, and Eloise's hair as they also waited, dressed in light purple gowns, for Claire to arrive. Fin waited next to the girls, smiling broadly. The servants hovered near the banquet table where they would retire as soon as the ceremony ended.

The minister stood on Jules's right. He cleared his throat. "Should someone go see what is taking her so long?" The man peered over his spectacles, his brow raised in question.

Jules took a step toward the door, when it suddenly opened. But instead of Claire walking through, Agatha appeared, followed by a man who carried Claire, bound and gagged, in his arms. She was limp and unmoving.

"This was supposed to be one of the happiest days of your life, Jules." Agatha smiled maliciously. "I am quite certain after I am done with you, it will be one of your worst."

David started forward, but Agatha grabbed Eloise about the neck and held a slim, silver blade to the young girl's throat.

Eloise's eyes widened in terror and she started to cry. Her soft sobs filled the sudden silence.

Jules went rigid. His stomach churned in fear. "If Claire is dead or if you harm Eloise, I'll kill you," he growled despite his audience. He no longer cared what would happen to him, only that Claire and the girls would survive.

Agatha shrugged. "Perhaps I killed Claire, perhaps I didn't. There is only one way to find out."

"Put her down," Jules demanded.

A new lackey Jules did not recognize dropped Claire on the floor at his feet. At the motion, her eyes opened, and she made a sound behind the gag in her mouth.

Dizzying relief poured through him as he knelt beside her. He jerked the gag out of her mouth. Claire instantly took a deep breath.

"For God's sake, she couldn't breathe, you barbaric monster." Jules couldn't resist the epithet.

"It might have been kinder had she died from suffocation . . ."

Penelope lurched forward, clutching her injured hand. "I won't let you hurt her."

Anna pulled her back. "No, Penelope. That won't help the situation."

The young woman was right. Jules needed them to fade into the background with the servants. He motioned to Anna, who understood his unspoken command, and she pulled Penelope farther away from Agatha and her henchman.

Jules's hands trembled as he smoothed Claire's hair away from her temples. "Did she hurt you?"

"Only my head." Claire's voice shook. "We hadn't planned on this today, had we?"

"No." Jules glared at Agatha over Claire's body. "You have me. Let the rest of them go."

Agatha's smile was terrifying as she stroked Eloise's neck with the knife blade. "I cannot do that, Jules, not when I've gone to all this trouble on your behalf. I've got everything planned, down to the last detail."

Rage darkened Jules's vision. "Go to hell."

Agatha laughed. "You first, and this time I won't give you a chance to harm me." She pulled Eloise back with her to the banquet table and forced the young girl to pick up a goblet that waited there. Together they moved back toward Jules and Claire. "I've prepared a drink especially for you, Jules, dearest."

To the young girl she said, "Go ahead, give him the goblet."

Still softly sobbing, Eloise did as commanded.

"You cannot force him to drink that," Claire said hoarsely.

"Oh yes, I can." In one swift movement, Agatha shoved Eloise forward into David's legs, while gripping Claire by the hair and holding the knife to her neck. The sharp blade pressed against Claire's flesh, causing a trickle of red to appear against her porcelain skin.

Despite the pain she must be feeling, Claire inhaled sharply and said, "Don't do it, Jules. Do not give her that kind of power over you."

"What's in the goblet?" Jules asked.

"My special blend of poison—cyanide made from apricot kernels, mixed with belladonna berries, and, just to make sure it's quite lethal, a touch of wolfsbane."

"Who else have you killed with your poison, Agatha?" Jules asked, his voice tight.

Agatha considered Jules, then smiled. "Why not confess? After today I will vanish to a place where no one will find me, so yes, I killed your brother by poisoning his whiskey. I killed your solicitor as well, but with my horse and carriage." Her eyes narrowed menacingly.

Jules held his shock and his pain in check as he pressed her for more answers. "There is something else I must know."

She frowned. "You expect me to reveal all my secrets?"

"This one, yes. If I am to go to my grave, then I need to know—was you who paid for my release from gaol?"

She smiled a terrible smile. "Yes, if you must know. I grew weary of waiting for you to die. If no one else would kill you for me, then I would have to do it myself." Her gaze narrowed on him. "I'd say things worked out much better this way. Now, take a drink and my revenge will be complete."

He had his answers; now he must do as she demanded. Jules lifted the goblet to his lips.

"Don't do it," Claire pleaded, her gaze clinging to Jules's. "Please, I beg you. Do not let her do this to you."

"I must drink it, Claire. That's the only way you will ever be safe." He smiled into her eyes, forced every sentiment he'd ever felt for her into that last gaze. "I love you."

"No," she whispered.

He lifted the goblet and drank.

"*Jules!*"

His face contorted with agony and the goblet fell from his fingers, crashing to the floor a heartbeat before he did.

Claire screamed. She wasn't certain exactly what happened next, but she felt Agatha's arm go slack. The knife slipped from her throat. Claire lunged toward Jules. "He's dead. You killed him."

Tears ran down Claire's cheeks as she lifted Jules's head and placed it in her lap. Her shoulders shook with silent sobs until David touched her shoulder.

Through her tears, she turned to see David holding Eloise to his chest. "It's all right, Claire. Eloise is safe. And you might want to see this for yourself," he said, pointing behind her.

Claire twisted around to see Agatha and her henchman struggling against their own bonds. Two servants held the henchman while a man she recognized as Arthur Cabot held on to Agatha.

"What?" she breathed. "But you are a debt collector!"

"A cover," he said. "I have been following Agatha and her many lackeys for some time. But I needed your help to get a confession out of her," Arthur said with a self-satisfied grin. "Today, I got what I needed to put her away for good."

"But Jules . . ." She looked down at the lifeless body in her arms. "He's—"

"Alive." Jules's voice was strong, vibrant. He opened his eyes and smiled. The most breathtaking, beautiful smile Claire had ever seen.

Her heart burst to overflowing. "You're not dead!" She brushed the moisture from her cheeks.

Arthur tied Agatha's arms behind her back. "Earlier this morning, I witnessed Agatha put poison into that goblet and made the switch to wine with bitters," Arthur said proudly. "I found Jules and told him of my plan to capture his stepmother. The rest of you had to be kept in the dark to make everything seem real."

Claire inhaled sharply. "She could have added more poison to that glass at any time."

Jules shrugged. "It was a chance I had to take, to put her away from us for good."

"No!" Agatha screamed in fury when she realized what had happened. "No, this cannot be the way it ends," she cried as Arthur dragged her toward the door.

"Oh, it will end differently," Arthur said with calm authority. "It will end for you with a hangman's noose."

Time stood still as the sound of Agatha's voice faded. Claire and Jules froze as the full impact of the moment hit them.

They were safe.

Agatha was gone, never to return.

Her heart pounding, Claire smiled. "It's over."

Jules nodded as he sat up and faced her. But as suddenly as his smile appeared, it faded. He held out his lace-cuffed sleeve to gather the sticky warmth of her blood that marred her neck. "I did not mean for you to be hurt, only Agatha to be caught."

She brought a hand up to cup his cheek. "I am unharmed, and I am so grateful this nightmare is finally over."

He turned and pressed a kiss into her palm. "Does that mean you will still marry me after all of this? If not, I have to find some other way to keep you in my life. Perhaps you will consider painting the ceilings and every wall of every room in this house?"

She stifled a grin. "And what happens when you run out of walls? Then what?"

"I would buy you more walls if only we had the funds."

She stared dreamily at him. "You know your lack of fortune means nothing to me. I am more than capable of supplementing our income with the occasional portrait or wall painting."

"And I intend to keep you quite busy so that you have no time to paint," he said suggestively as he traced his finger across the fullness of her lips.

Her eyes widened. "Milord, we have guests."

"Yes," he said, looking around him at the girls, David, Fin, the minister, and the servants, who regarded the two of them with interest. "You're right." He stood and extended her his hand. "Then what say you, milady. Do you care to continue with our wedding vows?"

"Oh, yes." Claire accepted his hand and allowed him to pull her not only to her feet, but into his arms. They were meant to be together. Jules held her close as the minister stepped before them and started the ceremony.

"Dearly beloved, we are gathered here this day in the sight of God to join this man and this woman in the vows of holy matrimony."

The minister's words faded into the background as a tingling, glowing warmth moved through Claire and into Jules, dissolving the sadness and the loneliness of their lives.

A fresh start, a new life as husband and wife.

Dear God, it was so simple, Claire thought as she gazed up at the man she loved and repeated her vows. Why had she not understood before what was so clear now?

The pain and turmoil of life was necessary in order to make moments such as this special. True love, true fulfillment, and true forgiveness was only given to those who had lived through the highs and the lows of life.

She and Jules had survived the worst, and now would revel in the best life had to offer, for the rest of their lives.

Author's Note

One of the plotlines in the Highland Bachelors series involves a group of men and women known as the Covenanters. The Covenanters were seventeenth-century Scottish Presbyterians devoted to maintaining Presbyterianism as the sole religion of Scotland. Covenanters were bound by oath to sustain one another in the defense of their religion and therefore signed covenants stating that fact.

These covenants that proclaimed the Covenanters' loyalty to God, as opposed to the king, began a chain of events that intensified in 1679 at the Battle of Bothwell Bridge on the River Clyde and set off a period in Scottish history from roughly 1680 to 1688 that was known as the Killing Times, when nearly 18,000 Covenanters, as well as the government forces who tried to control them, lost their lives.

In 1679, after the Scottish Covenanters' uprising was quashed at the Battle of Bothwell Bridge, around 1,200 prisoners were herded to Edinburgh. Some 400 of those ended up in an open space at Greyfriars kirkyard that became known as the Covenanters' Prison. Many of these prisoners were set free after making submission, while some were executed and others died of illness or wounds because of the horrendous conditions they were forced to endure.

What happened to the 300 prisoners who survived? That tale will continue throughout the Highland Bachelors series.

You were first introduced to the Battle of Bothwell Bridge in *A Laird for Christmas* as Nicholas Kincaid and Lady Jane Lennox dealt with the painful aftermath of war.

Jules MacIntyre and his wife Claire are forced to head into the historic and unsettling location of the Covenanters' Prison in Greyfriars kirkyard in *This Laird of Mine* in order to rescue Claire's wards.

Colin Taylor will need the help of Lady Portia Rothesay as they discover a past that links him to the Covenanters, a past that could get them both killed in *A Laird in Shining Armor*.

David Buchanan, Bryce MacCallister, and Jane's brother Jacob Lennox all have roles to play in what happens to the Covenanters as the government forces threaten not only their lives, but all they hold dear in upcoming adventures.

Acknowledgments

Many thanks to the very talented artist Kate Race, for all my beautiful covers and for sharing her knowledge of painting with me.

And to Pam Ahearn, who is everything an agent and a trusted friend ought to be. I am not certain what has meant more to me over the years . . . your confidence in me, your excellent advice, or your endless graciousness.

About the Author

© 2011 BARBARA ROSER/ROSER PHOTOGRAPHY

Gerri Russell's varied writing career includes stints as a broadcast journalist, magazine columnist, newspaper reporter, and technical writer and editor. Since deciding to follow her heart's desire and become a romance novelist, she has won two Romance Writers of America Golden Heart Awards and an American Title II Award sponsored by RT Book Reviews. Gerri is best known for her adventurous and emotionally intense novels set in the Scottish Highlands, including the series The Brotherhood of the Scottish Templars and The Stones of Destiny. She lives in Bellevue, Washington, with her husband and children.